SEEING IS DECEIVING

SEEING IS DECEIVING

Roderic Jeffries

This first world edition published in Great Britain 2002 by
SEVERN HOUSE PUBLISHERS LTD of
9–15 High Street, Sutton, Surrey SM1 1DF.
This first world edition published in the USA 2002 by
SEVERN HOUSE PUBLISHERS INC of
595 Madison Avenue, New York, N.Y. 10022.

British Library Cataloguing in Publication Data

Jeffries, Roderic, 1926–
   Seeing is deceiving – (An Inspector Alvarez novel)
   1. Alvarez, Inspector (Fictitious character) – Fiction
   2. Police – Spain – Fiction
   3. Majorca (Spain) – Fiction
   4. Detective and mystery stories
   I. Title
   823.9'14 [F]

ISBN 0-7278-5811-4

Typeset by Palimpsest Book Production Ltd.,
Polmont, Stirlingshire, Scotland.
Printed and bound in Great Britain by
MPG Books Ltd., Bodmin, Cornwall.

One

It was the evening of Good Friday and the Davallament procession. Alvarez, standing near the foot of the 365 steps leading up to Puig del Calvari, watched the descending column of penitent men – for obvious reasons, there were no women – who wore tall, conical hats with two eyeholes; many of them were barefoot and a few lashed themselves with scourges despite the papal prohibition of such a practice. A display of humility in others forced a man to have the courage to look into his own soul. He looked. He saw a sinner who always sought the easiest rather than the hardest route, was content to let others worry provided they did not worry him, who indulged his weaknesses instead of resisting them. All that must change. Would change . . .

As he turned, to ease his way out of the press of tourists who thought the procession was staged for their benefit, he noted a woman who stood several steps above him. Long blonde hair framed an oval face that was strikingly attractive; her lips were full, promising much; she wore a frock that moulded a richly formed body and was short enough to . . . He silently swore. He dedicated himself to leading a better life and a moment later allowed his mind to harbour lascivious thoughts. His penitence for such weakness would be to refrain from all liquor until Monday . . .

The walk back to his parked car took him past one

1

of his favourite bars and he automatically slowed as he approached the shaft of light that came through the open doorway. He squared his shoulders and strode on. Joy through strength; the joy of knowing his will power was strong.

He reached home and went through the front room, used only on formal occasions, to the dining/sitting room. Jaime was seated at the table, a glass in front of himself and a bottle of Soberano within easy reach. 'I've been wondering where you'd got to.'

'I had some work that had to be cleared up.' Alvarez sat.

'Working on a fiesta?'

'Duty comes before pleasure.'

'Not very often.'

'Depends how loud the superior chief's shouting.'

'You need a good stiff drink to take the taste away.' Jaime pushed the bottle across.

'I won't, thanks.'

'Won't what?'

'Have a drink.'

'What's up?'

'Nothing.'

'There's got to be something when you turn down a drink.' He called out. 'Dolores.'

She appeared in the doorway of the kitchen. 'What is the matter?'

'Enrique's ill.'

'I am perfectly fit,' Alvarez protested.

She ignored his denial. 'Do you have a temperature?'

'No.'

'Are you feeling sick?'

'No.'

'Where is the pain?'

2

'I've not broken my leg, I'm not suffering from a burst appendix or terminal heart failure. I just don't want a drink.'

She had an expressive face and her concern was obvious as she came forward to stand in front of him. 'Turn your head to the right.'

'Why?'

'I think your neck is swollen.'

He turned his head one way, then the other. 'Are you now satisfied I haven't developed mastitis?'

'It would not be your neck that was swollen if you had. Why don't you want a drink?'

'I just don't.'

'Perhaps you should go to the emergency centre and ask the doctor on duty to examine you.'

Alvarez was very reluctant to explain the cause of his abstinence, certain that to do so would cause more scornful amusement than admiration. 'If it's going to cause so much trouble, I'll have a drink.' He turned to his right, leaned over and opened the door of the sideboard, brought out a glass into which he dropped several ice cubes. He covered them with brandy, drank. 'Is everyone now satisfied I'm not about to collapse and die?' He put the glass down on the table with more force than was necessary and some brandy spilled over the rim.

'Am I not supposed to be concerned about the health of those who live in my house?' she asked sharply.

'All I was saying was—'

'I heard what you said.'

He inwardly sighed. One had to fly, not run, to keep up with her mercurial changes of mood. 'I'm sorry if you thought—'

'In this house, my thoughts are plainly of no consequence.' She crossed to the kitchen doorway, then stopped and turned. 'I am cooking llengua amb táperes and—'

He interrupted her, hoping to divert her resentment. 'Then we're about to have a meal that will make the gods envy us!'

'As my mother warned me, When a man speaks words of sugar it is to hide his thoughts of vinegar.' She spoke to her husband. 'You have drunk more than enough so you will not refill your glass.'

'But—' Jaime began.

'It is right and proper that I slave away my life in the kitchen to serve delicious meals while you drink until you don't care if it is uncooked tripe on your plate? Fool that I am to continue to do so uncomplainingly!' She returned to the kitchen, where, to express her annoyance, she banged a saucepan a couple of times.

'Uncomplainingly?' Jaime muttered. He turned to Alvarez. 'I suppose you were trying to be funny?'

'Just honest.'

'Saying you didn't want a drink was being honest?'

'In a sense.'

He was silent for a while, then said, his tone less abrasive: 'Can you see what she's doing?'

Alvarez looked through the doorway into the kitchen. 'Working at the table.'

'And not acting like she might suddenly return here?'

'I shouldn't think so.'

Jaime poured himself another drink, spoke more loudly than intended. 'When you never know where you are, it drives a man to drink.'

There was a call from the kitchen. 'As my mother used to say, No man has to be driven to drink, he runs to it faster than a racehorse.'

'Your mother—' Jaime stopped abruptly as she appeared in the doorway.

'My mother?' The two words were diamond edged.

'She knew a lot of sayings.'

4

'She was well read and very intelligent, which is why she was so surprised I married you . . . The meal will soon be ready and one of you can lay the table.'

'Why can't the kids do that?'

'Even a father with half his wits still about him would have realised they were having supper with Teresa. As I told you they would be.'

'You never mentioned anything about them being out.'

'My mother remarked that while a man would hear a bottle being opened a kilometre away, he would be deaf to his wife's call for help from the next room.' She returned into the kitchen, head held high.

Alvarez drained his glass, reached across for the bottle and refilled it, since to honour a half-broken dedication was clearly nonsensical.

The phone rang.

Dolores hurried out of the kitchen, came to a stop and stared at them; when neither moved, she continued on into the front room. On her return, she said: 'As you could have found out, it is for you, Enrique.'

He stood, went through to the front room. The telephone was on a small table to the side of the open fireplace and he lifted the receiver.

'Jacobo here, Enrique. Sorry to bother you at home, but I've just had an Englishman come in, name of . . .' He had trouble pronouncing the name, so spelled it out. Lockhart. 'Lives in the urbanización El Pi de Sant Antoni . . . D'you know, I've heard that one of the larger houses there has been sold for over two hundred million. Two hundred million for a house! Are foreigners mega-wealthy or just stupid? I can remember when you could buy a castle for one million . . .'

'And a worker earned a peseta an hour. What about Señor Lockhart?'

'Came in with his wife. I reckon she eats powdered

5

glass when she's hungry. Reminded me of Raquel Nolla. Do you remember her?'

'No.'

'She was an only child and her dad had a nice finca, but she still found it difficult to grab a husband, which wasn't surprising, since she was sourer than an unripe caqui. In the end, Pedro married her and I remember him saying some time afterwards that if the finca had been ten times the size it was, he'd still have had the worst of the bargain.'

'Marry for money and you sell your soul.'

'Marry for love and you won't be left with anything to sell.'

'How about telling me what the Englishman's problem is?'

'In a hurry? No time for a chat?'

'Dolores is cooking llengua amb táperes and if I'm not at table when it's ready, she'll make a fuss.'

'My cousin's husband over at Llubi grows capers. Sometimes gives us some of the special, small ones, but never very many because he's a tight-fisted bastard. They do say you never meet a man from Llubi who takes his hand off the money in his pocket while he's talking to you.'

'What's Señor Lockhart's problem?'

'If you're asking me, it's his wife.'

'Apart from her.'

'From the look of him, he doesn't get much chance to be apart from her.'

'What's he shouting about?' Alvarez asked with impatient irritation.

'He's not really certain.'

'Then tell him to clear off and not bother anyone again until he is.'

'And forget all about us being told we've got to be

more pleasant to foreigners even when they're being bloody rude to us . . . ? He claims someone was mucking around outside their house. He didn't hear anything, but his wife did so he had to go outside to find out what was going on.'

'And what was?'

'There was nobody there.'

'This happened last night?'

'Wednesday night.'

'It's taken him until today to report it? Then he's not in a panic.'

'I reckon he wouldn't have bothered, despite his wife, if it hadn't been for meeting friends they had lunch with. One of them mentioned they thought they'd had someone messing around outside their house during the night and, when she learned that, the Lockhart woman told her husband he had to come and tell us.'

'Have there been any recent break-ins in the area?'

'None reported.'

'Then in the absence of anything more definite, there's nothing can be done.'

'That's up to you. But it's been logged by us so, if something comes of it, you'll need to be able to cover yourself.'

'Are you saying you've put the report down in the books when it doesn't add up to a legless grasshopper?'

'Had to.'

'Only to cover yourselves.'

'The name of the game.'

'Obviously, some people's game.' Alvarez said a somewhat abrupt goodbye. Selfishness had spread until it had become a plague. Thankfully, there was one small crumb of comfort to be gleaned. It had taken Lockhart two days to report the matter, so he could hardly complain if it took twelve hours for there to be any response.

Two

The urbanización El Pi de Sant Antoni lay between Llueso and Port Llueso. For many years, permission to build on the hill had been refused – any development was bound to conflict with the natural beauty of rock, pine trees, and scrub grass – but a change of council had ensured there were those who could understand that, in the modern world, aesthetic appreciation had little value, since it was only in the mind, while capital appreciation had great value since it was in the pocket. That more than one member of the new council was a builder or had an interest in a building firm was purely coincidental, whatever anyone said.

Alvarez braked to a stop in front of a bungalow halfway up the hill. Here, the slope was not steep, nevertheless, the cost of building must have been considerably greater than had the land been flat. He crossed to the steps, climbed these to the small porch. The wind could be strengthening and clouds had gathered and he recalled that the forecast had been for the fine, warm weather of the past few days to give way to much cooler temperatures and possibly rain. Rain would be welcome, except to the tourists, because it had been a dry winter and early spring. The island had been blessed with large reserves of underground water, but as demands inexorably increased, these had begun to prove insufficient; now, water often had to be imported from the Peninsula in tankers and it was said that small desalination plants were

8

under consideration, or evaluation, or construction; it was possible someone had decided they might be a good idea once the island became dry.

The front door, in a typical pattern of squares and oblongs, was opened by a middle-aged woman. She identified him as a local from his appearance and said in Mallorquin: 'What is it?'

'Cuerpo General de Policia. I should like to speak to Señor Lockhart if he is here?'

'Come in and I'll tell him.' She stood to one side so that he could enter the hall. 'Is something wrong, then?' she asked, with open curiosity.

'That's what I'm here to find out.'

Her expression showed that his answer irritated because it told her nothing. 'Wait here.'

She returned in less than a minute and told him to follow her. He passed through a rectangular sitting room, furnished with dull sensibility, and out on to the patio. Because of the slope of the hill, this was long and narrow, ending with a swimming pool that was covered. Beyond the corner of the building, there was a view of the bay. As he stared out at the water and the surrounding mountains, he wondered if heaven had anything more beautiful to offer . . .

'Well?' said Dulcie Lockhart.

The couple were seated in deckchairs and she had a light blanket over her knees. Anyone with more common sense than the average foreigner would have remained indoors. She had features which he had often noted in English ladies of a certain type – a long, thin face, sharp nose, tight mouth, and square chin to complement the air of virtuous superiority. She also used considerable make-up when none would have been appropriate, since one could not make a good heifer out of an old cow. 'Good morning, Señora.'

She acknowledged his presence with a nod of her head.

'Good morning, Señor.'

'Hullo, there. Glad you speak English. Makes things so much easier for us.' Lockhart was rotundly middle aged and visually remarkable only for a thin moustache which looked more like a mistake than a feature.

'I understand you have made a report to the Policia Local—'

'Yesterday,' she snapped. 'Yet it has taken until now for anyone to be bothered to take notice of it.'

'Señora, we are very busy and as there did not appear to be any great urgency—'

'That we might be murdered in our beds is not considered a matter of urgency?'

'Had there been such a credible fear on your part, Señora, I feel certain you would have reported the matter immediately.' She had referred to beds, not bed. He was hardly surprised. When younger, she would have submitted, not enjoyed. He waited for one of them to suggest he sat; there was a silence. 'Would you mind if I sit?'

Lockhart said by all means he should sit, but made no move to provide a chair. He pulled one clear of the table and sat. From the look on her face, he should have known his place was uncomplainingly to have remained standing. 'Perhaps you will tell me what happened?'

'We were in bed, watching television—'

She interrupted her husband. 'I was not watching, since I do not enjoy mindless programmes.'

'This was on Wednesday night—' Alvarez began.

'Tuesday night,' she snapped.

'I was told Wednesday. The officer must have misunderstood what you said to him.'

'Very likely. His English was a mishmash.'

Poor Jacobo, who had been trying his best! 'You were both in your beds and you, Señor, were watching television. Then what happened?'

She answered. 'Someone tried to interfere with the shutters near my bed.'

'When you say "interfere with", could you be more precise?'

'Scratching sounds were coming from them.'

'What did that make you think was happening?'

'Obviously someone was trying to force them apart.'

Alvarez addressed Lockhart. 'And what was your impression of the cause of the noise, Señor?'

She said sharply: 'I've already told you, he was watching the television.'

'You did not hear the noise, Señor?'

'Not until I told him to take off the headphones.'

'And then you heard the noise, Señor?'

'Well, I—' Lockhart began.

'He did,' she said.

'So what did you do, Señor?'

'I told my husband to put on a dressing gown so he could go outside and find out what was happening.'

'And you did that, Señor?'

'Of course he did.'

Ever the compliant husband. 'Did the noise continue?'

'It stopped as soon as he got out of bed,' she said.

'After which, Señor, you went outside to check?'

'He did.'

'Did you have a torch with you?'

'Naturally, he did.'

'Was there anyone outside?'

Lockhart was finally allowed to answer a question. 'I couldn't see anyone.'

Which no doubt was a great relief. 'Was there any sign to suggest someone had earlier been around the outside of the house?'

'What do you mean?' she asked.

'Something might have been knocked over . . .'

11

'You wish to call me a liar?'

'Of course not, Señora. Why on earth should you think . . . ?'

'Why did you say "suggest"?'

'I don't understand.'

'Then I will explain in as simple terms as possible. "Suggest" denotes there is room for doubt. There was no such room. Someone was trying to force the shutters in order to break into the house and steal anything of value, probably after having murdered us.'

'I don't think one should be quite so positive.' When he noticed her expression, he spoke more hurriedly. 'Were there lights on in any of the other rooms?'

'Certainly not. We take great care never to waste electricity when it is so exorbitantly expensive.'

'Then I have to say I very much doubt the intention could have been to break into the house to steal. A would-be intruder would not choose to enter a room that was presumably occupied; he would go for one that was in the dark and therefore unoccupied . . . There is something I need to mention. I understand that at the time you were not so certain of events as you have since become.'

'What leads you to that conclusion, which would be insolent if you really understood what you were saying?'

'You didn't report the incident immediately; in fact, not for three days.'

'Because experience showed that very little notice, if any, would have been taken of what we said . . .'

'Steady on, Dulcie,' Lockhart said nervously.

'I always speak my mind!'

He nodded, then looked nervously at her to determine whether she'd noticed.

'It was only after we learned the Meyers had suffered exactly as we had that there was any point in reporting the matter.'

'Because you felt that their evidence would lend weight to what you said?' Alvarez asked.

'When someone is made aware of a second and exactly similar incident it becomes very much more difficult for that person to be able to ignore the matter.'

'If Señor and Señora Meyers heard scratching on their shutters, were they in bed at the time?'

'They did not say. As a person used to observing social etiquette, I did not ask.'

Perhaps the word 'bed' disturbed her? He stood. 'I will make further enquiries, but first perhaps I might be shown the shutters we have been discussing?'

'For what reason?'

'I should like to see how high above the ground they are.'

'Why?'

'The height may give some indication of what was intended.'

'I have already told you.'

'Nevertheless, I should like to see them.'

She spoke to her husband. 'I suppose you'd better show the man.'

Lockhart stood. 'Would you come this way, Inspector?'

Alvarez followed Lockhart along the narrow concrete path, on the outward side of which small pockets of stunted grass and wild herb bushes grew on the rising rock face, and around the corner of the house, beyond which was the swimming pool. They came to a halt by the second set of shutters. 'This is it.'

There was nothing growing that was more than centimetres high close to the path so that the scratching noises could not have been caused by vegetation's being blown against the louvres. 'Señor, you were in bed, listening to the television through headphones?'

'Dulcie won't watch anything she thinks might get a

13

little close to the knuckle, if you know what I mean, and she hates hearing the speech if she's not watching, so she likes me to wear headphones, which means she can switch off the sound of the set and read in silence.'

'Then you couldn't hear any noise outside until you'd removed the headphones?'

'That's right.'

'But after removing them, you did hear scratching noises?'

'I know my wife told you . . .' He was silent for a moment. 'Sometimes I can't hear as well as I used to.'

'So did you hear any scratching noises?'

Lockhart nervously rubbed the back of his neck. 'She doesn't like being contradicted.'

'That is a common female complaint. You didn't hear anything?'

'It's so much easier to agree.'

'There might well have been the noise your wife has described, but you didn't hear it?'

Lockhart nodded.

'When you came out here that night, was there a wind?'

He thought for a moment. 'As I remember things, there was just a bit of a breeze; much less wind than we're getting now. There often is a breeze up here even when it's dead calm down by the sea.'

'Would you judge it to have been strong enough to blow around a bit of rubbish – like a piece of paper or a plastic bag?'

'You reckon it maybe was something like that? I wondered at the time and looked for something caught up in the shutters, but there wasn't anything. Just as there was nothing on the ground – Dulcie wants everything very tidy.' He looked up at the sloping, rock-strewn land. 'Had a spot of trouble last autumn with neighbours because of plastic bags. Dulcie asked them to have the manners to keep their rubbish on their own land, which seemed to annoy 'em – they're French, so they couldn't understand what all the fuss was about.'

'Did you suggest to the señora after you'd come out here that she might have been hearing a bit of rubbish being blown about by the light wind and that whatever it was had gone by the time you looked?'

'She was too certain it was more than that.'

Alvarez thought for a moment, then said: 'I need bother you no longer, Señor, except to ask where your friends, the Meyers, live?'

Lockhart couldn't remember the name of the house so carefully described its position.

They returned around the corner of the house and Alvarez said goodbye to Dulcie. Her response was a brief nod of the head before she pressed a bell set in the wall. 'The maid will see you out.'

He understood that he could not be allowed to pass through the house on his own.

Standing by his car, he enjoyed the view once more. The clouds were beginning to thin, an occasional shaft of sunshine speckled the mountains and water, and the threat of rain seemed to be past; a yacht with multi-coloured spinnaker was making for the heads; a pair of ospreys soared overhead; distance mellowed the ugly development in the port. Could he not say, Bliss was it on this day to be alive . . . ? That depended. He was going to have to speak to the Meyers. This would not have raised a problem had it not been Saturday morning. There was no way of judging how long it would take to question them, which raised the possibility of having his weekend shortened. He decided that not even the superior chief could claim it was essential to question the Meyers immediately.

Three

W hen Alvarez entered the kitchen on Monday morning, Dolores said, quite good naturedly: 'It's been an age since I called you.'

'It takes my bones a long time to get going.'

'You'd find they'd respond more quickly if you drank less at night.'

'Drink helps me sleep.'

'Especially when you should be awake.'

He watched her heat some milk. 'Tell me something. Would you say that, generally speaking, women have sharper hearing than men?'

'Why do you ask?'

'I've been talking to a wife who claims the other night she heard rustling or scratching at the shutters even though the windows were shut and her husband couldn't hear a thing.'

'Perhaps he was hoping that, if he said that, he wouldn't have to move and find out what was causing the noise.'

Why were women always ready to put the worst gloss on a man's actions?

She poured milk on to the grated chocolate in a mug, passed that across. 'There was no coca left, so I've freshened up half a barra in the oven.'

'You've not been out to the baker's?'

'You expect me to get up even earlier than I do in order to rush out to buy you fresh coca or an ensaimada?'

'Of course not,' he hastened to assure her, as he wondered why she had been so lazy.

She brought the barra out of the oven and placed it on the bread board, which she put on the table.

'Is there any membrilla?' he asked.

'In the usual place.' She waited, then sighed as she crossed to the cupboard above a working surface. She opened the right-hand door and brought out the slab of quince jelly on a plate. 'My mother used to say that when a man's at home, he loses the use of his legs.'

'Did she really say all the things you say she did?'

'You wish to call me a liar?'

'Of course not.'

'Then the question is a nonsense.' She put the plate down on the table. 'I must go upstairs now and clean the bedrooms.' She looked at the clock, in the shape of a plate, on the wall above the refrigerator. 'If you don't hurry, you'll be so late for work it'll be time to return for lunch.'

'The superior chief is in Madrid at a conference, so there's no rush.'

'Would you know how to rush if there were the need?' She left the kitchen.

He cut the length of barra in half and spread membrilla over one piece. There were times when Dolores was far too sharp (Jaime should have taken charge of their marriage from the beginning); she was irrationally prejudiced against a man enjoying a drink; she had not bothered to go to the panaderia that morning; she did not control her tongue . . . Yet one had to remember that she was a very good cook . . .

He finished his breakfast, checked the time and was vaguely surprised to discover just how late the morning had become. Did he conduct the small experiment he had in mind, or did he postpone that and go directly to the

guardia post? He made his way to the foot of the stairs
and called out.

'What is it?' Dolores shouted.

'Can you come down for a moment?'

'Why?'

'I need your help to check something.'

She descended the stairs, her face pricked with sweat
because, although the day was not warm, she had been
working at full speed and with all her energy.

'I'm going to move a plastic bag and a wodge of
newspaper between the louvres of one of the shutters
and I want you to say if you can hear anything inside.'

'Why on earth are you doing that?'

'It could help me decide whether to believe without
question something I've been told.'

He asked her to follow him into the kitchen, where he
picked out an empty plastic shopping bag from the many
she kept, and removed the centre page of yesterday's copy
of *El Diario*. 'Will you stay in here with the window
shut? I'm going to go out and rub this bag and newspaper
between the louvres of the shutter and I want you to tell
me what, if anything, you hear.'

He went through the back doorway into the small patio.
The shutters over the kitchen window were clipped back
and he released and closed them. In turn, he brushed the
bag and newspaper between the louvres of the right-hand
one with, as far as he could judge, the force a light wind
would impart.

He returned inside. 'What did you hear the first time?'

'Very little.'

'And the second?'

'The same.'

'If you hadn't been deliberately listening, do you think
you would have noticed the sounds?'

She thought before she answered. 'It certainly wasn't

loud enough either time to have drawn my attention if my mind had been on something else.'

'What if you had been reading a book?'

'I'm sure it wouldn't have done.'

'How would you describe the noise you did hear?'

The question confused her. 'It was just a noise.'

'A kind of rustling?'

'I suppose . . . Well, more a kind of scratching.'

'I wonder if she'd make that distinction?'

'Who?'

'An English lady with blue ice instead of blood in her veins.'

'She ignored your clumsy advances?'

'My advances? I'd have to be crazy to take one step in her direction.'

'You sound as if that could be true so perhaps you will not be making a fool of yourself for once . . . Is that all?'

'Yes, thanks.'

She hurried through to the sitting room and upstairs.

He sat and lit a cigarette. It seemed it would need a fairly brisk wind to move bag or paper sufficiently to create much noise; according to Lockhart, the wind that night had been light. Of course, Dulcie Lockhart might possess more acute hearing than Dolores (surely very unlikely, remembering the times Dolores heard what was not meant for her ears?). Suppose plastic or paper had been caught up between the louvres and moved around by the wind, what had become of it? Had the wind freed it before Lockhart went outside and blown it well away?

Would what the Meyers were going to tell him answer the questions or show them to be irrelevant? That depended on the circumstances and he wasn't going to learn what they had been until he spoke to them . . . Life was go, go, go.

*　　*　　*

He had been seated behind his desk for no more than ten minutes when the phone rang. Hopefully, he ignored it and it did stop. Only to restart almost immediately. Reluctantly, he reached out and lifted the receiver.

The woman at the other end of the line had only to speak a single word for him to identify her as Salas's secretary, a lady of more years than charm who sounded as if her mouth were full of plums.

'The superior chief wishes to speak to you.'

'Then if you'll give me his number in Madrid, I'll phone him.'

'He is here.'

'I gathered he was at a conference.'

'He returned last night, since the conference ended early. Wait.'

A badly organised conference . . .

'Alvarez.'

'Señor?'

'Where have you been? I've been trying to get hold of you all morning.'

The morning had hardly begun. 'I had to conduct an experiment before coming to the office . . .'

'What experiment?'

'I needed to discover how much noise a plastic bag or a piece of newspaper would make when brushed between the louvres of a shutter.'

'What is the point of that?'

'It's an odd sort of a case . . .'

'Which will have become very much odder the moment you took charge. To what case are you referring?'

'An English couple called Lockhart claim that someone tried to break into their house. Actually, it's much more her claim, since he never really heard anything, and it is a bungalow, not a house . . .'

'Refrain from wasting my time with irrevelancies.'

'But I think it may very well be important that it is a bungalow, not a house, Señor. If it were a house with bedrooms upstairs, the shutters of a bedroom would be out of reach of the ground.'

'You think it necessary repeatedly to state the obvious?'

'I was trying to explain why it is important that the house is a bungalow.'

'I was under the impression that only a moment ago you were endeavouring to point out that they were totally dissimilar.'

'I was using the word "house" then in the general rather than the particular sense . . .'

'It would make my life more bearable if you could restrict yourself to common sense.'

'The Lockharts were in their bedroom, in bed, when they heard sounds coming from the shutters of one of the windows. At least, she heard them, but he didn't because he was watching the television and listening through headphones so that she could read in peace. She wasn't watching because she claims she dislikes any programme that is even the slightest bit risqué . . .'

'You find that a remarkable attitude?'

'Perhaps a little odd in this day and age.'

'Both my wife and I find much of what is shown on television to be disgusting. Morals are being forced along an ever-descending path. As Maldonardo wrote, "Purity of thought separates man from beast." I doubt you read Maldonardo.'

'I'm afraid not, Señor.'

'He also wrote, "The inquiring mind seeks light, the stultified one is content with the penumbra."'

Maldonardo sounded like a man who considered a feast to be bread as well as water.

'It would not come amiss if you took the time to read at

least a few of his writings . . . Now kindly make a proper report, omitting all irrelevancies.'

'The Lockharts were in bed when she heard sounds coming from the shutters; she was convinced someone was trying to break into the bedroom. Of course, this was unlikely, since that was the only lighted room in the house – the bungalow – and a would-be intruder would surely choose a room in darkness even if he didn't have the experience to wait until all the lights were out and he could reasonably assume the occupants were asleep. She made her husband remove his headphones and listen; he could hear nothing, although he suggested he could . . .'

'Why?'

'She's that type of woman.'

'I don't understand what you're saying.'

'She enjoys being contradicted even less than most women . . .'

'Refrain from such unwarranted comments.'

'At her insistence, he went outside and examined the land with the help of a torch and saw nobody or anything which might have caused the rustling or scratching noise. Whilst someone might have been trying to break in, as I said earlier—'

'Then there is no need to repeat yourself.'

'It was possible the sounds had been caused by something agitated by the light wind that was blowing at the time. To test the latter possibility, I carried out an experiment – which is why I was a little late arriving at the office. I scrumpled up a plastic bag and a sheet of newspaper and in turn pushed them between the louvres of a shutter and got Dolores – my cousin, though in fact she is rather a distant cousin—'

'I am uninterested in your family tree.'

'Only in one branch of it?'

'What the devil are you talking about now?'

'I asked Dolores to tell me what she heard. The answer was, in both cases, very little. It seems probable, in fact, that she only heard them at all because she was expecting to hear something . . . You know how it is: if there's reason to expect a result, one may persuade oneself that one is receiving it when there should be doubt one really is.'

'I know I am beginning to doubt it possible to discover any relevance in almost all of what you say. Did or did not someone try to break into this bungalow?'

'I don't think so. But I accept that it is possible someone did.'

'Would you care to suggest a third alternative; perhaps even a fourth?'

'What I mean is—'

'I do not have the time to allow you to attempt an explanation. At what time last night did this happen?'

'I'm not certain of the exact time. And it was Wednesday . . . No, Tuesday night.'

'I trust you do not feel too rushed, making your report a week later?'

'I was only informed of the facts on Saturday. Señora Lockhart, despite her present certainty, was clearly far less positive earlier and did not report the incident at the time.'

'Why not?'

'She says that in the circumstances she believed little notice would be taken.'

'She was aware that you would be in charge of the case?'

'On Friday, Señor and Señora Lockhart had dinner with friends and these friends mentioned they had experienced a similar incident and it was this fact which decided the Lockharts to speak to the Policia Local. I can't be certain

how similar this other incident was, since I haven't yet
spoken to the Meyers . . .'

'Why not?'

'It is my intention to do so this morning as soon as I
have completed all the work that should be considered
more important.'

'Señora Lockhart spoke to you on Saturday?'

'Yes, Señor.'

'What prevented you from questioning the Meyers
then?'

'It was the weekend . . .'

'You refrained from carrying out your duty merely
because of that?'

Alvarez wondered how he could have been so stupid
as to name the correct days? 'Señor, I drove to their
house Saturday afternoon and twice on Sunday, but on
each occasion there was no one there. They must have
gone away or perhaps they have a yacht and were sailing.'
The odds had to be that Salas would never bother to try
to establish the truth.

'Why haven't you found out if they are back this
morning?'

'As I mentioned earlier . . . But you will not wish me
to repeat myself.'

'What did you mention?'

'I conducted my experiment at home and then hurried
to the office to deal with any important matter which had
arisen. I was about to leave here to visit the Meyers' house
– of course, it may be a bungalow – when you rang me.'

'You will report to me as soon as you have spoken
to them.'

'Yes, Señor.'

The connection was cut.

Alvarez replaced the receiver. He wondered if Maldonardo had ever written, A quick tongue can make up for

a slow mind? He reached down to the right-hand bottom drawer of the desk and brought out a bottle of Soberano and a glass. He poured himself a generous drink. The phone rang. He swore.

'The superior chief wishes to speak to you,' said the secretary with a plum voice.

He drank. Whatever the problem, its solution would undoubtedly be made easier by the golden touch of the brandy.

Minutes passed, then Salas said: 'After speaking to you, I received a call from England, requesting our assistance. Unfortunately, in acceding to their demand, you will become involved. In order to avoid anything which might present the Cuerpo in an indifferent light, you will provide all the help that is called for without comment or, more particularly, any suggestion. Is that quite clear?'

'Yes, Señor.'

'We are to be advised later of Detective Inspector Fenton's date and time of arrival. I will meet him, since initial impressions may help to lighten later ones.'

A visiting policeman inevitably meant extra work. 'Señor, might it not be a good idea for a senior officer to work with him rather than me?'

'Of course. Unfortunately, due to administrative problems, that will not be possible.'

'Then I—'

'Will try your best to act the part of a competent member of the Cuerpo. Detective Inspector Fenton is coming here to talk to Señor Wade, who lives near Llueso. He was involved in a murder and fraud case, as yet unsolved, and we are particularly asked to note . . . Do you consider yourself capable of noting anything?'

'Of course, Señor.'

'We are asked to note that Wade is not a suspect in the case and the only reason for talking to him is the hope he might be prompted into recalling some further fact which will enable progress to be made in the case.'

'It sounds as if there won't really be any need for me to be with the English inspector when he talks to Señor Wade.'

'I obviously have to remind you that when an officer from a foreign force makes enquiries here, he must be in the company of a member of the Cuerpo.'

'But from a practical point of view, since this isn't strictly speaking an investigation . . .'

'It is a sign of incompetency to seek to evade rules.'

Alvarez drained the glass. The English detective was certain to provide uneasy company. He'd expect to work through the afternoon; he would demand every T be crossed, every I dotted; he'd look with distaste at a dish of snails, octopus cooked in its own ink, fried bull's testicles . . .

Four

A lvarez drove up the Laraix valley, past the elaborate gateway which marked a manorial estate that had been decaying until bought by a German who was spending a fortune restoring it, turned left into a narrow lane which passed through land that had once been intensively cultivated, but was now largely left fallow or tended by foreigners who put a great deal of effort – someone else's – into cultivating flowers and lawns instead of vegetables and fruit . . .

He was from farming stock and, should he ever win the lottery, would resign from the Cuerpo (having told Salas, as Maldonardo surely had written, that wealth separated the rich from the poor), buy a large finca with at least one deep well, and rear animals and grow crops, satisfying an inner longing. But he would not be harking back too far in time. In the past, farming had been a time of hunger, of illness without the means to consult a doctor. Ironically, when the Moors had occupied the island, peasants had been allowed to own their own land; after the Repartiment, when Christianity had returned, the land had been seized and divided between the nobles and the Church. A peasant could only own land if a large landowner would sell it to him; otherwise, he was a tenant without rights who had to share all he produced with his landlord. For centuries there had been hunger and misery, with accommodation often no more than a primitive hut; if one were lucky, one lived on beans, cabbage, olives, bread, and perhaps dried apricots; if one were unlucky, one died . . . He would farm, but the land would be his, the crops would be his; the house would be renovated, dry, cool in the summer, hot in the winter; he would eat meat and drink the best Rioja, and should he fall ill there would be skilled doctors and surgeons to help him . . .

He reached a circle of shade trees – planted a century before in the belief they would avert the Evil Eye? – and immediately past them turned into a short drive which ended in a turning circle. The bungalow was recently built and typical in that, although there was only the one floor level, there were several roof levels. He left the car and climbed two steps to the small porch, on the walls of which winter pansies were growing in pots.

The door was opened by an elderly man who held himself tall and whose clipped moustache and air of confident self-satisfaction suggested a service background. Alvarez introduced himself.

'Is there some trouble?' Meyers asked. His manner suggested he would cope with anything short of a pre-emptive atomic strike.

'I am here to ask you for your help, Señor.'

'Come on in.'

He stepped into the hall. On one wall was the large painting of a wooden warship, sails holed by shot, guns belching flame and smoke, injured and dead men lying on deck, naively executed yet offering the awful tension of battle which a more professional work might have missed.

'We reckoned it's just about warm enough to be on the patio, so we're out there.'

They went through the sitting room, divided by an open archway from the dining room, and out to a covered patio; beyond this was a swimming pool.

A woman was seated at the circular glass and bamboo

28

patio table. Meyers said: 'This is Inspector Alvarez, a detective who hopes we can help him.'

'Should we hope we can't?' She smiled at Alvarez. 'How d'you do.'

He had learned that nothing could more quickly arouse an English person's amused contempt than to react as a Mallorquin and treat the greeting as a question and list all one's ailments of the past months. 'Good morning, Señora.'

'What kind of help are you seeking?'

Meyers said briskly: 'First things first. Inspector, am I allowed to offer you a drink?'

'Indeed, Señor.'

'What will it be, then?'

'Perhaps I might have a little coñac with just ice?'

'Of course . . . Eugenie, will you have your usual?'

'Yes, please.'

'Have a seat, Inspector, whilst I organise things.'

As Meyers returned indoors, Alvarez sat and stared across the valley at the sharply crested mountains which looked attractively rugged in sunny weather, yet gathered a sense of foreboding when the clouds were heavy. 'It is very beautiful here, Señora.'

'We think so. But we know it's not everyone's cup of tea. We have friends who say that if they lived here, they'd feel penned in . . . My husband said you hope we can help you. Is it something to do with our residencias?'

'It is nothing to do with them.'

'I just wondered because we've applied and they're asking for so many papers, it's all become very confusing.'

'Our bureaucrats are dedicated to confusion.'

She smiled. 'Isn't it the same in every country? Eric decided to apply without getting help from a gestor. He won't admit this, but I'm sure he now knows that was the mistake of the year! I thought the Common Market was meant to make it possible to live wherever one wanted without any trouble, but it obviously isn't like that in practice. I suppose modern governments don't like people to have too much freedom.'

Meyers returned, carrying a silver salver on which were three glasses, an ice bucket, and a small bowl of crisps. 'I'll leave you to add what ice you want, Inspector.' He put the salver down on the table, passed one glass to his wife, one to Alvarez, sat.

There were a pair of silver tongs on the side of the ice bucket and Alvarez used these to pick out three ice cubes. It would have been much easier and quicker with his fingers. Sophisticated manners were time-consuming and largely unproductive.

'I was asking the inspector if his visit comes as a result of our application for residencias,' she said. 'Apparently, it doesn't.'

Accepting the hint, Alvarez explained the reason. 'I'm here because of something I understand was discussed when you and your husband were having a meal in the company of Señor and Señora Lockhart.'

'What kind of something?'

'It was a subject raised by one of them.'

'Then it was surely she,' Meyers said. 'He's only allowed to speak to agree with her.'

'You're being rather unkind,' she said.

'When one's talking about other people, the truth is rarely kind . . . So, Inspector, what did one of the Lockharts talk about which so interests you?'

'You had said one night you were in bed when you heard sounds which made you think someone was trying to break into the house.'

'Partly accurate, partly inaccurate. One of us mentioned hearing a noise and wondered what had caused it. Dulcie immediately said the same thing had happened to them and she proceeded to make high drama out of it – people trying to break into their place and she was so brave, she only screamed very quietly . . .'

'Really, Eric, you can be quite impossible!' She turned. 'Inspector, what happened is that conversation was proving rather difficult . . .'

'Because our hostess at the time suffers from the knack of inviting people who don't get on well together,' Meyers said.

'She tries her best.'

'Most of the problems of the world are caused by persons trying their best . . . Why else should I have ended up seated next to Dulcie throughout a five course meal?'

'You should learn to be tolerant.' She spoke once more to Alvarez. 'Conversation had become very laboured and, to try to move things along, I casually mentioned how one night we'd heard a strange noise when we were in bed.'

'When was this?' Alvarez asked.

'A fortnight ago?' She looked at her husband.

'More like three weeks,' Meyers said.

'Will you tell me what happened when you were in your bedroom?'

'After you explain why you're interested?'

'Because Señora Lockhart believes someone tried to break into her house, I have to investigate the possibility, but there is some doubt that she was right. If there has been a similar incident, then obviously it is far more likely she was.'

'No one was trying to break in here.'

'You can't be that certain,' she said.

'I can if, unlike Dulcie, I use my God-given sense. If someone's trying to break in through the shutters, he's going to make a sight more noise than we heard.'

'The noise was loud enough for you to hear clearly, Señor?'

'I may be old enough to remember when there was freedom of speech at home, but I'm not yet deaf.'

'How would you describe the noise?'

For the first time, Meyers appeared less than certain. 'Bit difficult, really.'

She said: 'I thought it was something rubbing on the wood.'

'Were the windows shut?'

'Yes, since it had been quite cold all day. In fact, we had the central heating on.'

'And you were both in bed at the time?'

'We were.'

'Who first heard the noise?'

'I did.'

'What did you judge could be causing it?'

'I couldn't think and neither could Eric when I told him to listen.'

Alvarez turned to Meyers. 'What did you do, having listened to the noise?'

'Got out the niblick.'

'Niblick?'

'An old fashioned golf club, used for getting out of a bunker. These days, they call it a number eight or nine iron. Doesn't sound half as effective.'

'You thought there was someone outside, even though you didn't suppose he was trying to break into the house?'

'Decided it was some sort of animal and a lofting stroke with the niblick would persuade it to bother some-one else.'

'So you went outside?'

'Of course.'

'Was there anyone in sight?'

'Not a soul.'

'Did you hear a car or a mobylette start up and drive away?'

'Everything was quiet except for the usual barking dogs.'

'Did you notice if any rubbish that might have been agitated by the wind to make the noise you heard had been caught between the louvres of a shutter?'

'Didn't think to do that at the time. And, as I remember things, there wasn't any wind.'

'You said you were both in bed when you first heard the noise – would the rest of the house have been in darkness?'

'Yes.'

'Have you heard anyone else mention this kind of thing happening to them?'

'I haven't, no.' Meyers looked at his wife. 'Have you?'

'I don't think so.'

'So what was it all about?' he asked Alvarez.

'It seems most likely, Señor, that something was caught up in the shutters.'

'As I said, there was no wind.'

'It can be very fitful.'

'And provide a useful answer!'

'Eric!' she said, alarmed by her husband's comment.

'That's all right, the inspector looks to be a man with a sense of humour.'

'I think a sense of forbearance would be more apposite.'

'Señora,' Alvarez said, 'the señor is right when he thinks I do not know what was happening. But I agree it is most unlikely anyone was trying to break into the house.'

'I suppose one can accept that as something of a relief.'

He drained his glass. 'Thank you for your help.' He stood.

'You haven't time to enjoy the other half?' Meyers asked.

'Perhaps, Señor, I am not so very rushed.' He sat once more.

Five

Alvarez awoke and stared up at the ceiling. One of life's gifts was the siesta; one of life's tragedies was that every siesta but the last had to end . . .

There was a call from downstairs. 'Enrique, it's after five.'

He looked at his watch and saw that indeed it was ten past five. Time was perverse – it sprouted wings when one willed it to saunter slowly. He reluctantly climbed off the bed, put on trousers and shirt.

As he entered the kitchen, she said: 'You haven't time for coffee.'

'Why ever not?'

'You're supposed to be back at the post long since.'

'The hours are flexible.'

'For you, they are double-jointed . . . Are you saying you do want coffee despite the time?'

He sat at the table and stared through the window. 'It's raining!'

'As you could have discovered much earlier.'

'The farmers will be pleased.'

'I doubt it.' She filled the base of the small machine with water, spooned ground coffee into the holder. 'Farmers are seldom pleased.'

'That's hardly surprising. So much over which they have no control can go wrong. Theirs is a hard life.'

'No harder than mine, that's for sure. When can I spend

half an hour leaning on a gate, talking?' She screwed the two parts of the machine together, put it on top of the stove and lit the gas. 'Do you want something to eat now, even though you ate enough for two at lunch?'

'When you cook escaldums de gallina, a man would have to be a shrivelled vegetarian not to enjoy his meal.' Her pleased expression showed his compliment had been accepted. As well it should have been. Chicken, egg, almonds, olive oil, garlic, parsley, saffron and salt had been transformed into ambrosia.

'What do you want, then?'

'I wouldn't mind a small slice of coca.'

'A "small" slice?'

'Maybe medium-sized.'

She laughed sarcastically.

Twenty minutes later, after draping a mackintosh over his shoulders, he left the house and hurried along the pavement to his car, parked fifty metres away. He settled behind the wheel, started the engine, switched on the wipers. The rain was heavy and might well become of tropical intensity, when small waterfalls would pour down the mountains, village streets would become awash as the drainage proved insufficient, fields would be flooded, and torrentes would flow again, some with dangerous intensity. . . And, no doubt, farmers would complain that their crops were being washed away.

To his annoyance he was unable to park near the post which meant he had a five minute walk through the downpour. The cabo on desk duty had a juvenile mind and said he looked as if it were raining. A smart reply only occurred to him after he'd reached his room.

He leaned back in the chair and stared at the telephone. He was going to have to phone Salas unless he could summon up a good reason for putting off the call. None occurred to him.

'Yes?' said the secretary, her abruptness carefully fashioned on her boss's manner.

'Inspector Alvarez speaking. I'd like a word with the superior chief.'

After several minutes – how better to signal one's seniority and superiority than to leave one's inferior waiting? – Salas said: 'Yes?'

'Señor, I have spoken to Señor and Señora Meyers and asked them—'

'How do you expect me to know what you're talking about when you merely quote names?'

'I didn't want to waste your time telling you something a second time . . .'

'Are you endeavouring to be insolent?'

'Of course not, Señor, but it was only this morning that you said—'

'Make a proper report.'

He carefully repeated all he had said earlier before detailing his meeting with the Meyers.

'What are your conclusions?'

'At first glance, there seem to be too many inconsistencies to come to any.'

'Since you are handling the inquiry, that is to be expected.'

'In each case there were scratching or rustling noises coming from the shutters, just loud enough to draw attention, nowhere near loud enough to suggest someone was trying to break into the bedroom. Would an intruder pick the one room that was obviously occupied? I think not. In both cases, was a piece of rubbish caught up between the louvres of the shutters and agitated by the wind? Neither party saw any rubbish in or near the shutters; Señor Lockhart says there was only a very light wind and Señor Meyers is certain there was no wind. So where does that leave us?'

'Well?'

'I think it is important to note that in each case the house was a bungalow . . .'

'You will not repeat that nonsense.'

'It is important to note that both buildings were bungalows.'

'Why should that be significant?'

'The bedrooms are on ground level.'

'What if that is so?'

'A person can see inside.'

'Ridiculous! With the shutters closed, that is impossible.'

'Not really.'

'Perhaps you will explain how one looks through wood?'

'Señor, if one gets down on one's knees, because all the louvres are angled downwards, one can look up between them and see the upper part of the room inside. Further, it is possible by using a kind of miniature periscope to see the lower part of the room as well.'

'I find it truly disheartening, as well as obnoxious, that one of my inspectors should not only possess such knowledge, but be prepared to boast about that fact.'

'Not boasting, Señor, but mentioning because it is necessary to do so.'

'The excuse of every purveyor of filth.'

'One reason for viewing a room in such a fashion would be to survey the interior with the intention of carrying out a break-in at a later date. But would anyone do that at night time and when he can be certain the bedroom is occupied, since the light is on? Much more likely is . . .' Alvarez became silent, reluctant to arouse Salas's over-developed sense of prudery.

'Is what?'

'The intention is to see the occupants of the bedroom.'

'What possible motive could there be for that?'

'The hope they'll be . . .You know.'

'I do not.'

'They might be . . .'

'Is it being unrealistic to ask you to speak coherently?'

'I think we're probably dealing with a peeping Tom.'

'What?'

'A man who gets pleasure from—'

'I am unfortunately aware of how such a person is said to gain his perverted pleasure. It seems there are also those who gain equally perverted pleasure from unwarrantedly discussing such matters.'

'Señor, when one studies the facts, only one conclusion makes sense.'

'To a certain type of mind, no doubt,' snapped Salas, before he slammed down the receiver.

With the swift change in weather which so often occurred on the island, on Saturday the sky was cloudless and the day was hot. Although the tourist season was not yet in full swing, bars and restaurants had raised their prices, memento shops had opened, straw Tahiti sunshades were set out on the beaches, and the vendor who had pedalled his ice cream cabinet along the front for very many years gratefully observed the first topless sunbather.

Alvarez leaned back in the chair, rested his feet on the desk, and closed his eyes. Life was as uneven as a roller coaster, so the wise man made the best of good times. His weekend lay ahead. After lunch, he would enjoy a prolonged siesta, untroubled by the need to return to work. On Sunday morning, he would awaken and lie in bed, enjoying to the full the pleasure of knowing he did not have to get up until he wished . . .

The phone rang, the plum-voiced secretary told him to wait, and eventually Salas said: 'Detective Inspector

Fenton is arriving at eleven fifteen tomorrow morning. Unfortunately, I cannot greet him.'

Because he would be playing golf?

'So I have detailed Comisario Garau to do so. Garau will drive him to the Hotel Gran Sol, in Port Llueso, where you will be waiting to greet him. Your task is to make certain he is not bothered by any problem. Thankfully, since everything is straightforward, there should be no call for you to show any initiative.'

'Señor?'

'What?'

'Why is Inspector Fenton coming here?'

There was a long pause before Salas said: 'Incredibly, you still have the capacity to astonish me. How few days is it since I informed you in great detail why he was arriving on the island?'

Memory lacked all consistency. A moment before, Alvarez could remember nothing about the inspector's visit, suddenly he could recall all he had been told. He tried to divert Salas's annoyance. 'What I really meant was, I wonder why the inspector is spending the time and money to come here when he could have saved both by speaking to Señor Wade over the phone or asking me to talk to him.'

'As to the first possibility, even you must be aware that direct contact is always likely to be more productive; as to the second, he must consider himself fortunate that it never occurred to him.' The line went dead.

Alvarez slowly replaced the receiver. Only moments ago, he had been enumerating the coming pleasures of the weekend; now he was condemned to working on Sunday morning. Life was a roller coaster that had only one short climb to a dozen precipitous descents.

Six

Alvarez looked at his watch, then across the reception area of the Hotel Gran Sol at the main entrance. If they did not arrive very soon, he would be late home for lunch . . .

He crossed to the desk and spoke to the reception clerk. 'The airport did say the plane was on time?'

'They did, so it can't have been more than half an hour late.'

'Are the roads solid with traffic?'

'Haven't heard they are and the coaches are getting through OK.'

'It's beginning to seem I may have to eat locally. There's a restaurant here, isn't there? What's the food like?'

'Never had to try it myself, but only a few tourists complain so it must be good enough for most of them.'

He wondered what Dolores had prepared? Oblades amb bolets? His mind conjured up the subtle taste of turbot, mushrooms, onion . . .

The portly figure of Garau entered the foyer and immediately behind him came a tall, lean man dressed in a suit. This sartorial elegance prompted Alvarez to remember he had forgotten to change his shirt before he'd left the house . . .

Garau imperiously beckoned. Short men liked to give

the impression of great authority, he thought ironically as he crossed the tiled floor, because they thought it compensated for their lack of centimetres.

'Detective Inspector Fenton,' Garau said, mispronouncing each word.

Fenton's handshake was firm.

'It is a pleasure to welcome you here,' Alvarez said with formal politeness.

'It's great to be here, especially on such a day!'

'You have been having bad weather?'

'Yes, even by our standards . . . I don't mind admitting I've been suffering visions of having to use my kitchen Spanish, so it's a great relief to find you speak such good English!'

'Thank you, Señor.' A compliment or an unguarded expression of surprise that a scruffy Mallorquin detective could adequately speak his own language, let alone anyone else's? Nationality often marked a man. That long, lean face, Roman nose, and square, firm chin were typically English. A nation of people who firmly believed democracy needed to be carefully graded . . . In one of those moments of self-honesty which could be so irritating, Alvarez realised he was allowing his resentment at having to work on a Sunday fashion his judgment. There was little, if any, hint of a sense of autocratic superiority in Fenton's features; indeed, even in repose, his mouth suggested humour. Alvarez's tone was considerably warmer when he said: 'I hope the journey was pleasant?'

'Not too bad, since it was short. I've long legs so that flying always fills my mind with pictures of sardines carefully lined up in a tin . . . Am I right in thinking you'll be helping me?'

'Yes, Señor.'

'That's good. And incidentally, the name's Hugh.'

41

Garau impatiently spoke in Castilian. 'You have arranged a meeting with Señor Wade?'

'Not yet, but I'll do that before I leave here so that I can tell our guest in good time.'

'What do you mean, "leave here"?'

'I'll be returning home for lunch.'

'Have you not understood that it is your job to extend every courtesy to our foreign colleague? You are to invite Señor Fenton to have lunch at a restaurant as a gesture of welcoming hospitality. Naturally, you will not choose anywhere expensive; you can explain you are certain he would prefer the local dishes found in a restaurant patronised by Mallorquins. And I warn you, the expenses you submit will be closely monitored.'

'I don't order a bottle of Vega Sicilia?'

Garau did not find that amusing. He tried to speak to Fenton in English, soon gave up and told Alvarez to translate – The full resources of the Cuerpo were at the service of the distinguished member of the world-famous New Scotland Yard . . .

'Actually, I'm in a county force,' Fenton said.

. . . a world-famous county force. Garau shook hands with Spanish vigour as he said goodbye. He left.

'If you book in,' Alvarez said, 'then if you like we can have a meal.'

'That's fine by me. I had to have a very early breakfast and the food on the plane looked even more plasticky than usual, so I gave it my best.' He picked up his suitcase before Alvarez could offer to do so and strode across to the reception desk.

There were two clerks on duty and Alvarez spoke to the younger one while the elder dealt with Fenton's registration. 'Do you know if Mendisol has reopened?'

'I don't think the renovation's been finished yet.'

'What about La Gavinat?'

'That's open, but if you're thinking of eating there, the chef left last week after a row with Pedro.'

'How could Pedro let him go? He is an artist in the kitchen!'

'He wanted a rise in salary and Pedro refused it, being so mean he'd underpay a guardian angel.'

'Where's the chef gone?'

'I've not heard.'

Alvarez noticed that Fenton was replacing his passport in an inside coat pocket and he moved along the counter. 'Is everything in order?'

'It is.'

'Then I think before we eat – and there may be a problem to decide where to go – I should phone Señor Wade and ask when it would be most convenient to visit him. So if you would like to go through to the lounge and order a drink, I will have a word with him.'

'I'll first go up to my room and freshen up.'

As Fenton crossed to the lift, Alvarez asked the younger clerk if he might use the phone for a local call. He brought out from his trouser pocket the piece of paper on which he'd written Wade's address and telephone number, dialled . . .

A man answered. 'Señor Wade?'

'Speaking.'

'Inspector Alvarez of the Cuerpo General de Policia. I should like to explain that Inspector Fenton has arrived from England and wishes to speak with you and—'

'About the murder of my wife?'

'I believe so.'

'And I hoped to God, never again . . . What's he want to speak about?'

'I cannot say, Señor.'

'I've told the police time and time again all I can remember.'

'Memory can be strange . . .'

'Bloody cruel!'

Years ago, he had had to learn that.

'I suppose I'll have to talk to him.' It was a statement, not a question.

'When will be convenient?'

'"Convenient" is hardly the word I'd use . . . Six o'clock this evening, here. Will that do?'

'Indeed, Señor. And thank you.'

After saying goodbye, Alvarez replaced the receiver. Life could be unbearably cruel. Having fought through the mental agony of his wife's murder, Wade had reasonably expected that he would be left to try to forget; because of the attempt by the police to learn something more that would enable them to identify the murderers, agonising memories must inevitably be re-ignited . . .

He made his way through to the lounge, a large room furnished in typically impersonal and unimaginative style, and sat at one of the tables; only two other people, an elderly couple, were present. Moments later, Fenton joined him. A waiter asked them what they'd like to drink – Fenton ordered a gin and tonic, Alvarez a brandy.

After the waiter left, Alvarez brought a pack of cigarettes out of his pocket and offered it.

'I gave up some years ago, thanks to my wife.' Fenton smiled. 'Not that at the time I would have said "thanks".'

'Do you mind if I smoke?'

'Of course not.'

'I often promise myself I'll stop.' Alvarez tapped out a cigarette. 'But promises to oneself are so easy to forget.' He struck a match and lit the cigarette. 'I have spoken to Señor Wade and we are to meet him at his house at six this evening.'

'That'll be a meeting the poor devil won't be looking forward to.'

'He said as much.'

'Justice often hurts the victim almost as much as the criminal; in truth, sometimes more.'

They had lunch in a restaurant at which Alvarez had not eaten for a long time, since it catered primarily for tourists, but Fenton had expressed a wish to be able to look out at the bay as he ate. Alvarez was pleasantly surprised by the quality of the food and glad that he had ordered a bottle of Domecq Domain to accompany it (the owner had agreed to list it on the bill at half its true cost, adding the other half to the main dish Fenton had ordered).

The waiter asked if they'd like coffee.

'You'll have a coñac with it?' Alvarez suggested.

'I've already drunk far more than I usually do.'

'As we say, that is when one drinks a little more.' Alvarez ordered two cortados and two brandies. As the waiter left, he said: 'I thought you might like to drive up into the mountains and see the other island; the part that's still largely untouched by tourism? Here, it is a totally different world from sixty years ago, up there it is much the same. Tourist buses pass along the roads, but only to get to somewhere else; no one builds shops, bars, restaurants, night clubs. A man can still find solitude.'

'Is that something you often seek?'

'Perhaps not as often as I should like.'

'You obviously love that part of the island!'

He tried to explain why the mountains meant so much to him. There was the emptiness, the fantastic shapes of weathered rock faces, the sharp crests which seemed to be trying to slice the sky, the pockets of fertile soil in small, hidden valleys which offered the sharpest possible contrast to the bleak infertility around them; there were the inhabitants of this wilderness, the feral goats who had learned to defy gravity, the genets now driven back to the remotest areas, the black vultures of majestic flight whose lives depended on death . . .

The waiter brought the coffees and the brandies.

As Fenton stirred sugar into his small cup of nearly dark coffee, he said: 'Do you know Charles Wade?'

'I have never met him.'

'One can't be hit harder by life than he was.'

Alvarez poured brandy into his coffee.

'One needs a very macabre imagination to think up a crueller death than his wife suffered . . . You'll know all too well how in our job we have to keep our emotions on hold because becoming emotionally involved with victims can only lead to disaster. But when I looked down at her body and saw how it had been scarred by red-hot pincers, I became so emotionally involved I swore I'd identify the bastards and see them slung into jail for life.' He cupped the small balloon glass of brandy in his hand. 'It's easy enough to swear an oath; the difficult task is to keep it.'

'Haven't you turned up much useful evidence?'

'I pride myself on being a good detective, but I've worked myself into the ground to get precisely nowhere. To be frank, my visit here is a last attempt to avoid having to admit defeat. Had a hell of a job getting the expense people to authorise the cost of the visit. Was I very close to solving the case? Could I guarantee I would learn vital information . . . ? They wouldn't have asked those questions if they'd stared down on that scarred body and tried, but failed, not to imagine the pain . . .'

Here was a very different person from the one Alvarez had initially – under the influence of resentment – presumed him to be. 'Why was she tortured?'

'As security officer at a high street bank, she possessed the information the villains needed to work their scam.

When there are millions of pounds on offer, compassion is a non-starter even if it was ever there.'

'Were millions of pounds stolen?'

'They were. So, somewhere, men are leading a luxurious life because they were prepared to torture a woman and then throttle the life out of her. We're civilised? The great myth.'

Alvarez braked the car to a halt. 'That's Laraix monastery down there.' He pointed.

Fenton stared down at the distant complex of buildings surrounded by pine trees and set in the broad valley that was ringed by some of the highest mountains on the island. 'What's its history?'

'Jaume the First reconquered the island and those inhabitants of Arabic origin had either to leave or become Christians. The young boy of such a couple saw a luminous light under a bush and, when he investigated, found a small wooden Madonna. He carried it back to his parents who, mindful that proselytes were advised never to miss the chance to prove their dedication to their adopted religion, showed it to a priest. The priest set up the statue on a makeshift altar, convinced that news of the miracle would bring people to pray to her – and ensure prosperity for a region which until then had suffered only poverty. The next morning, the Madonna had vanished, to be found later under the same bush. When carried back to the altar, she again returned herself to the bush. Eventually, it dawned on people that she wished to stay where she had been found and a small chapel was built over the bush. In time, the chapel became the monastery. For centuries, the faithful have come from all parts of the island, and many from the Peninsula, to pray . . . It is strange that when holy statues were found and removed to more luxurious surroundings – as seemed the respectful thing to do – they invariably took themselves back. Some say that was to teach people to understand that the trappings of wealth were of no true value. It is not a lesson which has lasted, as witness the national lottery.'

They became silent. The sky was partially clouded and there was sufficient breeze to rustle the garriga – the bush vegetation – and carry to them the scent of wild herbs.

Fenton was the first to speak. 'I've given more of myself to this case, Enrique, than any other I've ever handled. I've read and reread every scrap of evidence until I know it all by heart; I've persuaded the bank to offer a high five-figure reward for information leading to an arrest; I've turned over any villain whose record marks him as even a remote possibility . . . And I've gone nowhere. What's more, it's a thousand pounds to a penny that all this visit will do is confirm failure.'

Alvarez brought the pack of cigarettes from his pocket. 'Wouldn't you rather enjoy a smoke while we have a walk?'

He wouldn't, but Fenton's words made him realise he had to sacrifice himself. He opened the driving door and climbed out on to the road.

Twenty minutes later, they sat in a small natural clearing, fifty metres below the road. To their right, an outcrop of rock cut off any sight of the monastery, but they had a majestic view across the valley at mountains clothed with pine trees on their lower slopes.

Fenton said: 'It's total peace here. Yet it's a bitter fact of life that somewhere else there will be chaos and agony . . . I never knew the live Mrs Wade; only the dead Mrs Wade with a body marked by torture . . .' He continued to speak slowly, his tone remaining even when clearly his emotions were not. He was not a naturally gifted storyteller, but work had taught him to concentrate on the germane facts, since it was these which fashioned events. Alvarez had the imagination to clothe them with colour . . .

Seven

The postman stopped the van, picked up several letters, opened the driving door and cursed the early morning October rain, which was falling heavily. Already, his shirt collar was damp despite the towel he'd wound around his neck inside his mackintosh; before he completed his round, the whole of his chest and back would be damp and cold. His wife kept telling him to complain again about the foul-weather clothing that was issued, but no good had come from complaining in the past, so where was the point? And management already viewed him, he was certain, as a potential troublemaker. Management worked in dry, warm offices.

Having pushed two letters through the flap, he returned down the imitation-flagstone path and shut the wrought-iron gate with more force than was necessary. It was difficult not to feel resentful when others slept whilst he worked and it was raining as if the second Flood had started.

He walked twenty yards along the pavement to the next gate, this time wooden. All the houses in the close were of similar design and individuality could only be expressed in small ways. Here, there was a bay window. As he stepped through the gateway, a drop of water slid down the small of his back.

The flap of the letterbox of Nº7 always made a sharp metallic noise when he pushed it open and he couldn't understand why the house's owner didn't quieten it with some oil? Did the lucky sod manage to sleep through the noise? He pushed four envelopes through and, just before the flap dropped back, thought he heard a strange drumming sound.

Undecided whether in fact he had, he put his ear to the door and could just hear it once more; because the tempo was so uneven, he became certain it must hold some significance. He bent over, pushed the flap open, and called out: 'Anything wrong, mate?'

The drumming increased in tempo; something was knocked over and smashed. He hurried back to the van, opened the driving door, and reached across for the mobile phone which had been issued, as usual, before he left the sorting office. He switched it on, fed in the pin number, dialled 999.

A patrol car drew up outside Nº7. The sergeant and PC went up the path to the front door. A stickler for rules, the sergeant rang the bell and waited before he pushed in the lid of the letterbox and listened. After a moment, he shouted: 'It's the police. Hang on.'

The front door was locked. They followed the gravel path around to the rear door and that was unlocked. They found Wade on the floor of the front room, bound and gagged. When the gag was removed, he said, his words distorted by the dryness of his mouth: 'My wife. She was screaming. For God's sake, find my wife.'

'Cut him loose,' the sergeant ordered. 'I'll look around.'

Wade had been bound with professional skill – cord tied his elbows together behind his back; cord tied his ankles together and secured them to one leg of an armchair – and there had been only just enough slack to allow him to drum his heels. The PC cut through the bonds with his scout's penknife which until then had never proved to be of any practical use.

The sergeant returned.

'My wife?' Wade demanded hoarsely as he moved around, trying desperately to ease the pain of returning circulation.

'She's not in the house,' the sergeant answered, deliberately speaking in a non-committal tone.

Wade cried out that she had to be, he'd heard her screaming . . .

The sergeant tried to calm him down, told the PC to call for medical help and to advise CID.

After a while, Wade was able to ignore the pain sufficiently to give a very brief account of what had happened. He and his wife had been watching television when there had been a knock at the front door. He'd gone into the hall and, because of the time, had called out to ask who was outside. 'Maitland,' a man had answered. Since Maitland was his wife's immediate superior at the bank, he had wondered what was wrong but had seen no reason not to slip loose the chain, unlock and open the door . . . Three men, faces obscured by what were probably nylon stockings, rushed in. Shock so dulled his reactions that he was lying face down on the floor with one of the men kneeling on the small of his back before he fearfully thought of his wife. Seconds later, she had begun to scream . . .

Initially, the facts seemed confusing. The villains had used the name of Maitland to boost confidence, which meant they must have planned the job – why, when there was so little of any real value in the house? Mrs Wade was missing and the assumption had to be that they had taken her with them – why?

The answers began to surface when Fenton learned that

Mrs Wade was in charge of security at the local branch of one of the mainstream banks. Because experience had taught him the bitter lesson to distrust until honesty was proven, he closely questioned the sergeant and, more especially, the PC – could the cord have been self-bound? Impossible. Wade had been trussed up so expertly that he would have died from thirst before he managed to begin to break free.

'Would you reckon he'd been tied up since soon after eleven last night?'

'Yes, sir. He was in so much pain from returning circulation and cramp that the doctor gave him an injection to try to ease it.'

Detective Superintendent Norris announced that he would be taking charge of investigations. Fenton received the news without comment even though he placed Norris as a windbag who'd gained promotion through knowing what to say to please a superior. In the meantime, he was still in command and he organised the preliminary moves of the investigation. A description of Robina Wade and of the clothes she had been wearing was given countrywide circulation along with Wade's descriptions of two of the men – young, not noticeably tall, well built, wearing dark clothes, faces obscured by nylons, or something very similar, one might have been left-handed. Nobody was going to be in danger of being stopped and questioned on those descriptions . . .

The senior administrative officer of the bank – once he would have been called the manager – was informed of events while still at home. He left his breakfast half eaten and went in the police car to the bank to begin the task of assessing the possible fallout from events.

Fenton again questioned the sergeant and PC who had entered the house and freed Wade. Again, they confirmed that in their opinions Wade had been lying where they'd found him for just under seven hours, as claimed. He spoke to the doctor who had tended Wade. The condition of the patient had been what was to be expected in the named circumstances and there was very little, rather no, possibility of any deception.

Detective Superintendent Norris arrived and took command. He issued many orders to reinforce the impression of a thrusting, highly competent investigator.

A few minutes after four that afternoon, the two computer experts who had been flown down by helicopter from London traced a breach in bank security. There had been electronic movement at three in the morning after the relevant passwords had been provided, which allowed the overriding of normal time restrictions. Later, they were able to total the amounts of money involved. Seven million, four hundred and twenty-three thousand, two hundred and eight pounds. The money had gone to the Grand Elysian Bank in the Seychelles. Their spokesman confirmed it had already been electronically removed to the Idriss Mujber Bank in Tripoli. The Libyan bank denied any knowledge of the transfer.

Bank officials explained that, based on experience, the probable sequence of events was that each bank would have claimed a commission, but the Libyan bank would have transferred only roughly two-thirds of the money to whatever destination had been named and would keep the remaining third as their price for silence. So the villains would have ended up with approximately five million pounds. Unless, that was, the Idriss Mujber Bank had swindled them out of everything.

The body was found on a Wednesday by a man who was wildfowling at daybreak on the Sesham Marshes, a bleak, dangerous area of mudflats and fast tides. Moving to another hide, in the hope of better sport, he was crossing a narrow waterway when he noticed something unusual sticking out beyond a bend in the next mudflat. It proved on closer inspection to be a bare foot. It was not the first time he had come across a dead body, but that didn't make the experience any the less unpleasant.

The naked body lay on the PM table; in the harsh light from the overhead pod, it looked pathetic and ugly.

The pathologist said: 'Death was caused by strangulation, carried out with thin cord.'

The detective inspector carefully did not look at the distorted neck again; all his years in the force had failed to protect him from the horror of such scenes.

'Specific identification marks are a mole four millimetres in diameter below the right breast and a two centimetre irregular scar on the left thigh, the result of an accident many years previously. There are nine burn injuries. It is impossible to be certain exactly what caused these marks, but a best guess would be red hot pincers.'

The SOCO – scene of crime officer – swore.

'In each instance, the destruction of tissue is localised, but deep. The victim must have suffered greatly as the parts of the body chosen are those most susceptible to pain. There are extensive abrasions on the wrists which point to their having been bound and desperate attempts to break loose. In the mouth were several fibres which probably came from some form of gag.' The pathologist walked over to a stainless steel bin, pressed down on the pedal to lift the lid, stripped off his gloves and dropped them inside, pulled free his surgical cap and did the same with that. His assistant undid the tapes of his green surgical gown and, with a shrug of the shoulders, he freed it to join the gloves and cap.

He walked across to where the DI and SOCO waited. 'Would you say you have an identification?'

'That mole and scar have to be clinching evidence,' the DI replied.

Norris allowed he was a little overweight; others named him fat. As he slumped down on the corner of the table in the conference room – being used as his temporary office at divisional HQ – he began to resemble Michelin Man. 'The clothing matches Wade's description.'

'Except for the shoes and he did say he couldn't be certain about them,' Fenton said.

'I'm not overlooking that point.'

'Of course not, sir.'

'He mentioned the shape of the mole and its position, but initially not the scar. However, when specifically asked if his wife had any scars on her body, he recalled the one on her left thigh and was able to describe it. So do we have an identification?'

'An apparent one. But with seven and a half million quid missing, I'd suggest we need something more definite.'

'He'll be asked to view the body.'

'Poor sod! From all accounts, the damage is going to be difficult to hide . . . When I said something more definite, sir, I was thinking in terms of absolute evidence. Her fingerprints will be all around the house – it's only a few days since she was there – so a good set can be lifted and compared with those of the dead woman. And there's every chance of finding something that will provide her DNA, which can be matched with the DNA of the corpse.'

'You're not forgetting that under the new system of internal accounting, all lab costs will be put against CID?'

'No, sir, I'm not.' It was fairly certain that identity was already sufficiently well established and therefore any further tests could be called an unnecessary expense at a time when the government was, typically, demanding greater efficiency while cutting grants to county forces. But seven and a half million pounds surely called for absolute certainty?

Norris, having weighed up what was most likely to serve his interests, finally said: 'You'd better organise things.'

There were many who would have said Fenton was not an emotional man; his wife could have told them that he had had to learn to keep his emotions under sharp control or they would have proved too damaging to his work.

He stood in the hall of N°7 Rexley Close and wished himself anywhere else; wished he could have persuaded himself that a mole, a scar, and clothing were sufficient proof of identification. 'I'm very sorry, Mr Wade, but I'm afraid it is necessary.'

'She . . . I . . .' Wade turned away.

When a mind wanted to escape the present, it often concentrated on something irrational. Fenton stared at the framed print of a pastoral scene and wondered if the real world was ever quite so peacefully attractive?

'I'm sorry,' Wade said, as he turned back. 'It's just that . . . I understand the law has to take its course, but why so brutally?'

Fenton didn't try to answer.

'What exactly is it that you want?'

'We have to confirm identity.'

'Haven't I told you enough to do that? Christ, if she weren't dead, she'd be here! Why can't you understand that?' He turned away once more.

How did one explain to a husband whose only concern

was his own overwhelming grief that several missing
millions meant identification became far more important
than that grief?

'What exactly do you want now, then?'

'A visual identification by you.'

'Oh, my God!'

'I'm very sorry . . .' Fenton became silent. Even genu-
ine words could appear hypocritical.

'When?'

'Very soon. I will arrange for a police car to drive
you . . . There's something more.'

'That's possible?'

'I'll need your permission for a very small team of
officers to come into the house and search for your
wife's fingerprints and any material which will provide
her DNA unless this can be avoided. Can you suggest
anything your wife would have frequently handled that
normally wouldn't have been touched by anyone else?
Perhaps a toilet set?'

Wade did not immediately answer; then he said: 'They
were a wedding present from her aunt, who said they'd
been in the family for generations. Robina treasured them
because of that, so I never pointed out that, according to
the silver marks, they couldn't have been in the family for
more than forty-odd years. It's funny how . . . Funny?'

'Might I see them?'

'I suppose.'

They went upstairs and along a short corridor to the
front bedroom. On the small, reproduction, kidney-shaped
dressing table were silver-backed hairbrush, comb, and
hand mirror.

'Would you have touched these in the past few days,
Mr Wade?'

'No! I've touched nothing . . .'

Hoping that by some miracle she would return? 'If

I could take these for examination, it might well be that there's no need for anyone else to come here and bother you.' There were several hairs caught up in the bristles of the hairbrush and these would provide DNA samples; the mirror's silver back should have recorded prints well.

'Whatever you want,' Wade said dully.

'I'll give you a receipt and will make certain they're returned as soon as possible.'

'When . . . When do you want . . .'

'A visual identification? As soon as possible. Would tomorrow morning be suitable?'

'All right.'

They had managed to erase much of the damage to the neck and also the signs of agony on the face. Wade stared down at the body, covered in a green sheet up to the base of the neck. He pressed his lips together, screwed his eyes shut, turned away.

'Do you identify the deceased?' The coroner's officer bluntly asked.

Wade nodded.

'Who is she?'

'My wife.'

There was, the DC decided, a distinct aura of dust about Maitland, even though he was only in his middle fifties. 'The reason for asking is the need to learn all we can about Mrs Wade in the hopes that something will suggest who her murderers might have been.'

'You don't imagine her husband would be far better able to describe her than I?'

'He can't say anything about her here at work.'

'Any more than I can judge how criminals came to use my name,' Maitland said resentfully.

'Was it generally known you were Mrs Wade's superior?'

'Naturally, every employee knows I have administrative responsibility for security, although I am not concerned with the practical side. I am no computer expert.'

A man who didn't know a ewe from a RAM, the DC thought. 'What I really meant was, do you think a member of the public would know the working relationship between her and you?'

'I would not presume to judge what any member of the public knows. There are occasions when I tend to believe most of them know nothing.'

'Would it be difficult for an outsider to learn what her work was and the chain of command?'

'What possible point is there in asking me questions I cannot possibly answer?'

'Like I said earlier, the villains persuaded Mr Wade to open the front door by using your name. We'd like to know exactly how they learned of the advantage that would offer.'

'There should have been no such advantage. Mr Wade ought to have realised I would never call at his home that late at night. My wife and I go to bed early.'

Obviously only to have more time for reading. 'It was because it was late that he presumed there must be an emergency at the bank.'

'A most unwise assumption.'

Maitland had the warmth of a dead haddock. 'How did you find Mrs Wade?'

'She applied for a position in the bank in the usual way.'

'I meant, how would you describe her as a person?'

'Efficient, reliable, sensible and serious.'

Then she never kick-started a man's imagination. 'And trustworthy?'

'Her trustworthiness was such that nowadays one seldom meets its like; loyalty has become a forgotten word.'

'You never had any reason to doubt her honesty?'

'Certainly not.'

'Would you describe her as a friendly person?'

'At times too friendly.'

'Why do you say that?'

'An offer of friendship needs to be carefully husbanded, not carelessly given.'

The DC wondered if the other had a single friend?

'I have always been a very good judge of character,' Maitland said, with an air of satisfaction, obviously keen to explain his views, 'and, if I had been asked if *Miss Tait* would be a suitable person to work for the bank, I should have had little hesitation in saying that, in the light of her flippant character, she was not. My judgment was confirmed when her work became very slipshod . . .'

'I don't think we need bother with that . . .'

'. . . I naturally complained to Mrs Wade, her immediate superior,' continued Maitland, ignoring the comment and, like any mean-minded person, aggressively certain that what he said was worth saying. 'She informed me Miss Tait was under emotional stress following a broken relationship with a man – I think she referred to him as Keith, not a name to inspire confidence – who had promised to marry her as soon as he had divorced his wife. She should have remembered that "Whatsoever a man soweth, that shall he also reap".'

'But she was a woman!'

Maitland contemptuously ignored such mindless levity. 'Mrs Wade referred to Miss Tait as heartbroken. A more accurate description would surely have been, resentfully humiliated. Unfortunately – having regard to the circumstances – Mrs Wade made a point of befriending and helping Miss Tait, to the extent of

60

entertaining her many times at home. Compassion can become condonation.' He sniffed loudly, then continued speaking in his monotonous, surprisingly deep-pitched voice. He'd told Miss Tait that her work must improve. It had not. On the point of his making an official, condemnatory report to the manager of personnel, she had saved him the trouble by handing in her resignation. She was, she said, leaving to search for a new life. Not something she could ever find, since life was what an individual made of it. Her admitted adultery, her pert manner with its lack of even a hint of apologetic humility, her provocative form of dress and excessive use of make-up, had shown Mrs Wade's charity to have been sadly misplaced, falling as it had on very stony ground.

The DC was surprised Maitland had not shown sufficient insensitivity to tell Miss Tait so.

Later, he reported to Fenton. 'I've had a word with all members of staff except one who's away sick.'

'Learn anything?'

'Only that Maitland is even more of a prick than he looks.'

'It was always a long shot that one of them would know something.'

Several good fingerprints and thumbprints were found on the back of the mirror: these matched prints taken from the corpse. Many days later, the forensic laboratory reported that DNA extracted from hairs found on the hairbrush matched the DNA of the dead woman and it was many millions to one against their having come from different persons.

'We could have contented ourselves with the mole, the scar, and the visual identification,' Norris said to Fenton, who stood – not having been asked to sit – in front of the former's desk at county HQ. 'That would have saved a bloody fortune.'

'At least we can now be certain.'

'We'd have been certain then if you weren't someone who has to stick his finger in boiling water before he believes it's hot.'

During the winter, Fenton twice spoke to Wade, trying to glean some piece of information, previously missed, that would give the police a lead to identifying the men who had broken into the house, abducted Robina Wade and tortured her into disclosing the security details which had enabled them to spirit millions of pounds abroad.

On the second visit, Wade said apologetically: 'It all happened so quickly.'

'Yes, of course. And shock has far more effect on memory than most people think . . . I'll clear off now and leave you in peace.'

'You'll have a drink before you go?'

'I don't think . . .'

'Not just a quick one?'

Wade, Fenton judged, would sup with the devil to break his loneliness. 'You've persuaded me.'

They went into the front room, in a state of considerable untidiness.

Wade said: 'Robina called me the original litterbug.'

'My wife says the same thing about me.' A lie – he liked everything to be in its place. But by aligning himself with the other, he hoped fractionally to ease Wade's pain of having to accept the untidiness as a visible sign that his wife was dead.

'What would you like: whisky, gin, sherry, beer?'

'Would you have a lager?'

'Yes.'

'That'll do me fine.'

Wade left the room, to return with two tumblers filled with lager. He handed one to Fenton, settled on the settee. 'I've decided to move . . . I can't stand all the ghosts.'

Memories were ghosts. Fenton would have moved months earlier. To continue to live where he and his wife had found love, happiness, companionship, would leave him unable to look at, touch, do anything, without ghosts overwhelming him.

'I'm also leaving my job.' He looked out through the window, his eyes unfocused. 'People say one can lose oneself in work; all I seem to manage is to lose my way. The senior partner has been as supportive as he can afford to be, but it's been obvious for some time that his patience was wearing thinner than he liked. I handed in my resignation the other day to save him the embarrassment of having to ask for it. Financially, things may be tight, but hopefully not tough. I've a little capital and this house will surely fetch a lot more than I paid for it, so if I invest in high yield stock and inflation stays reasonably low, I should stay afloat until my pension clicks in . . . I'm sorry, Inspector, I must be boring you.'

'On the contrary,' Fenton denied quickly. 'Are you moving far?'

'I'm not yet certain. As a matter of fact, I'm thinking of possibly going to Mallorca.'

'That would be quite a change!'

'My sister and her husband went to Crete to live. Unfortunately, they had a very bad car accident and he was killed and she was injured; when she'd recovered, she decided to move, much, I suppose, for the same reasons as I. She couldn't face returning here because of the weather and plumped for Mallorca. We've kept in touch and when she heard of . . . of Robina's death, she suggested I leave England and move in with her and enjoy freedom from unwanted ghosts. I hesitated, and still do, because I'm going to have to budget very carefully and I'm not certain what the cost of living is like there. She keeps telling me that that's being silly. I suppose the biggest question is, can it work out? We used to get on well enough together, but at our age, living under one roof isn't the same as when young.'

'If you decide to make the break, how soon will you be leaving the UK?'

'When I find a buyer for this house, which may take some time because I'm not letting it go for less than it's worth, just for a quick sale.'

'I gather the market's quite buoyant at the moment.'

'As always, that depends whether one's a seller or a buyer.'

Fenton admired the way in which the other was facing life with hope rather than despair.

'As a matter of fact, I rang my sister yesterday. As you know, here it was raining cats and dogs and the wind was icy, she said that there it was sunny and warm. I don't think she was saying that just to egg me on to move, but that's the effect it had!'

'I'm sure you'll be . . .' About to say 'happy', he changed his words, '. . . glad you make the move if that's what you decide.'

'I think I will. But one can never be certain about anything, not even certainty.'

Fenton drained his glass.

'Do you think there's any chance you'll ever catch the men?'

'Yes.'

'But it's a long, long time since . . . since it happened.'

'There's been no let up on our part and there won't be. We are going to nail them.'

Wade spoke slowly. 'I used to pride myself on believing

in the sanctity of life, whatever the circumstances, but if I ever come face to face with the men who did what they did to Robina, I'll kill the bastards. And the law will hold me accountable. Justice ignores the innocent.'

Fenton agreed with that, but discretion kept him silent. He said goodbye and left. As he drove out of the close, he hoped Wade would eventually find a measure of peace wherever he decided to live.

Eight

Alvarez crushed a sprig of wild thyme between finger and thumb. 'You sound as if you have sympathy, even admiration, for Señor Wade?'

Fenton stared across the valley. Clouds had begun to drift in from the west and they were causing sunlight to play tag across the land. 'It would be hard not to. Thank God I've no idea how much inner courage it must take to live with the knowledge that your wife was tortured before she was murdered.'

The scent of the thyme, and the words, provoked in Alvarez's mind a memory that he would have preferred to have remained hidden. He, Juana-María, and one of her aunts – in those days, families had still believed unmarried daughters should be chaperoned – had been enjoying a walk through the woods which lay along Festna Valley. The aunt, large of body, had become so short of breath, even though they had been moving slowly, she had had to sit down by the side of an unoccupied charcoal maker's hut. Soon, she had fallen asleep and Juana-María and he had quietly walked on until out of sight, whereupon he had kissed her until she had drawn back, dismayed by the sudden surge of her own passion and also half ashamed because she had been taught that a woman never experienced such emotion until she was married unless she wished to be thought a puta. In stepping back, she had trodden on a small thyme bush and the hot, still

66

air had become suffused with its scent. She'd kissed him once more, without passion, led the way back to the hut. Her aunt had awoken several minutes later and, relieved to see them present, repeatedly asserted she had not slept. Not long afterwards, Juana-María had been pinned against a wall by a car driven by a drunken Frenchman and had died. Alvarez had had to find the courage to live with her death; he had never learned to forgive the driver . . .

Fenton looked at his watch. 'Is it time we moved?'

'It'll only take us twenty-five minutes to drive to the house.'

'Which surely will get us there dead on time?'

'I suppose he may not have lived on the island long enough to be dismayed by that!' He smiled as he dropped the sprig of crushed leaves on to the ground.

He was a slow driver in the mountains, very well aware that beyond the unfenced edges of the roads often lay steep, sometimes precipitous slopes. If brakes locked and the car went into a dry skid, it could spin off the road and hurtle down to slam into rocks with a force that made seat belts and air bags totally useless . . .

They reached the floor of the valley and he relaxed; he remarked how, years ago, every field they passed would have been intensely cultivated or heavily stocked, yet now so many were lying weedily fallow. 'It's usually only the older people who grow vegetables these days. And who can blame the young ones? Are they going to go out in the burning sun or biting wind and rain, bent double, plant, weed, irrigate, harvest, when they can work in comfort in the tourist trade and earn many times what their parents did? So much has changed.'

'More quickly here than in most countries, I'd guess?'

'In half a lifetime and in strange ways. A father used to leave his land to his sons according to how he judged them; the good son who worked hard all day received the rich soil that would grow three crops in a year and the deep well that never dried up, the lazy son, the shore land that was infertile and useless. Then the tourists arrived and shore land became worth so many millions of pesetas a mind could become dizzy at the thought. So the waster now does nothing because he has become rich and the worker tills the land until his bones cry out in pain, yet he barely makes enough to enjoy a beer at the nearest bar.'

'One more bitter irony of life!'

They reached the complex roundabout to the west of Llueso – so designed that it was an accepted hazard to meet a tourist car heading in the opposite direction – and took the Palma road; halfway to the Mestara crossroads, Alvarez turned off on to a track, surfaced with crushed rock, which ran through a belt of pine trees. A few hundred metres beyond the trees, the land rose and part way up the hill, the houses and bungalows of urbanización Beniferri lay in a curving line that went out of sight.

Ca'n Greix was a bungalow, with the usual plethora of roof levels, which stood ten metres back from the road. The garden consisted only of shrubs, set in gravel – the ideal garden in Alvarez's judgment, since it required the minimum of labour.

The panelled front door was opened by Wade. 'Good evening, Inspector Fenton . . . And you are Inspector Alvarez?'

'Yes, Señor.'

'Do come on in.'

Alvarez followed Fenton into the hall, in which the furnishings were a local, rather crudely made table in rustic style – on which stood the telephone – a chair, and a small oval carpet.

'It's kind of you to agree to see us,' Fenton said.

'I don't suppose you'll be surprised if I say my instinct was to refuse,' he replied, his tone harsh. He had a round face, its strongest feature a pugnaciously square chin, topped by greying hair which was beginning to recede; his trim build spoke of either a liking for exercise or moderation when sampling the pleasures of the table.

'I'm grateful that you didn't.'

'I've had to learn to do so many things I'd rather not . . . I hope that doesn't sound personal?'

'Of course not.'

'Good . . . By the way, my sister often plays bridge on a Sunday evening and she was uncertain whether she ought to cancel tonight and stay here. I told her to carry on as there was no way in which she could help you. That is right, isn't it?'

'Exactly right.'

'Then I don't have to ring through and ask her to leave the game and return even if she is holding thirteen spades . . . Come on through.'

The sitting room had picture windows and through them was a view across to the hills which lay on the far side of the Llueso/Mestara road. Both furniture and furnishings suggested comfort was held to be more important than style. On the walls hung four framed paintings by an artist whose local scenes were sufficiently accurate and pleasing to ensure he would never gain critical acclaim.

'What would you like to drink? I can offer most things.'

Fenton asked for a gin and tonic, Alvarez a brandy.

'I won't be a moment.' Wade left the room.

Fenton crossed to the nearer window and stared out. 'He's certainly found pastoral peace.'

Had this helped Wade find mental peace? Alvarez wondered. Experience suggested that for much of the time it would, but occasionally the contrast with memory would make that memory more painful . . . He briefly cursed the present which kept recalling the past.

As Fenton sat, Wade returned with a tray on which were three glasses and an insulated container. 'I forgot to ask if you both like ice; I didn't add it because it's not all that warm now.'

'As far as I'm concerned,' Fenton said, 'having just arrived from England, it's hot! So yes, please, ice.'

'And if I may have three cubes?' Alvarez asked.

Wade handed around the glasses, sat. 'Are you staying long, Inspector?'

'Since you've been kind enough to have a word with me so quickly,' Fenton replied, 'I'll be returning tomorrow unless something turns up.'

'What kind of something?'

'Anything that will give me an excuse for staying on which accounts will accept.' He smiled. 'In other words, a miraculous excuse.'

'I'm afraid I'm unlikely to provide that . . . I can't tell you anything fresh, much as I wish I could.'

'I know how difficult it is, but . . . I'll be frank, we're no further on than when I last spoke to you, back in England. So I'm here because there's always the hundred to one chance that after a period of time, a person's mind releases some fact that he'd no idea was being held.'

'Locked up in the subconscious?'

'The mind can do funny things.'

'And cruel ones.'

'I'm afraid so . . . I can maybe begin to guess what it must mean to you to be asked to recall events yet again, but I hope there'll at least be some slight compensation in knowing it might just help us to crack the case open.'

'The hundred to one chance?'

'The outsider sometimes comes home.'

Wade stared down at the glass he held in his hand. 'Hilary told me very bluntly I was crazy to see you because it would just reawaken all the pain . . . It's as well she's not here now or I'm sure she'd give her opinion in very forthright terms.'

'Being disliked goes with my job.'

'She'd express her disapproval, not dislike, in terms that might make it difficult to distinguish between the two. I'm sure there must be local expats who consider her rude. Robina used to say she—' He came to an abrupt stop.

It was only when memories hurt, Alvarez thought, that one really understood how much of the present lay in the past. He drank.

'Sorry about that.' Wade shrugged his shoulders, spoke to Fenton. 'You want me to do what?'

'To describe that night, recalling every single detail you can, even if it seems totally unimportant. It's the ignored detail that I'm hoping to hear.'

Wade quietly, in a voice almost devoid of variations of tone, began to recount the events of the night in October when there had been a knock on the front door and he had gone into the hall and asked who was outside and, when the answer was Maitland, had unchained, unlocked, and opened the door and men, faces concealed behind stockings, had rushed in and pinioned him to the floor . . .

Wade took a handkerchief from his pocket and ran it across his forehead. 'I need another drink. You'll both join me, won't you?' He stood.

An appeal that definitely needed to be met. 'Thank you, Señor,' Alvarez said.

'And you, Inspector?'

'I can't say no even though I seem to have been doing nothing but drink since I arrived on the island.' Fenton answered.

Wade took their glasses and left the room. After he'd returned and handed them the fresh drinks, he said: 'I'd like to offer you something decent to eat, but Hilary won't be returning for another couple of hours at the earliest; however, I could rustle up a scratch meal if you'd put up with that?'

'Very kind of you,' Fenton answered, 'but I ought to get back to the hotel. If I can get the flight I should, I'll have an early start tomorrow.'

'No miraculous excuse for staying on?'

'I'm afraid not.'

'Sorry I haven't been able to help provide one. No unlocked memories . . . I suppose that brings an end to the investigation?'

'No.'

'Then puts it on the back burner?'

'Not where I'm concerned, Mr Wade.'

'If you should learn anything fresh, I'd like to know . . . Or maybe I wouldn't.'

'If it were important enough, you'd have to know because there'd be a trial.'

'Yes, of course. Stupid of me.'

'I hope . . . Good luck. And thanks for putting up with us.'

They left after a brief goodbye. As they cleared the belt of pine trees and approached the road, Fenton said, 'My detective superintendent will listen to my report and then tell me at great length that he'd said I'd be wasting the force's money. If, on the other hand, I'd been lucky enough to learn something useful, he'd claim the credit for talking again to Wade. They say that an open mind is the secret of promotion. They don't add that it's a case of open in one direction, but closed in the other.'

Alvarez turned on to the road. 'Do you think you still really do have a chance of identifying the men who murdered Señora Wade and defrauded the bank?'

'About as good a chance as finding a politician who

means what he says . . . The job was slickly carried out and not a neighbour could provide anything useful. I've had my lads in CID tap every snout they're supporting, but not one has come up with as much as a whisper. No known villain is spending money like it grew on trees and he's inherited a forest. Now that Wade's been unable to recall anything fresh, the odds against any progress are sky high.'

They rounded a corner and very briefly, despite approaching darkness, the sea was visible beyond the Pla, the plain of Mestara, before both were hidden by hills.

'I hope you don't mind my refusing a meal without any reference to you?' Fenton said. 'The thing was, I had the impression the invitation was just good manners. What he really wanted, quite naturally, was me out of sight so I could soon be out of mind.'

'Added to which, on his own admission he is not a good cook.'

'A more practical approach!'

Alvarez smiled. 'Now your work is ended, it is time for a little pleasure. I should like to take you for a drink, or two, at one of the front bars. Of course, these are for tourists who are charged far too much, but I know the owner of one who does not wish it to be officially known that he puts Spanish gin into English bottles to increase his profits to a level that would amaze the tax inspector. To drink at a reasonable price as one enjoys the beauty of the bay in the evening is, as you intimated at lunch time, the perfect preparation for a meal.

'I suggest we eat at the Don Pedro, which is open for evening meals. Some would smile that it should call itself Don; Hombre Pedro would seem more appropriate as it is small, dark, and the pieces of old fishing gear on the walls are home to many cobwebs. But because of its appearance, few tourists go there and that is why the fish is some of the best a man can enjoy south of Galicia without bankrupting himself. I have eaten rap amb tomatigues there which would arouse the awe of the head chef at the Madrid Ritz.'

'It sounds every tourist's dream. What's the dish you've just mentioned?'

'In English, the fish is called, I think, monkfish. This is cooked with tomatoes, mushrooms, garlic, many herbs, and a flood of good white wine.'

'Doesn't monkfish look like someone's nightmare?'

'Indeed. But, as with women, beauty does not guarantee satisfaction. Have you ever eaten it?'

'Not knowingly.'

'Then let us hope it is on the menu tonight. If, of course, you would not prefer a steak?'

'I'm all for trying the local delicacies.'

'I knew you would be.'

Salas rang at twelve-thirty on Monday morning. 'Well?' was his only greeting.

'Señor?' Alvarez replied.

'I have been waiting all day.'

He stared through the window at the house on the other side of the road, its wall bathed in sunshine. Waiting for what? The farmers were waiting for rain that had been forecast, but had not arrived; he was waiting for his pension on retirement . . .

'Do I have to wait until tomorrow for an answer?'

He stared at the several letters delivered that morning which he had not yet opened. Was one of them from the superior chief and needing an immediate response? 'I have been so very busy this morning that it was not until you rang that I was about to read the mail, which is why I'm afraid I do not know to what you are referring . . .'

'Since I haven't sent you a letter, your failure is hardly relevant in this context.'

There was a silence.

'Are you still there?' Salas demanded.

'Indeed.'

'Then pull yourself together and make your report.'

'Report concerning what, Señor?'

'Has the English inspector yet spoken to Señor Wade?'

'We visited his house yesterday evening at six o'clock.'

'Then why was your report not on my desk for my arrival at the office this morning?'

'I was about to compile it . . .'

'That report should have been prepared last night and faxed to me first thing this morning.'

Gloomily he understood he was expected to work on a Sunday evening as well as morning and afternoon.

'What was the outcome of the meeting?'

'Señor Wade was unable to help Inspector Fenton . . .'

'I'm asking if you upheld the honour of the Cuerpo? Did you provide all the assistance the inspector requested? Did you refrain from any opinion, any advice, anything which might give offence?'

'I think so.'

'You can only say you think so?'

'Surely you would have to ask him to get a definitive answer?'

'Certainly to obtain a more coherent one. You will make a full report and fax it to me immediately.'

'But there's nothing more to tell you, Señor . . .'

The line went dead.

Nine

M ay proved to be a month of variable weather: days were hot and sunny, cloudy and warm, wet and cool. This indecision lasted through to June and on the fifth it even rained heavily. Then the Migjorn blew, clouds rolled away, and by the morning of the sixth, the sun shone so strongly that, having left the post, walked up to the old square, and crossed to Club Llueso, Alvarez was sweating heavily. 'A cortado and . . .'

'A small coñac,' interrupted the barman as he filled a container with ground coffee.

'Not what I was going to ask for.'

'You think you need to tell me you want a very large one?'

Alvarez crossed to one of the window tables and sat. He stared out at the moving throng of tourists in the old square and wondered why so many of them dressed with such little taste – a declaration or natural ineptitude? His interest became more focused. A tall, willowy blonde, in her middle twenties, wearing a very tightly fitting T-shirt which bore the single word 'Yes' on the front and shorts so abbreviated that had she possessed any sense of rectitude they would have had 'No' on them, crossed his line of vision.

'You're too old,' said the barman, as he put coffee and brandy down on the table.

'One is never too old.'

'You obviously need to wear glasses when you look in a mirror.'

'And, for the record, I was merely admiring an attractive picture.'

'And wishing like hell you could paint it.' The barman left.

Alvarez drank some brandy, some coffee, then poured the remaining brandy into the cup. People deliberately mistook the motives of others. Because by doing so they improved their own image? The barman refused to accept that he could look at a young and attractive woman and admire her physical beauty without a hint of lust. Dolores had only to see him speaking to a nubile female to believe he was erotically interested . . .

Before leaving, he had a second brandy to compensate for the small-mindedness of others.

Tourist buses had clearly recently dropped their passengers in the village and as he eased his way through the swirl of people now in the square, he momentarily made slight physical contact with a brunette who, when he apologised, smiled at him in such a way that for the next few minutes he wondered if she'd hoped he'd suggest a drink?

The flight of stairs up to the first floor were neither steep nor long, but by the time he reached his office, he was breathless. He sat. He really must drink less, eat less, smoke less, take more exercise . . .

Three-quarters of an hour later, the phone woke him.

'Is that the Cuerpo?' asked a man in a voice pitched high.

'Yes,' he answered bad-temperedly.

'You've got to come here. He isn't moving . . .'

'Steady on. What's your name and where's here?'

'Jorge Cervera. Don't you understand . . .'

'Where are you?'

'Cala Blanca.'

'On the south side of Parelona Peninsula, up near the lighthouse?'

'Yes. He may be seriously injured . . .'

'Who may be?'

'The man lying on the pebbles.'

'Is he still breathing, is there any sign of a pulse?'

'I don't know.'

'Put your finger on the side of his neck near—'

'I can't.'

'Why not?'

'I'm on my boat in the bay. It's Rosalía first saw him through binoculars and she says he looks bad because he hasn't moved all the time she's been watching.'

'Go ashore and find out if he's still alive.'

'I can't do that.'

'Why not?'

'The sight of blood makes me faint.'

Alvarez swore. 'Tell Rosalía to find out what's up with him. Get back on to me the moment you know. If he's alive, but injured, she must try to do something for him until the doctor arrives.'

'We can't stay here . . .'

'Leave the bay and I'll have you locked up on suspicion.'

'On suspicion of what?'

'Whatever I can think up. Are you using a mobile?'

'Yes, but . . .'

'Give me the number and then start moving.'

He listened, fed the number he'd been given into the memory of his own mobile, wondering as he did so what kind of person would want to leave the scene without discovering whether there was any relief he could bring to an injured person.

Cervera rang a second time. Rosalía thought the man must be dead.

Alvarez rang the emergency centre and asked that a doctor drove to Cala Blanca to examine a man who was reported dead, but might be seriously injured.

He left the post and walked in the shade to his parked car. The guide books called the drive which lay ahead of him a scenic delight; he called it mental torture. The road was a switchback, largely unfenced; mechanical failure or the slightest driving error could result in a fifty, a hundred metres' fall that ended in mangled agony . . . There were not many who understood how often members of the Cuerpo were called upon to display courage beyond the call of duty.

Cala Blanca was one of the few coves along the southern side of the Parelona Peninsula which could be readily reached. One turned off the road that continued on to the lighthouse, on the easterly tip of the island, and drove along a rough dirt track which ended a hundred metres from the edge of the bank that stood above the pebbly beach which ringed the water.

There was no need to feel for a pulse; the man who lay in a crumpled heap on the pebbles had clearly been dead for some time. He'd suffered injury to his head, but it was impossible visually to judge how extensive this was because of his long, black hair, matted with dry blood. He appeared to be in his early or middle thirties. Behind the grimace of death, Alvarez seemed to gain a hint of slyness.

He straightened up, shielded his eyes from the fierce sunlight with his hand, and studied the surrounding land. At a point level with the body this was some five or six metres high and its relatively sheer face spoke of winter storms carving away earth and rock. A first impression suggested the man had been walking above, had tripped, fallen, and landed on his head on the pebbles. Had death been immediate, or had he slowly died, on his own, knowing that hope had no place? . . . He hastily jerked his mind away from so depressing a question and studied the fairly large motor cruiser, her superstructure spelling gin palace, anchored in the mouth of the cove. He brought his mobile out of his hip pocket and was about to activate it when he heard someone approach. He turned and saw the doctor, case in right hand, making his way down. He crossed the pebbles to meet the other.

'What's the picture?' the doctor asked, his tone sharp, his words clipped.

'Almost certainly, he's been dead for several hours.'

'Then I needn't have hurried. Is the cause of death drowning?'

Wasn't it for the other to decide that? 'He has head injuries, so at the moment it looks more likely he fell from the path.'

'Drunk.'

Doctors never missed the chance to underline the perils of alcohol. Yet how many of them were tee-totallers?

'And if he was drunk enough to be walking up there and fall, he probably was a foreigner.'

'Not judging by the general look of him and the clothes he's wearing.'

The doctor abruptly resumed walking. 'If he is dead, you can call the hearse,' he said, having to speak over his shoulder because Alvarez was unable to keep up with him. 'I'll be finished long before it gets here. Warn them there'll be a walk, so they'll maybe need extra hands.'

Alvarez was grateful for the excuse to come to a stop. He used the mobile to speak to the undertakers in the village. That done, he continued the calf-straining walk across the pebbles.

Some time later, the doctor crossed to the water's edge and rinsed his hands.

'Are there other injuries than those to the head?' Alvarez asked.

'None is obvious.'

'Were they the cause of death?'

'He's dead.'

'What I meant was . . .'

'You'll have to wait for the post-mortem for answers.'

It seemed to be a rule of nature that small men were aggressively sharp. 'Would you think the wounds are consistent with having fallen from the path?'

'Perhaps.'

'You can't be more precise?'

'If I could, I would be.'

'It doesn't look as if there's been much bleeding, does it?'

'Doesn't it?'

'Can you give a probable time of death?'

'There is rigor in the face, shoulders, arms, trunk, and legs, which suggest around twelve hours since death, but in this heat it's even more unwise than usual to accept these symptoms as a good indication of time. Temperature of the body has dropped between four and five degrees, which again points to twelve hours, but is an equally unreliable guide.'

'But he almost certainly fell during darkness?'

'Yes.'

He stared up at the path. 'Why would someone be walking along there at that time of night?'

'That is not my problem to consider. But I can identify him, since he was a patient of mine some time back. His name is either Marcial or Mateo Ramos, I cannot remember which.' He sounded annoyed that he could not.

'Is there a family?'

'His father died several years ago, his mother is suffering from old age, and there is a sister. When I was treating him, he was unmarried.'

'What was his problem?'

'How do you mean?'

'Why were you treating him?'

'A question I am not prepared to answer at this stage.'

'It might prove to be important.'

'If it does, I will reconsider my decision.'

There was a shout. Three men, one of whom carried a rolled-up body bag, were descending down to the beach.

The doctor said: 'I am interested to know the extent of the injuries, especially what damage the brain has suffered. See I receive a full post-mortem report.'

Alvarez made a mental note to forget the order. The doctor left. The body was quickly bagged and carried away.

Alvarez activated his mobile and tried to recall from its memory the number Cervera had given him; on screen came the brief notice that there were no messages. He tried again with a different code and there was no response. He cupped his hands about his mouth and shouted and eventually attracted the attention of the couple aboard the boat; arm waving told them to come ashore. So much for modern technology, he thought, not without a degree of satisfaction.

He watched them go aft and climb into the inflatable secured alongside with less than nautical skill. The outboard started as an osprey began to cross the cove and it sheered sharply off to its left. The inflatable reached the beach, leaving behind churned-up water which only slowly returned to a poster-blue, glossy, smooth surface.

As they clumsily climbed out of the inflatable, Rosalía cried out because she missed her footing and was briefly in danger of falling backwards into the water; Cervera made no move to help her. She was no more than twenty, attractive, and still slim enough to wear a bikini that was more hope than substance. He was closing on forty and to call him slightly less than handsome was to flatter him; his build was pudgy. Son of first generation money, Alvarez judged, and a young woman seeking an ¡Hola! life and ready to pay the price.

'What is it you want with us?' Cervera asked petulantly as he stared uneasily at the spot where the body had lain.

'Some facts.'

'But I don't know anything about him.'

'No one's suggesting you do, but, since you made the report, I need to know the whys and whats. Your full name and address?' He was not surprised that Cervera's home was in the most expensive part of Cala Beston. 'What brought you to Cala Blanca and what first drew your attention to the dead man?'

He spoke reluctantly. He and Rosalía had driven in his Porsche to the marina at Mitjorn, on the south side of Llueso Bay, which was where he berthed his boat. They had sailed along the coast until they'd decided to have a swim, entered Cala Blanca, and anchored. She had been looking at the coastline through binoculars . . .

'Why?'

She looked uneasily at Alvarez. 'I was just looking,' she mumbled.

Idle curiosity was a good reason, but she had spoken so defensively that Alvarez was convinced she had had a specific reason. 'Were you expecting to meet someone here?'

'No.'

'Then why were you so interested in what was going on ashore?'

'She's told you.' Cervera spoke with as much belligerence as he could muster.

83

'Then she can tell me again whilst you keep quiet.'
Cervera's opposition crumpled.
'What were you looking for?'
'Someone,' she finally answered.
Now they were nearing the truth! Had there been a
sudden row between the two men in which she had played
a major part? 'Then why did you tell me a moment ago
you were not expecting to meet anyone?'
'I didn't want to see anyone.'
'Why would you visually search the shoreline if you
didn't want to see anyone?'
'Because . . . because I wanted to go swimming,' she
finally mumbled.
'And you wouldn't do that until certain you couldn't
see anyone?'
'No.'
'Why not?'
'Because . . . I wanted to swim without a costume on.'
Surprise gave way to silent sardonic humour. He'd
been mentally constructing a scenario in which the two
men had fought because of her and Ramos had fallen
to his death . . . And her only reason for viewing the
shore through binoculars had been to make certain there
was no one who might gain the briefest glimpse of
her naked body as she entered or left the water. The
human mind was an illogical maze. She was ready to
sell herself to a thoroughly unprepossessing man twice her
age, yet was overwhelmingly embarrassed at the thought
of being observed naked by someone who would never
know who she was. 'And it was when you were looking
at the shoreline that you saw the body?'
She nodded.
'You came ashore and judged him to be dead, then
returned to the boat. Since then, has either of you come
ashore until a moment ago?'

'No.'

'And throughout, you've seen no one else other than the doctor who was with me and the men who collected the body?'

'No.'

'Very well. If I need to talk to either of you again, I'll be in touch.'

'We can go?' Cervera asked.

'Yes,' he answered .

He watched them climb into the inflatable. He felt sorry for her even while he also knew contempt. When Cervera became bored with her, or age began to work its damage, he would discard her without a second thought.

Alvarez spoke to Salas over the phone. 'I have to report an accident, Señor.' He waited for a response.

'Then report it.'

'This morning, I was informed by a couple aboard a motor cruiser that they could see a body ashore in Cala Blanca. I drove there and ascertained that a man in his early thirties lay dead on the pebbles, having plainly suffered a head wound; it seemed probable he had fallen from the path above. The duty doctor examined the body in situ and said that the only apparent injury was the head wound and it would need the post-mortem to determine that this and this alone was the cause of death. The body has been taken to the morgue and I have arranged for a post-mortem to be carried out. The doctor was able to identify the victim as Marcial or Mateo Ramos and I shall be informing his mother of the sad accident; unfortunately, it appears that she suffers from old age and it may prove difficult to make her understand.' No one, he congratulated himself, could have delivered a more succinctly comprehensive report.

'Why did the couple on the boat notice the body?'

'The young lady . . . perhaps I should say, the young woman . . .'

'Why?'

'Her companion is twice her age and clearly wealthy.'

'Is their relationship of the slightest consequence except to a mind such as yours?'

'It explains why she didn't want to see anyone when she looked through the binoculars.'

'In that case, why did she look?'

'To make certain she couldn't.'

'Couldn't what?'

'Couldn't see anyone so she would know she wouldn't be seen if she saw no one.'

'You turn verbal confusion into an art form . . . Why didn't she want to be seen?'

'She intended to swim naked.'

There was a pause. 'Your mind is obsessed with peeping-Tommery.' He cut the connection.

Ten

In pre-tourist days, island families had formed tight units and all within had been cared for; aged parents were an accepted responsibility and when one or both ceased to be able to meet life's challenges, daughters, slightly less frequently sons, had given them food, drink, shelter, and company, even when to do so strained both finances and the bonds of blood relationship. It was ironic that as prosperity spread and made the lives of the young so much better, their sense of responsibility towards the old lessened until they no longer felt it shameful to consign a parent to a home.

Carrer de Picomell, in the oldest part of Llueso, was a narrow street with a bend halfway along, which had caused considerable congestion when mule carts had been a common form of transport and far more now that cars had superseded mules. Alvarez had to park well away from it and walk so that by the time he reached Nº14, he was hot, sweaty, and gauging how long it must be before he could return home and pour himself a brandy on ice.

He opened the door and stepped into the front room. It was in a mess and smelled – of cat, he judged, when a tabby appeared from under a chair, stared at him with cold dislike for a moment, then hurried through into the next room. He called out. There was no response. Earlier, the doctor had described Ramos's mother as suffering from old age, which probably explained the dust, the dirt, the smell, and the continuing silence. He called out again, more loudly.

A woman stepped inside from the road. 'What do you want?'

She didn't look like Dolores, yet she reminded him of her; perhaps it was the suggestion in both bearing and voice that whatever it was he wanted, he almost certainly shouldn't be pursuing it. 'I need to talk to Señora Ramos.'

'Who are you?'

'Cuerpo General de Policia.'

'Oh!'

'And you are?'

She hesitated, as if wondering whether it were wise to answer – a sure sign that she had been alive when one never answered authority's questions until one could no longer refuse to do so. 'Julia Miro . . . Is something wrong?'

'Are you a relation?'

'I live just next door. Do what I can to help, which isn't much, seeing I've my own family to care for. Frederico – my husband – is out with Luisa now in the car, looking for her Marcial who didn't return home last night.'

'I understand Luisa has a daughter – is she in the village?'

'Carolina? She lives in Inca.'

'A pity. It would have helped if she were here now.'

'That's not likely when she sees her mother as seldom as possible because of her husband. Their interest is money, not an old woman whose mind wanders . . . You haven't said why you're here. Is Marcial in trouble?'

'What makes you think he might be?'

'You.'

'Has he been in trouble in the past?'

'How would I know?'

The way in which she had spoken convinced him she knew very well. As a policeman, he was irritated by her stubborn independence; as an islander, he applauded it. 'Marcial had a very serious accident during the night. Sadly, he has died.'

'Sweet Mary!' She crossed herself. 'Haven't I said time and again that he should not have ridden around on that crazy motorbike? Yet for many years now there has been no man in the family to stop his stupidities and Luisa seldom knows what he is doing.'

Her words reminded him he had not determined what form of transport Ramos had used to reach Cala Blanca, something Salas was bound to ask sooner or later. 'As far as can be determined at the moment, it wasn't a road accident; he died from a fall . . . Why do you say he has a crazy motorbike?'

'How else to describe it? The young have always made fun of him because he can be slow of thought. One day, they promised him a present and made him very excited; then they gave him the bits and pieces of a motorbike one of them had crashed. They must have laughed and laughed when they saw his disappointment. Who can be crueller than the young? Yet, if he is not intelligent, he is really clever with his hands. He straightened out all the bits and pieces of the bike and put them together and made it work.'

'But not very well?'

'He set out for Palma to show everyone how wonderful it was and got no further than six kilometres short of Inca before it broke down. Took him hours to get it going again and return home. After that, he found enough sense to use it only locally, so that, every time it stopped, he could walk home to collect all the things he needed to mend it.'

'Could he have ridden it to Cala Blanca?'

'On that road?'

'You don't think he might have done?'

'If he couldn't get as far as Inca, how's he going to get over the mountains on a road that's like a snake in torment?'

'His accident was at Cala Blanca.'

'What was he doing there?'

'That is what I must ask his mother.'

'You'll not receive an answer. He tells her very little, but if he told her everything, she'd remember nothing.'

'You think she probably won't be able to suggest how he might have got there if he didn't ride his motor-bike?'

'I know she won't.'

'Can you say when your husband's likely to bring her back?'

'How can I possibly do that?'

'Does he have a mobile phone?'

'No.'

He looked at his watch and wondered whether to leave and return the next morning? But that would be to condemn the mother to more fearful uncertainty, however disturbed her mind. 'I'll wait here until they return.'

She took a deep breath and then spoke in a rush. 'Be patient and kind.'

'I can promise you I will, in so far as circumstances allow . . . You've said there's little communication between mother and daughter, but wouldn't it be right to phone Carolina and ask her to come here? She could help Luisa.'

'You think she'd do anything when she's hated Marcial ever since she was young and he . . .' She stopped abruptly.

He wondered what she had been about to say. 'You're

90

obviously a good friend of the family. Will you be here when I tell her about Marcial?'

'If I have to be.'

Disconcertingly, Luisa smiled most of the time; it was difficult to remember that this was a meaningless expression.

She sat on a wood and leather chair, a small, frail old woman with a head of thick, white, wavy hair. She worked at a small tapestry which, Julia told Alvarez in a whisper, she had started a long time before, days after her husband died, yet had never finished because she constantly undid what she had stitched.

Someone else had done something like that, Alvarez half remembered. 'Señora Ramos, I am afraid I have very sad news for you,' he said quietly.

She smiled.

'This morning, I was called to an accident in Cala Blanca.' Normally, that would have been enough to warn his listener of what was to come and she would have begun to know the bitter, overwhelming grief that would turn her life into darkness. But she continued to smile. The giving of bad news had never been so painful a task for him, even though it was possible it was affecting his listener far less.

Julia moved until she stood by the chair and could rest a hand on Luisa's shoulder.

'Marcial had a very nasty fall on to the pebbles on the beach and his head was so severely injured that, very sadly, he died.'

She smiled.

He felt the sweat of emotion on his neck and body. 'He must have died instantly and not suffered.' So often, a lie was kinder than the truth. 'I'm afraid there will have to be a post-mortem.'

She smiled.

He wanted to shout at her to cry, to shed many tears; he

accepted that this would be for his own comfort, not hers. 'Can you tell me, did Marcial often go to Cala Blanca?'

'He's a good boy,' she said.

'Did he tell you yesterday that he was going to Cala Blanca?'

'He looks after me.'

'Do you know why he went there?'

'He says he'll always look after me. He's a good boy. He bought me a lovely bunch of flowers in the market.' She suddenly looked to her right and her left. 'Where is he? I want him.'

'Luisa, Marcial has had an accident,' Julia said. 'He won't be coming back.'

Luisa smiled.

Alvarez spoke to Julia. 'Can the doctor help?'

'To make her understand? Isn't it kinder if she doesn't?'

'Can even a doctor answer that?'

'You're really knocking it back tonight,' Jaime observed, as Alvarez poured himself another brandy.

'I need it.'

There was a call from the kitchen. 'A man always says he needs what he knows he should not have.'

Jaime leaned forward until his stomach pressed against the edge of the dining-room table. 'I reckon she's got a high-powered microphone in her ear,' he murmured.

'And razor blades on her tongue.'

Dolores pushed her way through the bead curtain, hung because, in the heat, flies and mosquitoes were a nuisance. She folded her arms over her carefully constricted bosom – only putas and the famous lacked modesty – and spoke to Alvarez. 'I am preparing tonyina amb safrà.'

'Then royalty will have cause to envy us!'

She ignored his servile attempt to ingratiate himself. 'I am cooking it to a special recipe given to me by my mother.'

They waited, now uneasy.

'It calls for much effort and skill and sadly I now know both will be wasted, since there will be two at the table who will not know what they are eating.'

'This is only my second drink,' Jaime protested.

'You have a strange way of counting. Perhaps you have lost some fingers?'

'I assure you . . .' Alvarez began.

'An alcoholic assurance is as trustworthy as a politician's promise.'

'I'll appreciate every mouthful.'

'Did I not hear you say you needed another drink? Was that the fourth or the fifth, perhaps even the sixth? By now, can you tell the difference between sopes Mallorquines and a week old barra? I am a fool! I dedicate myself to serving two men and how do they respond? As always. With sottish indifference.'

'I am not tight.'

'That you can attempt to deny the obvious shows how much you have drunk. If you were stopped by Traffic and told to blow into a breathalyser, it would change colour with the speed of light.'

'There's a difference between having a drink or two and being drunk.'

'Perhaps fifteen minutes.'

'I've had one hell of a day . . .'

'And I, of course, have enjoyed myself in Palma, wandering from shop to shop along Jaime Three, looking at all the luxuries I cannot begin to afford.'

'I do my best . . .' Jaime began.

'Your misfortune is that that is never good enough.' She swept back into the kitchen.

Twenty minutes later, she served the tuna steaks, accompanied by onions, garlic, egg yolk, lemon, pine nuts, olive oil, parsley, bay leaf, saffron, pepper and salt.

Alvarez ate a couple of mouthfuls before he said, 'I have never tasted anything like this before.'

'Had you drunk less, you would recognise what it is you are eating,' she snapped.

'You believe I don't?'

'I believe drink twists a man's tongue yet lets him believe it is still straight.'

'This is delicious.' He ate another mouthful. 'It is perfection and my tongue is absolutely straight.'

Absolutely bloody crooked, Jaime said, but only to himself.

'You know, Dolores, it is a fact that I really did need that drink earlier because of what happened at work.'

'What was that?' she asked, her tone no longer critical. If there were trouble, she would rush to help.

Seeing her attention was on Alvarez, Jaime reached across for the bottle of wine and refilled his tumbler. He wondered how his wife, sharper than any needle, could allow herself to be bamboozled by false words of praise?

'I had to tell a mother that her son was dead,' Alvarez said.

'Sweet Mary, how terrible! Of course you needed a drink!'

Jaime drank deeply. A woman's mind was like the universe, unknowable.

'Whose son has died?' she asked.

'Luisa Ramos's Marcial. And for me, the tragedy was compounded because she has so few wits left that I could not make her understand what had happened. She will be continuing to wait for him to return home.'

She ate. 'Poor Luisa. She has been senile for a long while, thanks to her husband and her son.'

Jaime was unwisely prompted to ask: 'Why do you always blame the men?'

'Because they are always to blame,' she snapped. 'Did her husband not often get drunk and beat her . . . Just try to raise a finger at me!'

'For God's sake, do you think I'd ever dream of such a thing?' Jaime said, aghast.

'A man's dreams are not for any decent woman to know.'

'Why did you say it was also the son's fault?' Alvarez asked.

She speared a piece of fish on her fork. 'Perhaps it was even more Marcial's, but how does one judge? He was simple even in his cradle so perhaps he never understood what he was trying to do.' She raised the fork to her mouth.

'What was that?'

She swallowed. 'It is in the past and best forgotten.'

Julia had told him Carolina had hated her brother ever since . . . And then had become silent. 'Did he sexually assault his sister?'

'I do not wish such horrible things even to be mentioned in my house.'

How long would a hatred burn that had been triggered by such an experience? Would time damp it down or make it burn brighter? Was there now an explanation for Marcial's presence at Cala Blanca?

Eleven

The road to Cala Blanca possessed so much potential for disaster that to drive along it called for the suppression of the natural urge towards self-preservation. To repeat so hazardous a journey when it could turn out to have been unnecessary . . .

On Thursday morning, Alvarez braked his car to a halt ten metres back from the edge of the drop down to the pebble beach and stared out at the cove, quietly beautiful under the cloudless sky. He lit a cigarette. Julia had said Marcial possessed enough sense to understand after his abortive trip to Palma that his motorbike was fit for only short, easy journeys. Then would he have even considered, let alone undertaken, a ride to Cala Blanca . . . ? Of course, Marcial might have understood, yet not heeded that understanding. The sense of urgency might have been so great that he had ignored everything other than the need to reach Cala Blanca as quickly as possible, hoping that by some mechanical wizardry, the bike would get him there . . .

He climbed out of the car, dropped the butt of the cigarette and carefully trod it into the earth, started his search of the scrub. He soon found the motorbike, on its side athwart a wild rosemary bush. It was of ancient design and manufacture and, at a guess, no more than 125cc; its appearance suggested it had been fortunate to get anywhere near Inca that day. He used his mobile to phone Traffic and ask them to check out the registration number (would Marcial have bothered to register his ownership or insure?) and to send a recovery vehicle to collect and take it to the forensic laboratory for examination.

An hour and a half later, after a small low-loader had left with the motorbike, he drove back to the Parelona Hotel, a bastion of wealth, luxury, and privilege, much favoured by left-wing politicians. He asked several members of the staff if any had seen a rider on an ancient motorbike making his way along the road from Port Llueso to the lighthouse on Tuesday evening? No one had. People who worked in such a hotel noticed only Rolls Royces and Ferraris.

Life taught that one only appreciated something to the full when knowing one was about to lose it. To awaken from a deep sleep and not yet be fully awake, to drift weightless in a world of warm colours, was a sybaritic luxury . . . Yet soon he would have to return to the post to work.

'Enrique,' Dolores shouted from downstairs, 'you must move.'

'There's no rush,' he called back.

'For you, there never is. But I have to go out. There's coca in the cupboard and the coffee machine is ready to be put on the gas.'

Eventually, he rose, dressed, and made his way downstairs. He lifted the coffee machine off the stove and poured and only when nothing happened did he remember the coffee was not yet made; there was only one relatively small piece of coca; he could not find the cherry jam. Dolores should not have left everything in such a muddle.

He drove through the narrow, twisting streets to his preferred parking area, but it was fully occupied. When he did find space, he was faced with a long walk so that, by the time he reached the post, he was sweating and breathless. The young duty cabo, who lacked any sense of respect, said he looked as if he'd died five minutes earlier. Seated in his room, he felt his pulse, then panicked when he decided it was beating far too quickly, though he could not remember what the normal heartbeat was . . .

Half an hour later, cooled and to some extent calmed, he phoned Inspector Gual. Would Gual do him a favour? If he determined the married name of Carolina Ramos and her present address, would the other question her about her relationship with her brother when younger and ask her to establish an alibi for herself and her husband for Tuesday night? Gual replied that he'd far too much of his own work in hand to do anyone else's, but he wouldn't object to Alvarez's making enquiries within his territory.

'Lazy sod!' Alvarez said aloud, after he'd replaced the receiver.

In sharp contrast to Luisa's home, Julia's was clean and tidy. She watched Alvarez sit, then said, 'You ask if she yet understands? All I can say is, she knows Marcial is still not at home, but she doesn't seem to be as worried as she was yesterday. Perhaps she now believes he is away on holiday. Who can tell?'

'If you can't, I don't suppose anyone else can.'

'Occasionally, her mind clears a little and when next this happens, I am going to have to tell her yet again that Marcial is dead and perhaps she'll understand.'

'Friendship can offer a heavy burden.'

'Which has to be carried, however heavy.'

Initially, she had reminded him of Dolores, not in appearance, but in character. That similarity was being reinforced. Just as Dolores, she would do what she saw as her duty, come hell or high water. Women had their strengths as well as their weaknesses. 'I need to have a word with her daughter. Can you give me her married name and address in Inca?'

'Romaguera. And she lives in Carrer de Vivero which is close to the railway station; I can't give you the number of the house.'

'I'll find that easily enough.'

'As a matter of fact . . . Well, it didn't seem right, her not knowing about her brother, so I phoned and told her. I needn't have bothered. For all she cared, I might have been telling her a complete stranger had died.'

'You mentioned yesterday that she and her brother weren't on good terms.'

'Which is not to be surprised at.'

'Because of what happened when they were young?'

She said nothing.

'Is he older than her?'

'By six years.'

'Did he assault her when they were young?'

'I can't remember.'

'I'm sure you do.'

There was a long silence. Finally, she said: 'If certain things are to be told, it must be by her. I am not going to say.'

She probably had answered him; had the suggestion been nonsense, she surely would have said so. He thanked her and left.

In the past, the road from Llueso to Inca had been rough, seldom under good repair, and after torrential rain so rutted and holed that travel by coach or mule cart was physically exhausting and occasionally dangerous; now, it was a smooth, fast highway and always dangerous,

since every Mallorquin male considered himself to be
Schumacher's understudy.

Alvarez entered Inca from the west, a route that quickly
brought him to the railway station and, two roads on,
Carrer de Vivero. He stopped to ask an elderly woman
where Carolina Romaguera lived and she directed him
to Nº41.

Good food, medicine, and working conditions instead
of poor diets, old wives' remedies, and backbreaking
labour in the fields, had resulted in an increase in the
average height of younger islanders; Carolina stood a
centimetre taller than Alvarez.

'Someone told me about Marcial,' she said. 'I can't
remember her name.'

Carolina had attractive but hard facial features, similar
to those often seen on catwalks, and an aggressive manner.
Whether or not the past was as significant as he surmised,
he judged she would have met news of her brother's death
with indifference. 'Julia, your mother's neighbour and a
very good friend.'

She shrugged her shoulders, waited for him to explain
this visit. When he didn't, she said: 'What is it you
want?' She took care to be obvious as she looked at
her wristwatch.

'Perhaps I might sit?' He sat to show her that she would
not get rid of him by suggesting she was pressed for time.
The chair was contemporary – strangely shaped, covered
in brightly coloured material, and a shade uncomfortable.
'There will, of course, have to be a post-mortem.'

'Why?'

'The law demands it after this kind of fatality.'

She crossed to the small pinewood sideboard, picked
up a pack of cigarettes, did not offer it. 'So?' She struck
a match.

'Sadly, your mother is hardly capable of arranging the

funeral and burial, so it will be for you to do so. I will make certain you are immediately informed when permission is given.'

'I don't understand what all this has to do with the Cuerpo?'

'We have to investigate a fatality when there appears to be reason to do so.'

'That woman who phoned me said Marcial had fallen off a cliff.'

'I would describe it as a bank rather than a cliff.'

'What's there to investigate, whichever it was?'

'I am not certain.'

'Then why come here? My husband will soon be home and he'll want his meal the moment he's back.'

'Señora, when I say I am not certain, this means there is reason to question, but I cannot yet determine why. It would seem your brother rode from Llueso to Cala Blanca on his motorbike, which he knew to be in so poor condition it couldn't be relied upon to finish even a short journey on a good road. Doesn't that seem strange?'

'You don't expect him to have behaved sensibly, do you? If that's what happened, it happened.'

'But did it happen?'

'What's that mean?'

'I am not certain.'

She stubbed out the cigarette in an ashtray, even though it had only been half smoked. 'I don't understand what the hell you're really saying.'

'I am considering the possibility that your brother did not travel on so difficult a road on his motorbike; that the bike was left at the cala to make it seem he did.'

'Who's going to do something that stupid?'

'I hope to find out.'

'And you think I can tell you?'

'It is possible.'

101

'As far as I'm concerned, he could have gone from one end of the island to the other on a scooter and I wouldn't know why, or give a damn.'

'You and he were not friendly?'

'Isn't that obvious?'

'Why was this?'

'It happens with families.'

'Normally, only when there has been real cause. Did you have good reason for disliking him?'

'That's my business.'

'But, since your brother's death, mine as well.'

'Why?'

'Because the form of his death might not be as it has presented itself.'

'Are you saying it wasn't an accident?'

'At the moment, I simply cannot judge. Señora, please answer my question. Did you have active cause to dislike him?'

'And if I did?'

'Was this because of something that happened when you were young?'

She remained silent.

'He was six years older than you?'

'What if he was?'

'When you were six or seven, he was twelve or thirteen. That is an age when the questions in a boy's mind become loud and he thinks a girl should answer them. Is that not so?'

She crossed to the sideboard, jerked a cigarette out of the pack, and lit it.

'When you were young, did he assault you and is it that which causes you to hate him still?'

'What's it matter to you?' she demanded fiercely.

Not having heard anyone enter the house, they both were momentarily startled when a man stepped into the room. He stared angrily at Alvarez as he said: 'Are you bothering her?'

He had the build of a bruiser and the scowling features to go with that.

'He's the Cuerpo,' she said hurriedly.

'The Cuerpo?' He faced Alvarez again. 'What d'you want with her?'

'I'm here in connection with the death of your wife's brother, Marcial Ramos, and I am making certain enquiries concerning his death.'

'That woman who phoned said as it was an accident.'

'I have to establish if appearances are deceptive.'

She spoke breathlessly: 'He says that maybe someone put Marcial's motorbike near where he fell.'

'Why should anyone be that daft?'

Alvarez said: 'It would appear to explain how he reached Cala Blanca and so negate the possibility he went there in someone's car.'

Romaguera said angrily: 'You're trying to say it wasn't an accident?'

'I have to examine that suggestion.'

'Examine it somewhere else.'

'You're not willing to help?'

'Right.'

'Why?'

'Because I ain't interested, that's why.'

'Did you like Marcial?'

'Like that stupid bastard?'

Alvarez faced Carolina. 'When you were young . . .' He checked his words. Her expression was now one of fear. Terrified of the consequences of the question she was certain he was about to ask?

Romaguera stamped over to the outer door and pulled it open.

'Where were you Tuesday night?'

'Is that when he died?'

'Yes.'

'You're saying maybe I did him in?'

'Did you?'

'No. But if you're not out of the house bloody fast, I'll do you in!' He raised his arms, fists balled.

Alvarez, with as much dignity as he could summon, left. He settled in his car and, as he drove off, began to question himself as to why he'd not asserted his authority to pursue his questioning? Because Romaguera had been sufficiently incensed to carry out the threat? Or because he had been so certain that to question her with her husband present would not only cause Carolina immediate embarrassment and mental distress, but also future trouble?

Had he been motivated by fright or sentiment? As he turned on to the main road, he decided the latter. After all, it was better to have done the wrong thing for the right reason than the right thing for the wrong reason. Or so it seemed to him then.

Twelve

Alvarez drummed on the desk with his fingers. How could one gauge the actions of a man whose mental capacity made it unlikely he would respect logic? It was ridiculous to consider crossing the mountains to Cala Blanca on a motorbike that was totally unreliable. Why would Marcial have made such a journey, however he made it, at night? Had he gone to the cala to meet someone – his sister? Could she have lured him there by pretending she had finally understood that hatred had to end because what held siblings together must be stronger than what threatened to keep them apart? But why the cala? Because it was isolated, most especially at night, and her husband could brutally throw Marcial to his death without fear of any eyewitness; he was likely to agree to meet her there, since it held a special significance for both of them . . . ?

He dialled the local undertaker. 'Has the post-mortem on Marcial Ramos been carried out?'

'Not yet. There's only the one local doctor qualified for the work and he's ill.'

'When's he going to be back?'

'You'll have to ask him, not me.'

'In the circumstances, I think I'll ask for the PM to be carried out in Palma.'

'What's the rush? Is there a panic?'

'I don't know.'

'Toss a coin and find out.'

'If only it were that simple.'

'Then you are telling us to ship the body to Palma?'

'That's right.'

'We'll need the usual authorisation order to meet our claim for expenses.'

'Can't you—'

'No.'

The call ended and he replaced the receiver. Salas would have to issue the order. He leaned over and pulled open the bottom right-hand drawer of the desk, brought out bottle and glass and poured himself a large drink.

He phoned Palma and spoke to the plum-voiced secretary. 'Wait,' she ordered.

He waited.

'Yes?' Salas said bad-temperedly.

'Señor, as you will of course remember, the body of Marcial Ramos was sighted on the beach at Cala Blanca—'

'Get to the point.'

'A post-mortem was due to be conducted locally, but has not been . . .'

'Why not?'

'The only local doctor qualified to carry out such work is ill.'

'But probably still perfectly able to carry out a PM.'

When Salas suspected he might possibly be sickening for something, he remained at home until all danger had to be past. 'In all the circumstances, I think the PM should be carried out by Professor Fortunato at the Institute.'

'We cannot afford the extra expense that would be incurred merely on account of people's feelings. The family will have to wait until the doctor decides he's fit enough to do his work.'

'In fact, they are not pressing for a speedy funeral.'

'Then what grounds are there for your suggestion?'

'I am not satisfied everything is as it appears to be.'

'The strongest possible indication that it is . . . Did you not assure me that the death was an accident, due largely to a state of drunkenness?'

'There's no suggestion of drunkenness.'

'Then why did you claim there was?'

'I don't remember doing so.'

'Hardly surprising . . . Are you now telling me you regard the death as suspicious?'

'I think there are facts which have to be considered very carefully.'

'Such as?'

'Having spoken to a friend of the family, I've learned that Ramos built up his motorbike from what could be called a load of junk parts. Inevitably, it proved to be very unreliable even on good roads, so it seems most unlikely he would risk riding it over the mountains to Cala Blanca, a route that will test a vehicle in good condition.'

'Why do you assume he rode it to the cala?'

'It was in the scrub close to the beach where his body was found.'

'Why has there been no mention of this before?'

'The evidence is only just to hand . . .'

'I suspect it is the memory, not the evidence, which has suddenly surfaced. Is that your only reason for asserting the death was not an accident?'

'That possibly it was not.'

'Were you not a moment ago presenting evidence to show he could not have ridden his bike to the cala and therefore—'

'It's not quite that certain, Señor.'

'What isn't?'

'That Ramos would behave logically. He was not very bright.'

'One can assume that, since he is a Mallorquin.'

'So perhaps he did ride his bike over the mountains.'

Salas's voice rose. 'Have you not been putting forward the theory he did not as cause to doubt his death was an accident?'

'The facts suggest he would not consider riding it to the cala. But, being simple-minded, it could be he would not act logically and that he did. And the fact that the motorbike was there supports this assumption. But, although simple, it seems he had very considerable mechanical ability, and that raises the possibility of sufficient sympathy with some things to provide a sense of logic otherwise missing, and this would mean that although he would not directly recognise the stupidity of making the ride, indirectly he would and therefore would not make it. Accept that and logically—'

'Don't debase the word "logic" any further.'

'Then the fact the bike was found at the cala means the intention was to make it appear he had ridden it there when in fact it was carried by someone who did not know the mechanical condition it was in. You can follow what I'm getting at Señor?'

'You are far too optimistic.'

There was a silence which Salas broke. 'Are there any other facts, more readily detailed, which lend any weight to your assertion this may not have been an accident?'

'The head seemed quite severely damaged, but there was very little blood on the stones under or around it.'

'What did the doctor say about that?'

'He didn't comment on it, probably because he accepted the death as an accident and any apparent anomaly must be unimportant.'

'Clearly, you did not bring the point to his attention.'

'At the time, I did not know Ramos's motorbike . . .'

'Let us not enter confusion again. Are you saying it was murder?'

'That it might have been.'

'The possibility being based only on the grounds you have tried to explain?'

'There is one thing more. I have identified someone who may have had a motive.'

'Who?'

'His sister, Carolina. Over many years, she may have had very good reason for hating him.'

'May have, may have . . . Are these flights of supposition supposed to present an ordered investigation?'

'It's difficult to be certain.'

'A difficulty with which you are all too familiar. What is the good reason she may, or may not, have had?'

'He was six years older than her. So when she was five or six, he was eleven or twelve. A boy of that age is curious in a special way.'

'What is that supposed to mean?'

'He's a boy and she's a girl.'

'You feel there is merit in continually pointing out the obvious?'

'Boys become curious.'

'Are you suggesting . . . ?'

'It would explain why she hates her brother. And her husband might well have agreed to go along with her desire for revenge.'

'I presume it would not have occurred to you that you could very quickly end your obnoxious speculation by asking them if they had an alibi for Tuesday night?'

'I asked, Señor, but the husband was reluctant to give me an answer.'

'No doubt you framed the questions in such a way he had not the slightest idea what you were talking about . . . You will return at the first opportunity and question him to find out if he can establish an alibi for himself and his wife.'

'It may not be that easy because—'

'Confine yourself to simple words of one syllable, refrain from trying to explain anything which is in any degree complicated, and you may for once become comprehensible,' Salas said, before he cut the connection.

Thirteen

Alvarez braked to a halt, but remained seated behind the wheel as he tried to cheer himself up. It was later than he had intended because he had fallen asleep again after Dolores had called him, but Romaguera had not returned home until after seven the previous evening, so there should still be just under an hour's safe time.

He left the car, crossed to the front door, opened it and stepped inside. 'Señora?' he called out.

Carolina entered through the far doorway. Clearly, she had not identified him from his voice because her expression abruptly changed. She fidgeted with a corner of her dress as she stared down at the rough woven rug on the tiled floor. 'What is it this time?'

'I am here to learn the answer to one question.' He was saddened he should cause her fear; glad that, despite this, she remained defiant. Five hundred years before, she would have been one of the terrified, but redoubtable, women who, lacking any other weapons, had beaten off the Moors with frying pans (or so history taught). 'Were you and your husband in this house on Tuesday evening?'

'Yes.'

'Can anyone corroborate you were here?'

'Yes.'

'Who is that?'

'Eduardo and Eva.'

111

'Where do they live?'

'In the next road.'

He asked her to be more precise and she gave him the name of the road and the number of the house. Then she said, speaking uncertainly for the first time: 'Is this because of what you were saying yesterday?'

'That's right.'

'You asked if . . . When we were young . . .'

'Señora, after I have spoken to your friends and they agree with what you have just told me, the nature of the relationship between you and your brother will be of no concern to me or anyone else in the Cuerpo.'

She looked directly at him. 'You mean that?'

'Never more so.'

She murmured something which he imagined was a confused exclamation of relief. He thanked her for her help, left.

She had said her friends lived in the next road and it would probably be quicker to walk than to drive because of one-way roads, but he drove. Unnecessary exercise in the heat was dangerous.

Eva was a year or two younger than Carolina, of a far more sympathetic character to judge from her features, and possessed of a figure to make a man . . . Alvarez introduced himself. She was alarmed. There were those – of whom she was clearly one – for whom members of the Cuerpo were black goats with wall eyes, harbingers only of bad news. 'There's no cause to worry,' he assured her. 'All I want to know is where you were on Tuesday night?'

'Why are you asking?' She was reassured by his friendly manner.

'It's purely a matter of routine.' He noted that all the furniture in the front room – of which there was a considerable amount – was nearly new. Forty years before, a young couple would have had to be content with a very few pieces, and those hand-me-downs. 'So were you here, at home?'

She shook her head.

'Would you like to tell me where you were?'

She hesitated, finally said. 'We were with friends. Just having a meal, that's all.'

He smiled. 'I wouldn't imagine you were in a gambling den! What were the names of your friends?'

'What's that matter?'

'It could help them very much if you tell me.'

'Carolina and Miguel.'

'Precisely what I wanted to hear!'

She was plainly confused by this.

'When do you reckon you arrived at their place?'

'It wasn't until Eduardo had had a shower after returning from work.'

'And when did he return.'

'Just after eight.'

'So you arrived at their house maybe eight thirty to nine?'

'I suppose.'

'When did you leave?'

'Very late.' She was now completely at ease. 'I kept saying we must go because I have to start work early some days, but Miguel and Eduardo were going on about football and, once they start, they never stop.'

'And perhaps they were enjoying a drink or two?'

'They never talk football with dry mouths.'

'By the time you left, were either of the men in a fit state to drive a car?'

Her manner abruptly changed. 'We walked back.'

'I understand. But my question, which is very important, is not what actually happened, but whether you think either Miguel or Eduardo was capable of driving a car?'

'If they'd tried, I'd have refused to be in it and so would Carolina.'

'Then that is the complete answer.'

'What's all this about?'

'I had to make certain your friends could not help me with a case I'm investigating; you have done just that.'

Back in his car, he settled behind the wheel, swore. If he had not fled Romaguera's anger the previous evening, had remained until the alibi had been provided, he would have learned that Romaguera and Carolina could not have murdered Ramos (if Ramos had been murdered) . . . Perhaps Salas was right. He rushed to wrong conclusions because his mind sought the dark corners of people's minds rather than the light ones. It shamed him to remember how, the previous evening, he had congratulated himself on having nobly refrained from questioning Carolina in front of her husband. He should have cursed himself for considering the possibility that she and Ramos . . .

When he returned to Llueso, he ought to go straight to the post and report to Salas. But why do something today which could be put off until tomorrow? After all, an asteroid might blast into earth and destroy tomorrow so that no report ever had to be made.

There was no asteroid impact.

'I wish to make sure I have understood you correctly,' Salas said, with venomous politeness. 'You are now completely satisfied Romaguera could not have driven to Cala Blanca on Tuesday night?'

'Yes, Señor,' Alvarez answered.

'Then he did not murder Ramos?'

'No, Señor.'

'And your suggested obnoxious motive for murder can have no foundation in fact?'

114

'As a motive, no. But whilst it may be of no consequence in this case . . .'

'It will be returned to the dustbin of your mind.'

'I did seem to have reason—'

'You do yourself even greater disservice by continuing with a subject which could never have occurred to, let alone be accepted by, the great majority of people.'

'I thought—'

'One has to doubt the possibility. Since Romaguera will no longer concern you, is there anyone else you have identified as having a motive for murdering Ramos?'

'No, Señor.'

'Then one may finally assume his death was an accident?'

'Why did he go to the cala on a motorbike that he'd every reason to believe was incapable of making the journey . . . ?'

'In the cause of sanity, we will accept that, whatever his belief, lacking any evidence to the contrary, he did ride it there.'

'I'm sure we ought to make further enquiries.'

'Why?'

'I have the feeling we are still a long way from the truth.'

'Have I ever remarked on the value of facts as opposed to feelings in an investigation?'

'Yes, Señor. Often.'

'Yet the meaning of my words still escapes you?'

'It's just . . .'

'You prefer to ignore them.'

'Of course not, Señor.'

'Then perhaps from now on you will concentrate on what matters.'

'Is—'

'Well?'

'Is the post-mortem to be carried out locally?'

'Of course.'

'You don't think it would be a good idea still to ask Professor Fortunato to do it to make certain nothing is missed?'

'Because you have a feeling it might be?'

'Not exactly a feeling. . .'

Salas rang off.

Alvarez poured himself a drink from the bottle in the bottom drawer and gradually the morning seemed less bleakly hostile. And it was Saturday so that soon after midday, his weekend would start. Added to which, it was almost time for merienda. He drained the glass and returned it to the drawer as the phone rang. Normally, he would have ignored it, since he was on his way out of the office, but the caller might well be Salas, who had previously forgotten to mention some unnecessary detail and was now ringing back to press it home.

'We haven't yet received the authorisation for shipping the body of Marcial Ramos to the Institute for a PM by the professor,' a man said.

'That's not going ahead. The post-mortem is to be carried out locally.'

The speaker belligerently asked if Alvarez had the slightest conception of all the time and trouble that had already gone into making the preparatory arrangements for the transportation of the body? Advising each council through whose territory it would pass had demanded a mountain of paperwork, endless telephone calls . . .

'It's not my fault,' Alvarez said.

'Never is, I suppose!'

'It's the superior chief's ruling, not mine.'

'Then tell the silly bastard next time to make up his mind.'

What a pleasure that would be, he thought.

*   *   *

116

'You're very quiet,' Dolores observed as she looked at Alvarez.

'He's too busy stuffing his mouth to talk,' Juan said pertly.

She turned and regarded her son with – as Jaime had once unfortunately termed it in her hearing – her basilisk glare. 'You imagine that is clever?'

'I was just . . .'

'Just being rude and stupid. But perhaps I should not be too surprised. What can be more difficult than to be sensible and polite when those around you set such bad examples?'

'Who's that supposed to refer to?' Jaime asked.

'You wish to pretend you do not know?'

'If I did know, I wouldn't ask, would I?'

'Probably,' she said scornfully.

'Your father must have . . .'

'Yes?'

'Heard your mother say a lot of things.'

'And, unlike you, possessed sufficient sense to listen to them.'

Jaime went to drink, found his glass was empty. About to reach for the bottle of wine, he realised Dolores was staring at him. He raised his hand and scratched his neck.

She spoke once more to Alvarez. 'Are you feeling all right?'

'Couldn't be better.' She was like a hen, clucking around her family the moment she thought it possible one of them was not fit.

'Maybe he's got mumps, like Susana has,' Isabel suggested.

'I had mumps when I was your age,' Alvarez said, 'so I won't get it a second time . . . The fact is, I've been thinking about work.'

'Why should that cause you to worry about what you're eating?' she asked, a touch of asperity in her voice. She expected the diner's concentration to be on the food.

'I keep trying to decide if I've been as stupid as Salas obviously thinks me.'

'A wise man looks for wisdom, a fool for stupidity.'

'I feel certain things can't be as straightforward as the facts appear to suggest; the superior chief believes facts count, instinct doesn't . . . If you knew a motorbike was hopelessly unreliable, would you set out to drive it over the mountains to Cala Blanca?'

'Of course not.'

'But the bike was there. If Marcial Ramos was mechanically smart enough to build that bike out of a load of parts from a crash, wouldn't one think he had the mechanical sympathy not to ride it over the mountains? But would he? After putting it all together, he tried to ride it to Palma. Or was that a case of pride overcoming common and mechanical sense? Then what was he doing at Cala Blanca; why was he out at that time of night?'

Juan began to snigger, tried to turn this into a cough, ended up choking.

'Learn to eat politely instead of gobbling,' said Dolores.

'I finished ages ago.'

'Then why are you making so disgusting a noise at the table?'

'Because he hasn't any manners,' Isabel said.

'That is very true, but it is not your place to make the observation.' Dolores stood. 'You will clear the table, Juan, while I make coffee.'

'It's not my turn . . .'

'It may help you to learn to behave.'

'It won't.'

'Then you will be spending many days clearing the table after each meal.' She marched through to the kitchen, leaving the strings of beads clashing against each other for many seconds after she had passed through.

Muttering, while careful he could not be understood, Juan began to collect up the dirty crockery and cutlery.

'Let's be having the coñac,' Jaime said.

Alvarez poured himself a generous measure, passed the bottle across the table, used his fingers to lift out three half-melted ice cubes from the insulated container.

They drank.

By Wednesday, temperatures had risen until they were more akin to mid-July than June. Shallow wells had dried up, fields of wheat, barley, occasionally oats, had been harvested and were being grazed by optimistic sheep, lemons, oranges and tangerines were swelling, as were grapes, lettuces were bolting, and air-conditioner engineers were working overtime.

Alvarez adjusted the angle of the fan on the desk to try to gain more comfort from its draught, settled back in the chair. In front of him were several letters which needed answering – he would provide the answers in good time – a long memorandum from Palma – he would read this in good time – a note from a fellow inspector, asking for the information urgently needed in an important case – he would provide this, if possible, in good time . . .

He hadn't fallen asleep, but the ringing of the bell did cause him to start heavily.

'Inspector Alvarez, this is Doctor Zamora.'

'Good morning, Doctor.' A pleasant man, Alvarez thought, who, unlike some of his colleagues, did not assume an air of omniscient authority.

'I have completed my PM examination of Marcial Ramos. The extent to which the outer table of the skull was deformed and thrust into the diploe, the nature of the surrounding fissures, the damage to the brain, and the considerable subdural bleeding, make it certain that death was caused by the head coming into sharp contact with a large, solid object.'

'When you say that, presumably the object could in fact have been several stones?'

'My judgment would be, not.'

One did not lightly question a doctor's verdict. Alvarez said hesitantly: 'The beach at Cala Blanca, at the point where the body lay, is composed of pebbles, some of which are quite large. If pebbles were clumped together, could they cause this injury?'

'It might be possible.'

'But unlikely?'

'However closely clumped, I would expect the indication of more than one point of impact.'

'Would you have expected much bleeding?'

'I presume you mean external bleeding. That would to some extent depend on how soon death intervened, but in general, yes, there would have been a fair amount.'

'There were very few bloodstains on the pebbles.'

'And you want to know if that could be significant?'

'Yes.'

'Since one can only generalise, one has to accept that a particular case can prove anomalous. Conditions may have caused less external bleeding or traces of bleeding to be less visible than one would normally expect. However, you may decide there may be significance when I tell you that wedged into the brain was a small piece of plant, forced there by the blow.'

'But the beach is all pebbles and the nearest vegetation is up on the bank from which he presumably fell.'

'Quite. However, bear in mind that, following a severe blow to the head, there can very occasionally be what is termed a latent period during which blood accumulates, the victim appears to recover, and for a brief period even engages in further activity; then he collapses and dies.'

'That means Ramos may have been up on the bank when he fell and his head struck a rock, but he regained sufficient control to pick himself up and move; and it was when he was on the edge of the bank, climbing down it, or even on the beach, he collapsed and died?'

'I have one further piece of information which seems to complicate the picture even further. The plant section struck me as unusual. I have a friend who is a very keen amateur botanist and I asked him if he could identify the plant. He did so. It's an orchid, name of *Italica*. He was very interested and wanted to know where it had come from; when I said Cala Blanca, he was surprised. *Italica* normally grows on acidic ground, amongst bushy areas and pine woods. As he pointed out, the ground around the cala is not acidic, there are no pine trees, and the vegetation is scrub rather than bush.'

'Is he saying this orchid couldn't be growing around the cala?'

'He wouldn't go that far; to quote his own words, "Say something doesn't grow somewhere and you're at risk of being proved totally wrong." But the orchid apparently is relatively rare on the island and becoming rarer and there are no records of its ever being found between Llueso and Cap Parelona and only one instance between Llueso and Mestara.'

'Then how do I find out if these plants are growing around the cala, but no one's previously recorded them?'

'You search, surely?'

'When I don't know what I'm looking for?'

'You have a point! I suggest you speak to my friend, Benito Fiol. You'll find him very keen to help you search – did I not know him to be as sane as myself, I'd doubt the sanity of a man who flew to the north of the Peninsula and spent days searching on the foothills of the Pyrenees for a plant, declared extinct half a century ago, merely on a report from a source acknowledged to be unreliable. Naturally, he failed to find it.'

When the call was over, Alvarez sat back and glumly stared through the window at the sun-washed wall of the building on the opposite side of the road. A third trip to the cala and an exhausting search in the heat? If the piece of orchid had been small, battered, and stained, as it must have been, Fiol's identification could have been mistaken. Experts were often wrong. Yet if in this case correct, if *Italica* did not grow anywhere near the cala, then several facts could be tied together to show Ramos had almost certainly not died where his body had been found. The pleasure to be gained from informing Salas that he'd been right to suspect a faked scene – and therefore by implication that Salas had been wrong to dismiss his doubts – must surely outweigh the physical discomforts of the search?

Alvarez wiped the sweat from his forehead. Could he have been so misguided as to believe that the pleasure of mentally sticking up two fingers at Salas was worth the trauma he was suffering? Fiol was like a mountain goat, inexhaustibly energetic. He raced from side to side of the valley, scaled steep slopes, blind to the possibility of missed footholds or rockfalls, courting heat exhaustion and constantly calling on Alvarez to hurry to where he stood to look at some plant. Each time, Alvarez had responded, supposing *Italica* had been discovered; each time, he found himself looking not at their quarry, but at some totally insignificant plant which Fiol tried to glamorise with a long, incomprehensible name . . .

Fiol hurried up to where he stood. 'I think one can say

that section of *Italica* did not come from here. There's not been the shadow of a single plant.'

There had not been the shadow of anything. After seven in the evening and still the sun bored into a man's mouth until his mind was tortured by images of iced drinks. . .

'I've been meaning to have a wander around the lighthouse area to check on what's growing there these days, so being so close we might as well drive there now.'

'I do have a lot of work waiting.'

'Then count yourself lucky. Work is what keeps a man alive.'

Zamora had claimed Fiol was as sane as he, which made for one crazy doctor.

Politeness, and the fact that they had used Fiol's car, as he disliked being driven, meant Alvarez could object no further. It was almost nine before Fiol braked the car to a halt near the roundabout at the eastern end of Llueso. 'You can walk from here, can't you?'

Could he?

It was while he was enjoying his merienda on Thursday morning that Alvarez realised he had forgotten to ask Fiol to name the known habitat of *Italica* between Llueso and Mestara. Twenty minutes later, receiver to his ear, he sat back in the chair in his office and listened to a prolonged dissertation on the iniquitous members of the public who had only to see something rare and beautiful to trample it or to pick it and then later, when bored, throw it into the dustbin. There had been an established colony of *Italica* and the dense conical clusters of pink flowers with their magnificent pointed helmets (How could anyone become so responsive about so unresponsive a subject?) had brought delight to every botanist; then the local council, as empty-headedly indifferent to nature as their ilk always were, had given permission for the urbanización Beniferri to be developed. Naturally, the fervid pleas of all botanists had been ignored. Mammon always triumphed. Houses had been built, people, dogs, cats had roamed, the colony had ceased to flourish and now was in danger of extinction . . .

Fiol offered to show him where the largest known colony of *Italica* was growing. Fearing this might turn out to be a frantic scramble on some hideously dangerous mountain peak, he explained that he couldn't be certain when, if ever, the pressure of work would ease sufficiently to allow him the pleasure. But if the other would just indicate where the plants were . . .

Fourteen

It was after five when Alvarez turned off the road on to the track which led through the belt of pine trees and, once clear of them, parked the car. He stepped out and stared up at the first of the bungalows and houses which ringed the hill in an uneven arc. He wondered if Wade was yet enjoying the easing of memories which time could offer?

He began to search the area Fiol had delineated. The sun was burning hot, he sweated profusely, and his throat became parched. If, he thought resentfully, Doctor Zamora had been less thorough and so had not found that piece of *Italica*, he would not now be suffering. Those who showed too much zeal were responsible for most of what went wrong in the world.

As he slowly combed the land between the trees and the hill without success, he came to the conclusion that *Italica* had died out, never grown there, Fiol had given the wrong directions, or he had mistaken what those had been. In truth, it didn't matter which – the result was the same. He tottered across to a large rock with a flat top, half a metre in diameter, which was by the track and sufficiently close to the trees to be in shade, and slumped down on this. He lit a cigarette. How much longer must he continue before admitting defeat? Would it not be better – for the project as well as himself – to harness Fiol's insane enthusiasm and ask him to carry out the search on the grounds that an expert's eyes were needed? There should be no need to accompany him; a young cabo could be detailed (the sargento owed him a favour).

A car came down from the urbanización and along the relatively level road until it slowed and then stopped abreast of where he sat. The driving-side window slid down and a woman stared out at him. Her beaky, craggy face, with the dusky line of an embryonic moustache, reminded him of an ancient aunt who had been credited with either supernatural powers or a hoard of hidden pesetas, else how had she ever persuaded a man to marry her?

'What do you want?' she demanded in strangulated Castilian.

The pronunciation, raised voice, and arrogant tone identified her nationality. 'Can I help you, Señora?' he asked in English.

'What do you think you're doing?'

He pondered the question.

'Are you struck dumb?'

'I am sorry, I don't quite understand what it is you wish to know.'

'This is private property. Trespassers are not permitted.'

'I'm causing no harm.'

'Quite immaterial. If you are not off this land immediately, I shall call the police and tell them to remove you.'

'I am the police.'

'Impossible,' she said, as she surveyed him.

'My name is Inspector Alvarez of the Cuerpo General de Policia.'

'You mean someone like you . . . Good God!'

Did she imagine she looked like Venus reborn? He dropped the cigarette butt on to the ground.

'What do you think you are doing?' she asked a second time.

'Señora?'

'Are you incapable of understanding that your irresponsible stupidity may well cause a fire?'

'The cigarette is on bare earth and I am about to put my shoe on it.' He moved off the rock, stamped the butt into the soil. 'I think a fire is now somewhat unlikely.'

'If I thought you knew what you were saying, I'd report you for dumb insolence.'

'Then I must be grateful I do not.'

'What's that?'

'I would not wish to be thought insolent, whether dumbly or vocally.'

'It is a great pity that you people are not taught to speak coherently.'

'It can be difficult to do so in a foreign language.'

'Only if one is too lazy to try. I have lived here for only a few years, yet I speak Castilian perfectly.'

'Then surely it will be less difficult for you to understand me if we continue in Castilian?'

'Your attitude is unacceptable.'

'Then I'm sure it will be better if I move on.'

'You will not do so until I've told you exactly what is my opinion.'

'Which is, Señora?'

'That, living here, one expects everything will take twice as long as in a civilised country because people do not know what hard work means, but it is totally ridiculous for the police to need over a fortnight to respond.'

'To respond to what?'

'You admit you do not know?'

'I don't think "admit" is quite the right word . . .'

'You are hardly capable of determining that with your

poor knowledge of the language. You admit you have no idea why you are here?'

'I know precisely why I am here. To look for a flower.'

'If you believe you are being in any way amusing, rather than insolent, you are thoroughly mistaken.' The window began to rise.

'Señora.'

The window came to a stop.

'Perhaps you will be kind enough to explain what it is the police have not reacted to?'

The window dropped to the fully open position. Her voice loud and laced with the irritation which came from having to explain to a half-witted foreigner, she said: 'A fortnight ago, late in the evening, I rang the police in Llueso to tell them a man seen acting suspiciously had run away after being challenged. Naturally, we expected there to be an immediate response, but no one appeared. You claim to be a policeman, yet say you know nothing about the incident and are looking for a flower; if true, there has still been not the slightest response to my phone call. And that after two weeks!'

'You saw this man?'

'I did not. My husband and I were at home when we heard the shouting. He went out to discover what was the trouble, I stayed inside.'

'Then your husband saw him?'

'No.'

'Did anyone see him?'

'Would there have been cause to report the incident otherwise?'

'Then who did see him?'

'One of our neighbours, Gaines. He tried to chase the man, fell over, and hit his chin on something. It was only a slight injury, but one would have imagined it was a fatal wound from the fuss he made. His type always make a ridiculous fuss. No stiff upper lip.'

Under her moustache were very thin lips; made for extra stiffness?

'It was obvious the police should be called, so I phoned them. The man to whom I spoke was clearly far from intelligent, but I made the mistake of supposing he would at least make certain a policeman came out immediately, not a fortnight later. And then you have the gall to tell me you are here to look for a flower!'

'Señora, I can assure you that when you phoned, had you been understood—'

'I have told you, I speak perfect Spanish. I am not prepared to put up with any further insolence.' The window slid up and she drove off.

He watched the car until it went out of sight behind the pine trees. It was easy to guess what had happened. She had spoken in fractured Castilian and been too arrogantly certain she was word perfect to realise she might not have been intelligible. When the duty member of the Policia Local had tried to get her to speak more slowly and simply so he could understand her, she had ignored him and rung off. He would have shrugged his shoulders and returned to reading his girlie magazine . . .

The lack of immediate response to the phone call must surely have bred a sense of annoyance even in those more balanced in their social and cultural values. Was it now up to him to do what he could to lessen or eliminate such resentment? Regretfully, he decided that it was.

He returned to his car and drove up the track to Ca'n Greix. The door was opened by a woman. 'Señora Palmer?'

'Yes?' she answered, perplexed.

He introduced himself.

'My brother naturally mentioned meeting you. Do come in.'

He entered the hall.

'I imagine you want a word with Charles? I hope you won't mind my asking for a favour?'

'Of course not.'

'Could you be . . . as measured as possible? Inspector Fenton's visit reopened and sharpened memories and although that was nearly two months ago, it's still affecting him. If you have to ask more questions—'

He interrupted her. 'Señora, I am not here because of what occurred in England, so I will not have to mention that terrible tragedy. What has happened is, I was searching the land below when a car stopped and the señora who was driving told me that a fortnight ago a man had been skulking around the properties, was chased, and escaped. She complained that she reported the matter to the police immediately, but no one has ever come along to investigate the incident. I am certain that the officer to whom she spoke could not understand what she was saying and that was why no action was taken. In the circumstances, I should like to show there has been a mistake and if anything can still be done, it will be.'

'You obviously met Anthea Wyatt . . . Come on through. Charles is out by the pool.'

He followed her through the house and out on to the pool patio. Wade, in a swimming costume, was seated in the shade of a sun umbrella. He lowered the newspaper he had been reading and came to his feet. Clearly, he recognised Alvarez immediately.

'I am sorry to bother you, Señor . . .'

'I hope it isn't . . .' He checked the words.

'It isn't,' she said quickly. 'The inspector's here because he ran into the dreadnought and she told him what happened a couple of weeks ago when that man was lurking around the place and she complained the police never bothered to turn up.'

'If you have met the dreadnought, you are a shaken – and probably stirred – man. Inspector, after a dramatic event, a drink helps to restore normalcy. What can I offer you?'

'May I have a coñac with just ice?'

'Indeed . . . And do sit.' He moved a third chair to bring it within the shade. 'A little cramped, but better touching elbows than burning them . . . What for you, Hilary – the usual?'

'Yes, please.'

He turned and walked briskly around the pool to the house.

She sat, waited until Alvarez was seated, then asked: 'Have you heard anything from Inspector Fenton?'

'No, Señora.'

'Does that mean they're making no progress?'

'It may. On the other hand, it's rather doubtful he'd have been in touch with me if they had.'

'It seemed he must have come here as a last resort, which was such a pity, because, if he hasn't gained anything from the visit, Charles suffered renewed and sharpened memories for nothing.' She stared unseeingly at the rock face which rose to her left. 'I worry and worry, seeing him depressed for so much of the time. He puts on a good face when others are around – as you've learned – but when we're on our own . . . it's a very different picture. I do what I can to help. A couple of times, I've persuaded him to go on a trip somewhere, but I don't think he's really enjoyed it, because I've had to meet most of the costs. I've said time and again, I can afford the occasional luxury, because I'm reasonably well off, Frank having always been very careful moneywise, but I'm certain it makes him feel uncomfortable when I pay for him. Pride can be such a damned nuisance.

Wade returned, carrying a silver salver on which were three glasses. He passed these around, sat, raised his glass. 'May our pleasures grow as our problems diminish.' He drank. 'And mentioning problems, I gather you've met Anthea. A refugee from the beginning of the last century . . . So, following what she told you, you are making enquiries and would like to hear what, if anything, we can tell you?'

'That is so, Señor.'

'I start with a proviso. We only know much of the story from hearsay and, since Bert was the provider, one has to remember it was sufficiently late in the evening for him to have shaken hands with the Widow Clicquot many times . . .'

Hilary interrupted her brother. 'Flora says there definitely was someone messing around with the shutters.'

'Did they hear a scratching sound from the shutters?' Alvarez asked sharply.

They both looked at him, clearly surprised.

'I ask because this may be important.'

Wade said: 'I don't know exactly what Flora said was happening – do you, Hilary?'

'She did mention a scratching noise and—' She stopped, sneezed, then sneezed again even more violently. She hurriedly stood. 'Excuse—' A further sneeze cut short her words. She hurried past Alvarez and went indoors.

'She suffers from hay fever, although it can't be hay which triggers an attack out here,' Wade said. 'She's gone for her patent puffer, which usually stops an attack dead in its tracks.'

'I should very much like to know the name, Señor. I have a friend who suffers severely every year when the wild olive trees are in flower, and nothing the doctors have given him stops the attacks. There are days when he cannot work.'

'I'll get her to show you the puffer when she comes back . . . Here she is.' Wade called out: 'Hilary, bring the puffer to show the inspector, will you?'

She turned back. A moment later, she brought out a puffer, similar to those used by asthmatics, with a small nose shield attached to the square pressurised spray can. She put it down on the patio table, sat. 'I can't recommend it sufficiently. Nothing else works so quickly or effectively – for me, at any rate. You heard me begin to explode: two puffs from this and no more sneezing or itching eyes.'

'I don't think we have anything like this out here or I'm sure my friend would have tried it.'

'It's only appeared in the States so far and, when I made enquiries in England, they said it hadn't yet been approved there for sale. Here, they haven't brought it in either, so I have it sent over from America.'

'I must make a note of its name.'

'He has a friend who suffers badly from hay fever,' Wade explained.

'Then the simplest thing is for him to have this puffer which I've only just started.'

'No, Señora . . .' Alvarez began.

'For heaven's sake, I've three spare ones and, if needs be, can easily have some more sent out. So give this to your friend and, if it works as well for him as me, he'll be a fortunate man!' She pushed the puffer across.

'You are very kind, Señora.'

'It's not kindness to help a fellow sufferer, it's a duty!' She smiled.

There was a brief pause, then he said, 'Señor, you were telling me what happened that night.'

'It started when Bert and maybe Flora heard this noise at

the shutters. He rushed outside to discover what was going on. He says he surprised a man and started to chase him – one must allow for the trouble he would have had deciding which of the three images to chase – fell over and cut his chin on a small rock. He decided he was dying – a prospect to bring a smile to Anthea's lips, since she believes people like he should be confined to zoos – and Flora drove him to the emergency centre, where they stitched him up. Ever since then, he's been dining out on his miraculous escape from extinction.'

'You're very unkind,' she said.

'Pure jealousy speaking. Here am I, a working lifetime spent with nose to the grindstone and nothing to show for it but a little capital and there is he, by his own account a survivor from ten dozen and one doubtful enterprises, drinking champagne by the bucket and sailing his sixty-foot yacht with a nubile blonde.'

'If ever a nubile blonde stepped aboard, Flora would make very certain it was a case of look, no touch,' Hilary said.

'A typical wifely attitude!'

'Either before or after this incident,' Alvarez said, 'has anyone else heard scratching or rustling noises at their shutters?'

'I've not heard so. Have you, Hilary?'

She shook her head.

'Would you expect there to have been similar incidents, Inspector?'

'I am not certain.'

'Police talk for "I'm not saying"?'

Alvarez smiled.

Thirty minutes and one drink later, he left.

He drove up the road and around the curve of the hill to a very large bungalow, which had not been visible before, set on a stretch of reasonably level land. Because of the rocky nature of the area, soil had been imported to make raised flower beds. What had that cost? he wondered as he climbed out of the car. What did the watering cost?

The porch had columns of marble. The front door, in traditional style, was made from a very expensive, dark wood. He rang the bell and the door was opened by a middle-aged woman to whom he introduced himself and said he wanted to speak to Señor and Señora Gaines. Silently, she led the way through the hall into the very large sitting room – furnished luxuriously – and out to the patio. A man in open neck shirt and shorts sat at an elaborately shaped wrought-iron, marble-topped table; a large woman, sufficiently ill-advised to wear a two piece swimming costume, lay on a lilo in the middle of the pool.

'He is of the police,' the maid said in barely recognisable English.

Gaines, about to drink, held the flute in front of his mouth. 'You're a copper?'

'Yes, Señor.'

'Been walking backwards, have you?'

'How do you mean?'

'It's taken you so bloody long to get here, you've either arrived via the pole or been walking backwards . . . D'you want a drink?'

The transition from critic to host was so abrupt that it was several seconds before Alvarez said: 'Thank you, I should like one.'

'What's your poison?'

'Coñac with ice, Señor.'

He indicated the bottle of champagne in an ice bucket. 'Bubbly not good enough for you?'

'Too good.'

Gaines laughed, a short, barking sound.

'Who is it? Flora called out.

'A copper.'

'Then wait until I'm there.' She began to paddle towards the stone steps at the shallow end of the pool and, becoming too energetic, capsized and plunged into the water. She surfaced, quite unfazed, and walked the remaining two metres to climb the steps.

As Gaines leaned over to press a button set in the wall, she came to a halt in front of the table, water streaming down on to the tiles. Her chin was thrust forward as she said to Alvarez: 'So you've finally managed to arrive!'

'Señora, I must explain that until earlier this morning . . .'

'You lot couldn't be bothered.'

The maid stepped out on to the patio.

'Brandy and ice for the visitor and another bottle and a glass for the little lady,' Gaines said.

The maid returned inside.

Flora sat. She said pugnaciously: 'You just don't care about us foreigners. And you can't say you do!'

'On the contrary . . .'

'You think I'll be taken in by a load of flannel? The police were called at the beginning of the month and it's taken until now for anyone to turn up.'

'Señora, we are as concerned with the problems of foreigners as with those of Mallorquins. I can assure you that, had the report of the incident been intelligible, immediate action would have been taken. But the officer who answered the telephone could not understand what was being said. He asked the señora several times to identify herself and to speak more slowly, but she would not and, becoming very angry, rang off. Without knowing who had called, or why, there was nothing he could do. It was only this afternoon when Señora Wyatt stopped her car and demanded to know why her phone call had been ignored that I first learned what had happened. Naturally, I then spoke to Señor Wade and his sister and it was they who gave me your name.'

136

'That's straight?'

'That is the truth, Señora.' Perhaps he had taken a little for granted, but it was in a good cause.

'It's not you people ignoring us?'

'Far from it.'

She reached for a towel and rubbed the back of her hair to try to prevent more drips of water sliding down her neck and back. 'I should have known. Can't leave anything to that woman except being rude. I was too worried about my Bert or it would have been me what called you lot. I ain't no linguist, but I'd have talked until the policeman understood me.'

Alvarez had little doubt that she would have done just that.

'She's only herself to blame, then. I'll tell her so.'

'Best not,' Gaines said.

'I'm not scared of the likes of her.'

'Course you ain't. But why stir up trouble?'

'To give her a bit of her own back.'

'You won't get through, not with her thinking we should all curtsy to her. You'll be wasting your breath.'

'I've plenty to spare.'

The maid returned with the drinks; she took the empty bottle out of the ice bucket, replaced it with the full one.

The brandy was of excellent quality. Rough diamonds, Alvarez thought, might not sparkle in society, but they possessed their own charms.

'So what exactly is it you want with us?' Gaines asked. He drained his glass, picked out the bottle from the ice bucket, removed the wire, twisted the bottle around the cork until there was a satisfactory pop. He filled one flute and passed this to her, refilled his own.

'I should be grateful if you would tell me what happened that night, Señor.'

'Not going to get you anywhere now, is it?'

'Don't be soft, Bert,' she said firmly. 'If you don't tell, how's he to do anything?'

'All right. All right.' He drank deeply. 'As I remember, we was getting ready for bed when I heard something outside, on the shutters. I asked Flora if she could hear anything and she said no, she was thinking of Harry. That's our son. Doing very well, he is, but seems to think we're happy to make up the difference between what he earns and what he spends . . .'

'Enjoying himself, he is, and it don't hurt you,' she said. 'And the detective don't want to know all about our Harry.'

Gaines drank. 'I told her, listen. And then she said, yes, she could hear something, what could it be? I told her I didn't know, but, if it carried on, I was going to find out so as it stopped annoying us. Not sleeping so well these days, neither of us. Getting old.'

'Don't bother with what he can see for himself,' she snapped.

He drank. 'This noise did keep on. Wasn't all the time, like, but it would be there, then it wouldn't.'

'Can you describe it?' Alvarez asked.

'Not so easy.'

'Please try.'

'It was a kind of scratching, coming from the shutters . . . Here, don't you like that brandy?'

'It is by far the nicest I have drunk for a long time.'

'Should be, seeing what it costs. But, if it's all right, why ain't you drinking?'

Alvarez hastened to make his appreciation more obvious. Gaines pressed the button on the wall. Alvarez replaced his glass on the table. 'Was there a wind that night?'

'How would I know?'

'You wouldn't,' Flora said. 'There wasn't none; still as a corpse.'

The maid stepped out on to the patio. 'Bring the gent another brandy and make it large enough for him to see,' said Gaines in English.

'Another coñac,' Flora said in kitchen Spanish.

The maid took Alvarez's glass, left. Gaines picked up the bottle. 'Pass your glass, love.'

'No more for me,' she answered.

'Come on . . .'

'One of us has to know where we are.'

'It's what I'm doing ain't so certain.' Gaines guffawed.

'When you went outside, did you have a torch?' Alvarez asked.

She answered. 'He wasn't going outside without one, not with the ground so uneven. I said, if you can't see where you're going, you'll fall and damage yourself. I was dead right even though he had the torch and ought to have been able to see.'

'Didn't need a torch,' Gaines said, 'not with me switching on the outside lights. And if you hadn't gone on about me having to have one, I'd maybe have caught the man.'

'And what could have happened to you then?'

'I'd have given him something to think about.'

'What happened when you went outside?' Alvarez asked.

'I saw the man running away. Didn't stop to think . . .'

'Couldn't,' she said.

'And I just started chasing him. Next thing, my foot catches on something, I go sprawling, and my chin hits a bit of rock and my jaw's busted. I shouts for help and, after a couple of hours, Flora turns up . . .'

'Had to put something on, didn't I? Wasn't turning out in me nightie.'

'It ain't transparent.'

'You think I'd wear one that was?'

The maid returned and handed Alvarez a refilled glass, left.

'You made such a row, everyone comes out to see what's up and they'd all of seen me. You'd of complained fast enough.'

'When I was in agony?'

'If you didn't, you should of done. Are you saying you'd of liked all of 'em to see more of me than's decent?'

'I ain't saying anything of the sort.'

'That's just as well!' She turned to Alvarez. 'They was all standing around so I told the old bitch to call the police, since she always says she speaks Spanish perfectly, and I took him to the emergency centre in the village, where they stitched up his chin. And, when we got back here, I said it was best he laid down, but he wouldn't. Know what he did?'

'No,' Alvarez answered, though he could guess.

'Got a bottle of bubbly out of the refrigerator and got stuck into that.'

'I really needed it,' Gaines said.

'Would you like to tell me when there's a time you don't?'

'I can't stand needles. And there was this man sewing away as if he was putting a button on a shirt . . .' The memory was so traumatic that he had to refill his glass.

'Did you recognise the man you saw running away?' Alvarez asked.

'Can't say I did,' Gaines answered.

'By that time of night, if he looks in a mirror, he asks me who's called,' she said.

'There's no need to talk like that.'

'Someone's got to tell the truth.'

Alvarez said: 'Can you describe him?'

'Wasn't in a fit state to describe his own foot,' she said.

'That's where you're wrong!' Gaines said. 'He looked back before I tripped and he was still just visible in the house lights. And I had me torch on.'

'What sort of age was he – twenties, thirties?'

'Wouldn't like to be that certain.'

'Was his face round or oval?'

'Wasn't really one or the other; just ordinary.'

'What kind of hair did he have?'

'The light wasn't good enough to make that out.'

'You couldn't even judge the colour of it?'

'No.'

'Was any feature of his face particularly noticeable?'

'Wouldn't say so.'

'Was he tall or short, fat or thin?'

'Wasn't anything special.'

'What was he wearing?'

'Shirt and trousers.'

'What colour and pattern shirt?'

'Couldn't make that out.'

'Was he carrying anything?'

'Can't say I noticed. I mean, the next thing after seeing him was, I fell and bust me jaw . . .'

'You didn't bust it,' she said.

'It felt like I did.'

Gaines's description was useless and failed utterly to determine whether that man could have been Marcial Ramos, Alvarez thought despondently.

Fifteen

Dolores put the dish of oranges, bananas, and apples down on the table. Tradition had it that dessert was not an important part of a meal and she was a great traditionalist: while she could serve a fulles de llimonera or xulla del cel that would please the most discerning palate, she usually spent all her skill and energy on the main dish.

For once, they all ate in near silence. When they'd finished, she reminded Juan and Isabel that once more it would be the task of both of them to clear the table and then went through to the kitchen to begin the washing up. After finishing his second digestion-promoting brandy, and some ten minutes after the table had been cleared, Alvarez made his way through the front room to the road, where Juan was skateboarding with one of his friends. Alvarez called him over.

'What is it?' he asked, resentful at being interrupted.

'There's something I want to ask you.'

'But me and Bernado are busy.'

'A couple of minutes won't make any difference.'

'It will to me and Bernado.'

Alvarez put his hand in his pocket and jingled the coins that were in it.

Juan put one foot on the skateboard and, while standing still, moved it backwards and forwards.

'Do you remember during a meal some time ago I

started talking about Marcial Ramos and how I couldn't think why he should have gone to Cala Blanca?'

'No.'

'You began to laugh and then decided you shouldn't have done, tried to stop, and ended up coughing. Why was that?'

'Don't know what you're talking about.'

'What had you heard about Marcial?'

'Hadn't heard anything.'

Bernado, on the other side of the road, called out to know if Juan was ever returning to play.

'I'm coming now,' Juan shouted back.

'Hang on,' Alvarez said.

'I can't.'

'Because you're in such a hurry to buy a granissat?'

Juan hesitated, then said: 'I haven't any money.'

Alvarez jingled the coins again. 'You're in a hurry and I don't want to hold you back. So just tell me quickly what you were thinking that day I mentioned Marcial, then go off and enjoy a double-sized granissat.'

'I can't remember.'

'Think back really hard. Do you suppose you'd been told Marcial had been up to something that would have made your mother angry if you'd mentioned it because she might have thought you were showing an unhealthy interest?'

Juan moved the skateboard more rapidly.

'This is just between you and me. No one else will ever hear what you say.'

'I don't know if it was for real . . .'

'Of course you don't.'

'I mean, I wasn't interested.'

'Of course you weren't.'

'It's just Tomás said . . .' Juan stopped.

'What did he say?'

143

'That Marcial was watching . . .'

'People undress?'

Juan stared briefly and uneasily at him. 'How did you know?'

'It's my job to know.' One should always try to appear omniscient in the eyes of the young. 'How did he go about doing that?'

With the secret out, Juan spoke eagerly. Marcial had been doolally in most things, but working with his hands, he'd been brilliant. He'd bought, or acquired, a miniature TV spy camera and fixed that on a flexible probe which would take it up between the slats of a shutter; when in position, he could alter the angle of the camera and view whichever part of the room was interesting; he'd watched on a small TV monitor and had also been able to record on tape. He'd shown several people in the village what he'd taped and on more than one occasion . . . Juan became silent.

'I'm glad you've told me because this is very important.'

'You won't mention it to Mum?'

'I've told you, it's our secret.'

'What about the granissat, Uncle?'

Alvarez brought coins out of his pocket, selected two five peseta ones and passed these across.

Juan spoke with contempt. 'You think that'll buy anything?'

'It's not enough?'

'It's a hundred now for a small one and you promised me a large one. That's two hundred.'

Alvarez reluctantly handed over two one hundred peseta coins, took back the five peseta ones.

'What about Bernado?'

'He'll have to fund his own expensive lifestyle.'

Juan skateboarded away.

Alvarez watched the two boys disappear around the nearby corner. Could the price of a granissat really cost two hundred or had he been suckered? He was only able to dispel the irritation that question prompted by telling himself that had Juan realised the value of what he'd said, he would have claimed that the delicious lemon drink now cost a thousand pesetas.

Vehicles in Palma rang.

'You've learned something from that motorbike?' Alvarez asked.

'Yeah. If you offered me a hundred thousand to ride it across town, I'd tell you to stuff your money.'

'Could it have gone from Llueso across the mountains to Cala Blanca, just short of Cap Parelona?'

'Could you walk across the bay?'

'It was owned by a man who reputedly was pretty expert mechanically.'

'He'd need to be a genius to get it halfway up the first mountain.'

'So you don't think he could have made that journey?'

'Isn't that what I've been trying to tell you?'

Alvarez thanked the other, rang off.

Alvarez rang Fiol on Friday morning. 'I've had a really good search for an *Italica*, but didn't come across a single one, maybe because I was in the wrong area. Is there a chance you can show me exactly where it grows?'

'I remember offering to do just that and you refused,' Fiol replied.

'I know, but I simply couldn't find the time then. Things have eased off very recently and it is important. I'd be most grateful.'

'Very well. In truth, I'm far from averse to making

an up-to-date survey of the region. What shall we say – tomorrow afternoon?'

Tomorrow was Saturday. 'I was hoping we could go today.'

'Impossible. As it did you, time defeats me. But if Saturday's too difficult, we'll make it Sunday morning.'

An ancient hero had been offered the choice of being eaten by a monster or sucked down in a whirlpool. If only he could remember how both fates had been avoided. 'Sunday's out so it'll have to be Saturday.'

'Four in the afternoon all right?'

'Six would be a lot easier.'

'You think that'll leave us enough time?'

'I'm sure of it.' He was not going to give the other the chance to extend the search to the foothills of the Sierra de Mos.

To watch Fiol this time was just as exhausting as it had been before. The man hurried even when he climbed slopes, seemingly oblivious to the heat, which had not yet begun to diminish. Alvarez soon ceased to try to give the impression that he was helping and retired to the shade of the pine trees and sat. There was a sense of peace – if one did not look in Fiol's direction – and for once not even the barking of a dog disturbed this. It gave a man the chance to recharge his batteries . . .

There was a shout and he opened his eyes and looked across to see that Fiol was waving at him. He stood and slowly crossed to where the other stood.

'Eureka!'

He looked down at the small plant and thought it hardly warranted the trouble that had had to be taken to find it.

'We must very carefully extend the search,' Fiol said.

'Now I know there is one here, we needn't . . .'

Fiol's enthusiasm swept on. 'But is it the sole survivor? Is it the last witness to the destruction by humanity? We'll start with an intense search in this area; then we will move over there.' He pointed to the side of the curving hill to their right.

'Don't you think . . .'

'Keep within an arm's length to make certain we're checking every centimetre of land.'

Twenty minutes later – by which time Alvarez was cursing his decision to enlist the help of a madman – he came to a rock, roughly half a metre at its widest point, one irregular face of which bore greyish looking stains. Blood, when exposed to various elements, one of which was bright sunshine, changed colour. He studied the lie of the land. A few metres from where he stood, it began to rise, quickly becoming quite steep. A corner of the first building in the urbanización was visible. If a man were running, too panicked to judge where he was going, and he fell . . . By the rock was a crushed plant that might have been an *Italica* – Fiol could hopefully identify it despite its state. He shouted to Fiol that he had to check what he'd seen, crossed to the track, went along through the belt of trees to his car. From there, he brought out a blanket and a torch.

Back at the rock, he knelt and used the blanket to cut out as much sunlight as possible, shone the beam of the torch on the greyish stains, continually altering the angle at which the light struck the rock face. One stain resembled glossy varnish and convinced him this was blood and he must return to the post to collect the kit which would provide a simple, rapid, on-the-spot test to decide whether he were right.

Watched by Fiol, momentarily more interested in what he was doing than searching for more specimens of *Italica*, he

147

rubbed a filter paper on the stain which had responded
to torch light and, when certain some of the substance had
been transferred, treated the paper with three reagents in
turn. The paper showed pink. Blood was present . . .

'Well I'm damned!' Fiol exclaimed.

'What's up?'

'Look at that.' He pointed at the crushed plant.

'I wanted to ask you, is that an *Italica*?'

'Surely that's obvious? People are barbarians! Deliberately destroying nature's jewels.'

That had hardly been Ramos's intention.

At the post, Alvarez spoke to the sargento. 'I want three
or four men.'

'What for?'

'To pick up a rock in a field and bring it back here.'

'Why can't you do it yourself?'

'It's far too heavy.'

'Must weigh a couple of kilos,' sneered the sargento.

On Monday morning, Alvarez reached across the desk to
the telephone, lifted the receiver and dialled.

'Yes?' said the secretary in a voice filled with plums.

'Inspector Alvarez here. I should like to speak to the
superior chief.'

'He is not in his office.'

'Not turned up for work yet?'

'Hardly a remark he would appreciate.'

Of course not, lacking any sense of humour. 'Can you
say when he'll be around?'

'Superior Chief Salas is attending an important meeting
which is expected to end by ten.'

'Then I'll ring back some time after half past.'

'If you think that necessary.'

*   *   *

'It's odd,' said the barman in the Club Llueso, as he poured a drink, 'but you're looking almost happy.'

'Then enhance the impression by making that a decent sized coñac.'

'If I'm supposed to pour any more, I might as well pass the bottle across.'

'There'll be no complaint from me.'

'I think I prefer it when you are your usual miserable self!'

Alvarez carried coffee and brandy over to the window table and sat. It was true, he did feel cheerful even though it was a Monday. Why? Because he was convinced he was about to solve not one, but many cases. Ramos, whose past had hinted at unwelcome traits, was the peeping Tom who had been prowling the land using a homemade TV camera to view intimate bedroom scenes. So far as was known, he seemed to have stopped in April, but more probably had continued without being noticed. Just under three weeks ago, he had been peeping into the Gaines's bedroom when, once again, he had caused sufficient noise to be noticed. Outside lights had been switched on. The shock of being suddenly caught in their glare had probably delayed his reactions, with the consequence that he was still in view when Gaines had come out of the house. His escape had been fortuitously helped by the latter's fall.

It might be thought that this would have persuaded him to lie low for a long while or even give up his perverted pleasure, but fear could be a stimulus rather than a deterrent; it was with the added zest which came from known danger that he had set out on the night of the fifth. During his peeping, something or someone had so alarmed him, he had again taken flight, his luck had finally run out and he had fallen, rolled down the slope and struck his head on the rock at the foot of the hill as the piece of *Italica* became embedded in the wound.

Doctor Zamora had said it was possible to suffer a blow to the head which caused a large clot of blood to form beneath the skull, yet did not appear to have any effect until hours later when some unusual exertion, or even emotion, caused the victim to collapse and die. Had Ramos fallen and struck his head, picked himself up, returned to where he had hidden his motorbike, and driven across the mountains to Cala Blanca where, walking along the edge of the slope, he had collapsed, fallen on to the pebbles, and died? Having suffered the first injury, would he travel anywhere but home? Vehicles denied the possibility of the motorbike's crossing the mountains. What possible reason could there have been for him to go to Cala Blanca?

He heard the church clock strike and realised he'd spent far longer at the bar than he should have done, considering his declared intention to ring Salas again. He stood and began to cross to the door.

'Hey!' the bartender called out.

He turned.

'You've not had a second coñac.'

'I can't wait to drink it.'

'It'll rain frogs any minute!'

He left and crossed the old square, impeded by the endless throng of tourists who had nothing to do. Back in his office, he rang Palma.

'The superior chief has not yet returned,' the secretary told him.

'When he does, tell him to ring me.'

'I will mention that you have called,' she answered sharply. A lowly inspector did not tell his superior chief what to do.

He replaced the receiver. He should have remembered the old saying, To hurry is to be delayed. He could have enjoyed that second brandy.

Salas rang at a quarter past eleven. His greeting was typically abrupt and to the point. 'What do you want?'

'Señor, on Wednesday, Doctor Zamora, who conducted the post-mortem on Ramos, told me that embedded in his wound was a piece of plant. This was identified as an orchid called *Italica* which has a flower with a tight cluster—'

'You imagine I am interested in the appearance of a flower? Stick to matters which have at least a modicum of relevance.'

'In fact, Señor, it does.'

'What does?'

'This flower.'

'What about this flower?'

'It has a relevance.'

'Which is a damn sight more than can be said for all you're saying. Have you any more idea of what you are talking about than I have?'

'The orchid does not grow anywhere around Cala Blanca.'

'And perhaps neither on the summit of Mount Everest?'

'It's important it doesn't grow there because this suggests Ramos did not die there.'

'You have searched the whole area?'

'Not quite.'

'Yet, typically, are prepared to make a claim you cannot justify.'

'An expert botanist has assured me—'

'Had you ever been capable of learning from experience, you would know that experts are expert at arriving at wrong conclusions.'

'In this case, I don't think that that matters . . .'

'I am not too surprised to hear you claim a wrong conclusion is of no account – your work all too frequently supports that contention.'

'I did say, Señor, it didn't matter in this case. When I understood the only area between Cala Blanca and Mestara where it was known to grow was close to the urbanización Beniferri, I decided to find out if there was anything to indicate that that was where Ramos had suffered an injury. On my first search, a car drew up and an English lady asked why—'

'What is the point of all this?'

'The peeping Tom has been active again. He was peeping on that Tuesday evening. Something or someone disturbed him and he ran off, fell, rolled down the hill and hit his head on a rock. The doctor has told me it is feasible to suffer a severe head injury, yet continue to behave reasonably normally until later collapsing and dying. That might suggest Ramos had picked himself up, returned to his motorbike, ridden over to Cala Blanca, and there collapsed.'

'Having suffered the first injury, why would he not have sought immediate medical help which one can presume would not have involved him in an investigation, since Mallorquin doctors no doubt treat the law with the same contempt as everyone else?'

'I don't know.'

'Why should he ride over to Cala Blanca?'

'I don't know.'

'Is there anything you do know?'

'While searching for specimens of *Italica* with Señor Fiol, I came across a rock at the foot of the hill on which the urbanización stands and on this were stains which preliminary tests identify as blood. I have arranged for the stone to be lifted up, together with surrounding earth, and taken to the forensic laboratory in Palma. If they confirm that it is human blood, they will compare it with Ramos's. Given a match, we can be certain he was a peeping Tom. Señor, a moment ago, you asked me questions to which I don't know the answers.'

'A not infrequent occurrence.'

'Not only do I not know them, I cannot suggest logical, or even illogical, ones. Which makes me believe they do not need to be asked.'

'I do not waste my time asking unnecessary questions.'

'Assume Ramos was peeping. He'd given himself away more than once by the noise made when he inserted or moved the tiny camera between the shutter slats; had been chased once, but escaped. He tried to run and escape a second time, missed his footing, fell, hit his head on the rock and suffered a fatal injury. Someone who had been alerted to his activities found him dying or dead. This presented a problem. If his death was reported and he was left where he lay, his equipment would reveal whom he had been recording and what he had seen; if it was missing, in the course of an investigation it must become obvious someone had removed it. This had to be prevented, so his body and motorbike were driven to Cala Blanca where an attempt was made to set the scene of accidental death . . . A deception which in part failed because it was so unlikely he would have driven over the mountains on his motorbike – Vehicles have confirmed this. Such a scenario would explain why there was so little blood on the pebbles at the cala.'

'As obnoxiously repellant as it must be to anyone for whom decent, honourable behaviour is sacrosanct, it has to be accepted that what occurs in a bedroom sometimes gives what can be misguidedly called pleasure to a perverted onlooker. Yet a justified sense of embarrassment on the part of those surveyed can hardly be sufficient to explain why someone should go to the lengths you suggest to hide the truth, when to do so places him in danger of criminal proceedings.'

'That depends.'

'On what?'

'On what actually was going on in the bedroom when Ramos was watching. Some people . . . For some people, their idea of fun breaks normal boundaries and I'm wondering . . .'

'I have absolutely no wish to listen to the many obscene possibilities you so obviously have in mind.' Salas slammed down the receiver.

Sixteen

Friday was heavily overcast. Mallorquins in homes, streets, and shops, assured each other the weather had never before been like this in the last part of June and the climate was indeed changing; in truth, being an island, there always had been and always would be short periods when the weather was quite contrary to the time of year. In the hotels, gift shops, bars, restaurants, and on the beaches, tourists complained at having spent good money on a day that was warmer, yet otherwise little different from the one at home; they wondered whom they could sue.

Because of the cloud cover, the humidity was high. Alvarez fractionally redirected the fan, but gained no extra benefit. He used a handkerchief to mop his forehead and neck and daydreamed of living in Galicia amidst green fields and cool breezes until the telephone disturbed his wishful thoughts.

An assistant at the Laboratory of Forensic Sciences said that both rock and earth had been stained with human blood; that this blood and that of Ramos had been typed and the two had proved similar; that further and more detailed tests had been carried out and these proved conclusively that the blood on the rock had come from Ramos.

Alvarez settled back in his chair after yet again altering the angle of the fan. He was seldom given to self-congratulation, being too conscious of his own short-comings, but he now allowed himself a measure of satisfaction. It was his imaginative perseverence which had brought the case this far (he was certain he would have found the bloodstained rock without Fiol's insistence he continue to search); now, it was going to take him further. Did he still accept the possibility that Ramos had ridden to Cala Blanca after falling and hitting that rock? No. Ramos had been peeping, had alerted someone, had been pursued, lost his footing and tumbled down the side of the hill, hit his head, and died. His corpse and his small, ancient motorbike had been carried in a vehicle to Cala Blanca, where the scene had been set for the accident to have happened there. The unknown had to be someone from the Beniferri urbanización so it was now necessary to speak to everyone who had been there on the night of the fifth to try to identify who had so dark a secret that extreme measures had had to be taken to try to conceal it.

He had not actually counted how many houses and bungalows made up the urbanización, but at a guess there were a dozen. Not all would have been occupied on the fifth, but it was possible the majority had been. It was going to take time and energy to question everyone . . . What a pleasure it would be to prove that the Wyatt woman was involved! He poured himself a large brandy to drink to that fantasy . . .

Wade opened the front door of Ca'n Greix.

'Good morning, Señor,' Alvarez said. 'I must apologise for troubling you yet again.'

'No need to apologise.' His manner was pleasant, but reserved. He held the door wide open and as Alvarez stepped inside the hall, called out: 'Hilary, it's the inspector.'

'Shan't be a moment,' was the answer from the room to the right.

He spoke to Alvarez. 'I think you like brandy with ice?'

'Indeed, Señor.'

'I'm sure I've said before, the name's Charles.' He raised his voice again. 'Can you bring drinks out to the patio, please?' he called out to his sister. 'One brandy with ice, one gin and tonic.'

He led the way out to the covered patio where table and chairs had been set out. When they were seated, he said: 'Is the weather going to clear?'

'The forecast is for sun by the late afternoon,' Alvarez replied. 'And, by the look of things, that may prove correct.'

Wade's tone sharpened when he said: 'Are you here because you have finally heard from England?'

'No. They have not been in touch.'

He stared out. 'Then you haven't brought any fresh news. Am I grateful for that, or bitter? Grateful because, if you had, I might well have lost all sense of peace; bitter, because I want the bastards punished. Retribution. One can be reasonably certain that the person who questions the validity of that has never been a victim. Victims want eye for eye, tooth for tooth . . . How does the quote continue?'

'I think it mentions wounds.'

'In those days, they were more realistic than we have become. Liberalism arrived later. But enough . . . Especially as it sounds as if refreshment is on its way.'

A moment later, Hilary stepped through the doorway on to the patio, a brightly coloured tin tray in her hands. 'Hullo, Inspector.' She looked enquiringly at Wade.

'There's no news from England.'

She put the tray down on the table, handed out the drinks.

'Are we allowed to know what's brought you here?' she asked as she sat.

157

'Of course, Señora. We now have reason to believe that the man Señor Gaines chased was not casing the properties, trying to identify which would be the best and easiest to break into, but was a peeping Tom.'

'Ye gods! Never expected to hear of one of those pests out here.'

'I am afraid we suffer the same problems as anywhere else.'

'Of course you do. And it's stupid to reckon otherwise. But it's so peaceful here that one is lulled into thinking there can't be any nastiness around.'

'If only,' Wade said. He turned to Alvarez. 'Do you know who this man is?'

'A Mallorquin, regrettably.'

'I gained the impression you weren't too certain who he was, but what you've just said surely means you do?'

'We are certain, but still lack absolute proof. He died at the beginning of this month, apparently in an accident at Cala Blanca, on the Parelona peninsula.'

'Why do you say "apparently"?'

'We now know that he was severely injured when he fell, probably while being pursued, and struck his head on a rock at the foot of this hill.'

Wade drank. 'I'm sorry, but you've lost me. If he was injured here, how could the accident have apparently happened anywhere else?'

'Because that is what we were meant to believe.'

'It all sounds complicated.'

'It is!'

'If he was being pursued when he fell,' she said, 'wouldn't whoever was chasing him have given the alarm?'

'That seems reasonable, so perhaps his pursuer did not know he had fallen. His pursuer might have tripped, as Señor Gaines did, and, by the time he'd picked himself

158

up, there was no sign of Ramos; he may have been unable to run quickly and was so far behind he just gave up and returned to his house.'

'You're here to try and find out exactly what did happen?'

'I am, yes.'

'Then the odds are, Bert wasn't chasing alcoholic shadows. Surprise, surprise!'

'That's being cruel,' she said.

'Why do you always rush to defend him when someone suggests he might just drink a little heavily?'

'Because he's never obnoxious in his cups, like one or two names I could mention, men who develop wandering hands after the fourth glass.'

'It's an old Scottish custom because the winters are so long.'

'I wasn't meaning Cyril.'

'Can you say that without crossing your fingers?'

'You're becoming impossible. Perhaps you've been drinking all morning whilst I was doing the shopping.'

'Should I stand on one foot and count backwards from a hundred to prove I've drunk only half a gin and tonic?' Wade picked up his glass and jiggled it so that the melting ice swirled around. 'I take it, Inspector, you're here to ask if we've ever been peeped upon?'

'Yes, I am.'

'Then I'm afraid yours is a wasted visit. We've had no indication of such activities. In any case, surely someone of his ilk would be interested in couples, not a brother and sister?'

'Perhaps. But there are those who are content merely to watch a person undress.'

'But wouldn't that be in the hopes—'

She said: 'Let's leave it. Can't you see, the inspector doesn't want to go into details in case I start worrying about some slimy little man watching me take my clothes off? You ought to have more nous.'

'Mea maxima culpa . . . Inspector, before we change the conversation, to everyone's relief, is there anything more we can tell you?'

'I should like to know if there has been a time when you've been in a bedroom and have heard rustling or scratching noises at one of the shutters which drew your attention and perhaps made you wonder what caused these?'

'I don't think so.' Wade turned to his sister. 'I take it you've never heard anything when you've been in your bedroom or you'd have shrieked for help.'

'Called, not shrieked.'

'Were you in this house throughout the evening and night of the fifth of the month?' Alvarez asked.

'Living here, time gets lost and I'm not certain I could say where we were three or four days ago, let alone way back.'

'I'll check.' She stood. 'If we didn't go out to dinner, we were here . . . Whilst I'm inside, shall I refill glasses?'

'An unnecessary question.' Wade drained his glass, placed it on the tray; Alvarez did the same.

She carried the tray indoors.

'Our mother used to say that Hilary and I were so unalike in character as well as appearance that it was difficult to believe we were siblings. Hilary is methodical, I am not; she notes down anything that can possibly be important, I commit everything to memory and consequently forget. So, right now, it's a pound to a penny that she's reading through the appointments book she keeps with the fervour of someone who'd rather break a leg than a dinner date.'

'My superior chief always seeks such precision.'

'While foregoing it on his own account, no doubt?'

'He doesn't have to bother; he has a secretary who, I'm sure, never misses anything.'

'Thereby delegating both responsibility and blame.'

Hilary returned a couple of minutes later, passed the drinks around, sat. 'There's nothing down in the book for the fifth, so we were here.'

'And, as you have said, you heard and saw nothing to alarm you or arouse your curiosity?' Alvarez asked.

'I certainly can't remember anything.' She looked at Wade.

'Ditto. Clearly, we are mines of no information, but surely that's better than of misinformation . . . ? Inspector, will you tell me something?'

'If I can, of course.'

'We were talking to friends the other day who'd been told they should watch the Eagle Dance in Llueso as that was the only village still carrying on the tradition and perhaps it will soon die out and be lost. They aren't the kind of people really to be interested in local customs so weren't sufficiently interested to ask about it, but I am. Does it take place around now?'

'At the beginning of this month.'

'So we've missed it. Blast! Is it held every year?'

'Yes, it is.'

'Then I'll catch up with it next year. What happens?'

It was many years since he had watched it and he had difficulty in remembering the details. 'Two young women with cardboard figures of an eagle on their dresses dance in company with John the Baptist in the streets. They wear jewellery – necklaces, bracelets, rings – which is loaned by the villagers and this can weigh as much as five kilos and, of course, is worth a great deal of money.'

'It is to be hoped the donors get it back.'

'In very many years, not a single piece has gone missing.'

'Which says everything for the honesty of the islanders. Try doing that in England and by the end of the dance, the girls would have lost even their good resolutions.'

'It's not that bad,' she protested.

'Tell that to the people who've just been mugged in broad daylight.'

People were mugged on the island, Alvarez thought, but he wasn't going to point that out. 'When I leave here, I have to talk to anyone else living in the urbanización – do you know which houses are occupied?'

'Hilary's the one to answer that question.' He turned to her. 'Right?'

'Perhaps,' she answered. 'There are certainly three families, excluding us. I'm not certain about Beatriz. She went back to Holland two weeks ago and I haven't heard she's returned, but she tends to lie low, so she may have done.'

'It will all depend on whether or not she's been able to sort out the affairs of her no-good son.'

'You're always so harsh.'

'From the little she lets slip, probably lenient. He's forever asking her for financial help and she's precious little to spare. On top of which, every time she goes back to Holland and the weather's bad, she suffers another nasty bout of bronchitis.'

'I expect she reckons the problems are less than the pleasure at seeing him.'

'Some pleasures come too expensively.'

'That's for the person concerned to decide. Mother always said you had the typical male arrogance of judging what other people should, or shouldn't, do.'

He laughed.

Alvarez said: 'Were the families you know are here now also here on the fifth? . . . Of course, I already know that Señora Wyatt was.'

'I'm reasonably certain, subject to Beatriz, they all were,' she answered.

He stood, thanked them for their help and the drinks, said goodbye. Wade accompanied him to the front door. He began to walk towards his car, then veered over to the left and came to a halt before a bush in flower. 'This is very attractive.'

'Isn't it?'

'What is its name?'

'I haven't the foggiest. Hilary is the gardening fundi, I'm just the dogsbody labourer. You'll have to ask her the next time.'

He turned back and crossed to his car, settled behind the wheel. By walking over to the flowering bush, he had been able to look into the integral garage and identify a battered Peugeot 306, the later model with the larger tailgate that eliminated the sill. With the back seats down, the tailgate up, and some cord, it would probably be possible to carry Ramos's motorbike in that . . .

He drove on to the next building, a house with many roof lines. All shutters were closed and the garden was overgrown with weeds, nevertheless he repeatedly rang the front doorbell and walked around the house before accepting it was unoccupied.

The third building, considerably larger than the previous two, was the Gaines's.

Gaines, seated at the table on the covered patio, did not bother to stand or offer a greeting, and his first words were: 'Keeping up with local tradition, then?'

'Señor?'

'Turning up at drinking time.'

'It's always drinking time here,' his wife commented from the seat on the opposite side of the table.

'Who's complaining?'

'Who's listening?'

163

He turned to Alvarez. 'Sit down and tell us what you want. A drop of champagne?'

'I should prefer a coñac with ice.'

'I remember now, my champagne isn't good enough for you.'

'As I think I said, it is too good.'

'Never trust a man with a smooth tongue is what my dad used to say.'

'It was, Never trust anyone,' she corrected.

'You and him used to have some right old barneys. He said to me, "You've picked a tough one who'll always be ready to argue." He was dead right . . . Here, don't let's waste valuable time. Give Victoria a buzz and tell her to bring a brandy. And whilst she's about it, there's no harm in another bottle of bubbly.'

'Harm for whom? And her name's Inés.'

'Don't seem to suit her, so I'll stick to Victoria. That's a proper name.'

'Too proper for you, wasn't she?'

'There's no call for history.'

'Unless you've written it.'

He said to Alvarez: 'Got a tongue sharper than a razor!' He sounded pleased, not resentful.

Flora leaned across the side of the table to press the bell set in the wall. Gaines emptied the bottle of Veuve Clicquot into his flute, put it down by the side of the ice bucket. 'I reckon you're here to admit you can't find the sod what made me break my chin?' he said challengingly to Alvarez.

'It was only a bit of a cut,' she said.

'Then why did they have to sew me up like I was a bloody handbag? Two dozen stitches.'

'Four. And you made such a fuss, they were laughing at you.'

'It was agony.'

164

'If you'd had a baby, you'd know what that word really means.'

'If I had a baby, I'd be headlines in the Guinness Book of Records.'

'That's all he wants, to be in the records. Gawd knows why.' She nodded at her husband. 'And if he keeps drinking, that's where he'll be, marked down as the biggest boozer in the history of mankind. We throw out more empty champagne bottles in a week than the rest of 'em put together.'

The maid stepped through the doorway, listened to Flora, returned inside.

'Come on,' Gaines said, 'admit you haven't a clue who the bastard was who nearly killed me. You lot would have trouble finding sand in the Sahara.'

She spoke hurriedly to Alvarez. 'He's only talking like that because of the booze.'

'We have identified who the man was whom you were chasing,' Alvarez said with satisfaction.

Gaines leaned forward until his ample stomach pressed against the edge of the table. 'You know who he is, do you? So he's in jail?'

'No.'

'Why not?'

'Because he's dead.'

'That'll teach him!'

'You shouldn't talk like that when someone's died!' she snapped.

'I'll talk what I want when he tries to break into my house and then bloody near kills me.'

'He wasn't intending to burgle your house,' Alvarez said.

'So what was he doing?'

'He was a peeping Tom.'

'Well I'll be—'

She cut short his words. 'Are you telling me he was looking into the rooms?'

'I'm afraid so.'

'When it's warm, I always take a shower before I go to bed. So was he looking at me with nothing on?'

'It is impossible to be certain one way or the other.' It could hardly have been a very rewarding peep.

'The dirty old man – deserves to die!'

A moment ago, she had been reprimanding her husband for a similar sentiment. A strong sense of modesty often outweighed a liberal viewpoint.

The maid returned, handed Alvarez a glass with a large brandy in it, put an unopened bottle of champagne in the ice bucket, picked up the empty one at the side, left.

'Señor,' Alvarez said, as Gaines began to unwind the wire cage over the cork, 'have you been troubled a second time by the possibility that someone was outside the house?'

'If he was dead, he wasn't going to be mucking around here again, was he?'

'There was time between the night you chased him and were injured and the night he died, for him to have returned. Did you again hear sounds from the shutters?'

'If I had, I'd of taught that bastard a lesson.'

'Don't talk like that,' she snapped.

'Why not?'

'Because the inspector may think you killed him.'

'Don't be daft.' He grunted as he finally freed the wire.

'Why d'you think he's here now, asking questions, if it's not to find out who did him in?'

'How should I know? Come for the free booze, like as not.' He released the cork too suddenly and champagne frothed out and over his trousers before he could fill his glass. He swore.

166

She faced Alvarez. 'How did this man die?'

'In what appeared to be an accident.'

'Why "appeared" to be?'

'He suffered a serious injury to his head when he struck a rock on the ground in front of this hill. Yet his body was found in a cove near the lighthouse, many kilometres away.'

'So how could that happen?'

'That is what I'm trying to find out.'

'We can't help.'

'In fact, Señora, you can by telling me where both of you were during the evening and night of the fifth of this month.'

'You don't really think Bert could . . . Just because he said what he did . . . Every evening, he gets so boozed he couldn't kill a mosquito on the end of his nose. Why d'you think he fell when he was chasing that man?'

'I put my foot in a rabbit hole,' Gaines said loudly.

'There ain't no rabbits here.'

'I saw one the other day . . .'

'With a long pink trunk?' She spoke once more to Alvarez. 'If you think he could have done anything, you're so very wrong.'

'Then you'll want to tell me where you and he were that evening.'

'You reckon I can remember that day good enough to know what we was doing?'

'I'm hoping so.'

'Where were you and what was you doing then?'

'That is of no importance . . .'

'You don't remember, so why should I be able to?'

He changed the subject. 'What car do you own?'

'I've a Mercedes and he's got an Audi.'

'Is either an estate or a hatchback?'

'Mine's an estate,' she said. 'So?'

167

'A small and unimportant point, Señora.'

'When you talk like that, I know it's bloody important . . . What else do you want to know?'

'I don't think there are any more questions, so I'll leave you in peace.'

'You think there's much peace in this house?'

'Sit down,' Gaines said loudly. 'You've only had one drink.'

'Thank you, but I must return to work.'

'Kills a man quick, returning to work.'

Alvarez drained his glass, stood. She followed him into the sitting room. 'You must understand something.'

'Señora?'

'It's daft, thinking like you are.'

'I'm not certain how I'm thinking.'

'Don't give me crap. You're a lot smarter than you like to make out.'

'There are many who would disagree.'

'Because there are more fools than wise men in the world. I should know. I'm married to one. Made his way up from nowhere, worked himself silly, but never done anyone dirt unless they tried to do it to him first. Made a fortune. We come out to enjoy the rest of our lives and the money and what happens? Most of the Brits here don't come from where we did and they reckon that makes 'em superior. The worst is that Wyatt bitch. Acts like there's a bad smell under her nose and don't realise it's herself what stinks . . . I've said to him time and again, laugh at 'em, tell 'em if they'd been you, they'd still be down in the gutter. He won't. His ma was in service until she was chucked out for being in pup and he can't never get over his beginnings. So, instead of fighting, he lowers his head and takes to the bottle, not understanding that the more he drinks, the more them lot sneer. D'you know why I'm telling you all this, things I don't normally say to anyone? Because you ain't sleepy-eyed, like you appear, and there's something funny about the peeper's death. You're wondering if my Bert could have had anything to do with it, wondering harder, since he as good as told you he'd croak anyone he found peeping on me. I'm saying now – and it hurts to tell it – by the middle of any evening, my Bert falls over his own feet because he's boozed enough to think he's got four. If he tried to do anyone in, it would be him that went. Can you understand?'

'Yes, Señora.'

'I was told the other day that *señora* was a kind of mark of respect, so I suppose you're laughing at me.'

'I am showing my respect.'

She was confused.

'Over the centuries, we islanders have had to meet many invaders and sometimes we have fought with our hands, sometimes only with our minds. You have so much fight in your mind that soon you will persuade your husband to start fighting with you and together you will win.'

'I . . . I don't know what to say to that, straight, I don't.'

'Let your silence speak for you.'

He said goodbye and walked through to the hall. She remained where she stood.

In his car, a look at his watch showed it was just after half twelve. Since it would take roughly fifteen minutes to return home, were he to have plenty of time in which to relax before the meal, his investigation must come to a temporary halt.

Seventeen

Dolores had just passed around the apples when the phone began to ring. She remained standing, her hand on the earthenware bowl. 'What an unfortunate family I have! It seems my husband is deaf, my two children are deaf, my cousin is deaf, and I alone have the ability to hear.'

'It won't be for me,' Jaime said.

'But it does not occur to you to go and find out who the call *is* for?'

'If it's not for me, which it isn't, that'll waste time and the phone costs a fortune every second . . .'

'But if you're wrong and it is for you and someone else answers, will that not waste equally as much time? More, since you are not someone who hurries even when you should?'

As he sought an answer, the phone ceased ringing.

Alvarez refilled his glass with wine. Dolores sat, began to peel an apple with her knife.

The phone rang again.

She looked around the table, her lustrous dark-brown eyes in challenging mode.

'It won't be for me . . .' Jaime began, proving he was a man of small imagination.

'But it will be you who finds out who the call is for,' she snapped.

He reluctantly came to his feet, went through to the

front room. When he returned, he said resentfully: 'Didn't I tell you?'

'Who is it for?'

'Enrique.'

'Who wants me at this sort of time?' Alvarez asked.

'If you'd answered, like Dolores said you should, you'd know. It's someone at the post.'

'What does he want?'

'Why ask me?'

Alvarez stood, made his way through to the front room, picked up the receiver. 'Yes?'

'Woken you up, have I?' asked the duty cabo.

'You've interrupted my meal and ruined my digestion. So what's your problem?'

'I haven't got one. You have. Matilde Pino has rung to say her Pablo is missing and she wants you to find him.'

'What's "missing" mean?'

'He didn't return home last night, hasn't been back this morning, hasn't been to work, and María's had no word from him.'

'Who's she?'

'His girlfriend. Matilde was upset because she thought he'd spent the night with María, but it seems he didn't. Can't think why the possibility should have worried her.'

'There are still some people who have moral values.'

'And can't talk about anything but the day they had tea with King Alfonso and Queen Ena . . . It seems no one's had sight of him since midday yesterday. If you ask me, he struck lucky yesterday evening and met a long-legged blonde on the beach who wanted to learn about local customs.'

'She'll have found out they don't differ from anywhere else . . . Wherever he is, it's up to you to find him.'

'Not according to the sargento.'

'Tell him from me—'

'He said that if you started arguing, he'll have a word with the teniente.'

'The lazy sod will do anything to get out of work.'

'Now there's a case of great minds! He said the same thing about you.'

'What's Matilde's full name, address, and does she have a telephone?'

The cabo gave the details.

'I'll get in touch with her.'

'I expect the sargento will want to express his appreciation of your willing cooperation.'

Alvarez swore, knowing this was senseless, but finding some relief in doing so.

He returned to the dining room, sat, lifted up his glass and drank.

'Was it important?' Dolores asked. She deplored intrusive inquisitiveness, yet liked to know what was going on.

He began to peel an apple. 'A mother's reported her son's been missing from home since yesterday morning and his girlfriend's not seen him.'

'And I've seen six fairies dance the cancan on the head of a pin,' Jaime said.

'When was that?' Isabel asked.

'Remember that your father has even more nonsense on his tongue than in his head,' Dolores snapped. She spoke to Jaime. 'When you have nothing sensible to say, keep quiet.'

'All I was suggesting—'

'Only a father with no thought for the minds of his children would suggest such a thing to their ears.'

'I thought you said they were deaf? If you ask me—'

'I would receive a worthless answer.' She faced Alvarez. 'Has she not spoken to his friends and asked if they know where he is?'

'I can't answer.'

'Why not?'

'I haven't yet had a word with her.'

'A mother suffers the cruellest pain she will ever know, believing her son has come to some terrible harm, and you sit there and drink instead of moving heaven and earth to find him?'

'My middle name's not Atlas . . .'

'Have I suggested anything so ridiculous?'

'When you said I ought to be moving heaven and earth . . .'

'You think that this tragic matter is a time for infantile joking?'

'Look, there's no real reason to believe he's in trouble.'

'That he has not been home is no cause?'

'Ten to one, he's found himself a . . .' He hurriedly stopped.

'You were going to say?'

'That he'll turn up when things are back to normal.'

'What is abnormal for him now?'

'How do I know?'

'Then why suggest something disgraceful when you are ignorant? Who is this poor mother?'

'Matilde Pino.'

'From the other side of the village? And is her son's name Pablo?'

Alvarez noticed the brief look – had it expressed slyness? – which Juan gave his mother. 'That's right.'

'Then one need not be surprised!' she said.

'Surprised at what?' Jaime asked.

'He has been wild since his father died when he was young. Little is more likely than that he has spent a night away from home in circumstances one does not talk about.'

'Hang on,' Alvarez said, 'didn't you go for me moments ago because I suggested . . .'

'We do not talk about it.'

Ten minutes later, the two children cleared the table while Dolores prepared coffee and started the washing up. Alvarez and Jaime poured brandies to aid their digestions.

'You heard her, didn't you?' Jaime said in a very low voice. 'She goes at you for daring to think this Pablo was having it off with a tourist, then says the same thing and doesn't like it when that's pointed out.'

'Ternell wrote that woman is controlled by emotion, man by logic.'

'Is that supposed to explain anything?'

'Everything.'

Dolores swept through the bead curtain and came to a stop, arms akimbo. 'Well?'

The two men questioned their immediate pasts.

'Have you phoned the mother whose agony one would think would soften even the hardest heart, yet perhaps not yours?' she asked Alvarez.

'I was just about to.'

'If men did even a tenth of what they say they are just about to, not a home would have a shutter with a broken slat, a shelf that needs repairing, or a blocked drain.'

'I said—' began Jaime.

'That you were just about to mend the shutter and shelf and clear the drain?' She uncoiled her arms and returned to the kitchen.

'See what I mean?' Alvarez asked. 'It's emotion that fuels them. She's so certain Matilde is suffering horrors when probably Matilde's jealous because her Pablo has found a bit of skirt and, if he's not careful, he'll be snared, which means she won't be the matriarch any longer.' He finished his drink, thought about pouring himself another, decided that in her present, aggressive mood, Dolores might well find further cause for complaint if he did so. He went through to the front room, searched in his pocket for the bit of paper on which he'd written the telephone number, dialled that.

Matilde spoke so quickly the words jumbled into each other. Pablo had been home for lunch the previous day – the restaurant was closed on Thursdays – and had left without any word that he would not be back that night. She always went to bed early – at her age and without a husband, God rest Félix's soul, what else was there to do? – and so seldom heard him return. This morning, she had prepared his breakfast, but, when he had not come down to the kitchen, she had gone up to his bedroom to find the bed unused. Immediately, her mind had been flooded – as any mother's would – by horrific possibilities; he had had a crash in his car, had been run over while crossing the road, gone swimming and drowned . . .

'So you got in touch with his friend, María, to see if she knew where he was?' he said, cutting short a list of the calamities which could befall man.

'He was going to see her, but never turned up. She decided he'd met friends and had had too much to drink – even though he had promised never to do that again after the last time – and had forgotten her. Now, she is as frightened as I am. He drives so fast that he must have had a terrible crash . . .'

'What restaurant does he work at?'

'The Rocamar. I thought he must have gone straight there to work so I rang and asked to speak to him; they said he had not turned up and, if he did not do so soon, he would be without a job. I told them, he is a good boy and something awful must have happened. If he has had a crash . . .'

'I'll find out if there has been a report of a road accident in which he was involved.'

'Or maybe he has . . .'

'It'll all take time, so don't expect to hear from me again until fairly late this afternoon.'

'Please find him.'

'I'll do my very best.'

His eyelids were heavy and his mind drifting, but he had promised her he would do his very best. Before he went upstairs for a delayed siesta, he phoned the accident coordinating centre and asked if Pablo Pino had been involved in any incident. He had not. Alvarez then phoned the three local hospitals to find out if Pino had suddenly collapsed and been taken to one of them. They had no record of him.

'Phone now.' Dolores put the ensaimada on the table.

'There'll be nothing lost or gained . . .' Alvarez began.

'Now!'

He went through to the front room. Tearfully, Matilde told him Pablo had still not returned, no one had seen him, María was having hysterics, the restaurant said that if he did not turn up for the evening meal and did not have a doctor's certificate, he would be sacked . . .

'Does he have friends he sees more often than others?'

After a while, she said: 'There's Arturo.'

'Where does he live?'

She thought he lived in Estart; she could not provide an address, but his surname was Luque. Before he rang off, Alvarez once more told her she must not assume the worst just because so little was yet known. Most people eventually reappeared and, in view of the lack of any accident, there was no reason to think Pablo would not be one of them.

The telephone directory listed subscribers' names under

towns and villages: there were two Luques in Estart. The first woman he spoke to thought he was trying to sell something; the second said her son and Pablo were good friends, having been to school together, but she didn't think they'd seen each other since the weekend.

In all honesty, he had now done all that could be done. A person was not officially missing until a reasonable time had passed or there was good reason to believe it unlikely he or she had voluntarily disappeared; it needed the circumstances or the time to assume that . . . It was, therefore, with an easy conscience that he returned to the kitchen.

'Well?' demanded Dolores.

'There's still no sign of him.'

'The poor woman!'

'She shouldn't be quite so convinced it's a tragedy. Far more likely, he's . . .' He hesitated.

'Found some foreign puta who couldn't uncross her legs quickly enough. What are you going to do now?'

'There's very little can be done until more time has passed except contact the hospitals again and have a word with Matilde.'

'You must make her understand you are doing everything that can be done.'

'I've told her so several times.'

'Over the phone, but not face to face. You have no conception of what a woman suffers because of her son. He is her life until he grows up, then he forgets her for another woman, because that is the thoughtless way of man. Yet let him be in trouble and it is her heart which pains the more.'

'I'll go to her place and talk to her as soon as I possibly can.'

He should not have expected to be praised for his projected kindness.

'And why not now . . . ? That I have to plead and plead for you to do something that, were you not a man and therefore infinitely selfish, you would rush to do!'

In the urbanización Beniferri, the D'Avours lived in a house, which answered many of the questions Alvarez needed to ask; that they were an elderly couple might answer others.

They possessed that touch of complete assurance which spoke of wealth and power. They were careful not to display any sign of a feeling of superiority, yet one had to be in their company for only a short while to become aware that, for them, equality had an unequal meaning. Perhaps it was their studied politeness which most clearly revealed their inner certainties.

'Please sit down, Inspector,' D'Avour said, indicating one of four very ornate chairs.

Alvarez settled very carefully. If the chair was not reproduction, it was possibly worth almost as much as his salary for a year.

'Now, please say how we may assist you.'

Tall, thin, with a neat white moustache to complement white hair that was carefully brushed to hide growing baldness, dressed in casual clothes of great style, D'Avour looked every inch the retired diplomat he might well have been. Alvarez spoke in French, certain they would understand he meant this as a subtle compliment and, unless Parisian, would overlook his rough accent and occasional misuse of words. 'I am investigating the death of Marcial Ramos.'

'A very unfortunate occurrence. More especially if that which is being said about him is true.'

'He was a peeping Tom.'

'It is sad,' she said.

He wondered if she meant it was sad a man could

labour under such an objectionable compulsion, sad he should have been so weak as to give in to it, or sad it could have happened in the midst of such calm beauty? But then perhaps her response had been no more than a conventional one to something objectionable. Her manner gave no indication which.

'Are you here now to ask if we can tell you anything that might concern what has happened?' D'Avour asked.

'Yes, Señor.'

'Then the answer has to be extremely brief. We know nothing.'

'Have you had any reason to think someone might have been skulking around this house, particularly at night?'

'No.'

'Are all the bedrooms upstairs?'

'They are.'

'Then it is very unlikely you would ever have been bothered.'

'Why should that be?'

'Unless Ramos used a ladder – and where would he easily find one? – he would have been attracted only to bungalows, since they enabled him to peep while remaining on the ground.'

'Lacking any knowledge about such matters, I should like to learn how a person can look into a room on the ground floor if shutters are closed? Was this man hoping to find them left open?'

'He built a unit which enabled him to see inside when shutters were closed. I haven't seen it, but I've reason to believe it was a spy TV camera fitted on the end of a flexible rod. The camera was wired to a small display unit. He inserted the camera between two slats of a shutter and used the flexibility of the rod to position the camera to provide a good view of the room; in the heat and unless there is air conditioning, windows and curtains are usually left open to allow as much circulation of air as possible.'

'Ingenuity put to a very regrettable use.'

'I am grateful we sleep upstairs,' she said.

'Señor, I hope you will appreciate that I need to ask you questions which may seem intrusive, perhaps impertinent, but I assure you they are not meant to be.'

'We quite understand.'

'Do you own a car and, if so, what type is it?'

'A Peugeot, a saloon model.'

'Can you tell me where you were on the evening of the fifth of this month?'

'I cannot, but I don't doubt my wife can.'

She stood. 'One moment, please.' She left the room, her walk touched by grace even though age had attacked her body. When she returned, she sat before she said: 'We met friends who had sailed here from Nice and we stayed the night in a hotel.'

'You wish to know the name of the hotel?' D'Avour asked.

'I hardly think that's necessary,' Alvarez answered.

'I am surprised you do not consider it essential.'

He was uncomfortably aware that even though it appeared very unlikely they could in any way be concerned with the case, he should have asked for the hotel's name so that, if necessary, their stay could be confirmed.

'We stayed at the Hotel Parelona,' D'Avour said.

'Thank you, Señor.'

He left a couple of minutes later, escorted to the door by a maid in uniform, not – he was convinced – to make certain he did not help himself to any of the small and no doubt valuable objets d'art that were in evidence, but because in this house even an uninvited guest was treated with all possible courtesy.

He settled behind the wheel of the Ibiza and switched

on the fan to maximum power, tried and failed to think up a valid reason for not visiting the last house on his list. He drove out, turned left, and, during the very short journey, was so concerned by the coming meeting that he failed to scare himself with thoughts of going over the outer, unfenced edge of the road.

He had presumed the Wyatts must live in the largest and most luxurious home in the urbanización: it proved to be one of the smallest and plainest. Proof that a puffed-up frog made the most noise.

He knocked on the front door and this was opened by a middle-aged woman. 'Are Señor and Señora Wyatt here?'

'Who wants to know?'

'Cuerpo General de Policia.'

'Are they in trouble?'

'Not as far as I'm concerned.'

She did not try to hide her disappointment.

He followed her through the small hall, into the sitting room, and out to the patio. Wyatt, rotund in face and body, sat on one side of the patio table, Anthea on the other; he was reading a newspaper, she a magazine. There was a filled glass in front of each and between them a tray on which were bottles and an ice bucket.

'Good evening,' Alvarez said.

'Don't think we've had the pleasure,' Wyatt responded.

'Hardly a pleasure,' she said.

'How's that, my dear?'

'It is the policeman who was so impertinent.'

'He's a local, so he'll have spoken from sheer igno-rance.' He turned to Alvarez. 'You are who?'

'Inspector Alvarez of the Cuerpo General de Policia, Señor.'

'Of the Keystone Kops,' she snapped.

'That's rather amusing, what?' Wyatt chuckled.

181

'What do you want?' she demanded.

'I should like to ask a few questions, Señora.'

'Why?'

'I am investigating the death of Marcial Ramos . . .'

'We know no one of that name.'

'Almost certainly not, but it is possible he knew of you.'

'There are many who know of us and whom we have no wish to know.'

'He was a peeping Tom . . .'

'Do you have the slightest idea what that objectionable term means?'

'Yes. And as I have to try to discover the extent of his peeping, I need to ask you if at any time you have heard or seen anything to suggest he was bothering you? For instance, after dark, have you been in the bedroom and heard rustling or scratching sounds coming from the shutters . . .'

'Are you suggesting anyone would presume to attempt so disgusting a thing where I am concerned?'

'Señora, one has to accept that his tastes were probably eclectic.'

'Walter, see he leaves immediately.'

Wyatt hesitated.

'Now!' she snapped.

Alvarez decided he had done all that could be expected of a reasonable human being. He crossed to the French windows, went into and through the sitting room, opened the front door and left. It would take a direct order from the superior chief to force his return.

Eighteen

M atilde Pino lived on the west side of Llueso, in the shadows of a block of recently built flats which cost so much to buy they brought a feeling of despair to younger Mallorquins who wanted a home of their own when they married. One of over twenty side-by-side houses, in the summer, with all shutters closed to keep out the sun, it looked from the outside to be bleak and to offer few comforts; prosperity had made appearances deceptive and inside it lacked no modern comfort.

'Have you found him?' Matilde asked, anxiety pitching her voice high and thin.

'I'm afraid not, which is why I'm here to see if you can help me,' Alvarez answered.

'How can I help when I don't know where he is?' She suddenly swung round and pointed at a framed triptych of photographs, framed in green leather. 'I only know he's dead before his time, like his father was.'

'You know nothing of the sort,' he said forcefully. 'He has not returned home, that is all that is certain. Every day of the year, people disappear for a while and then come back and all is as it was; were your daughter missing, then you might have cause to worry, since much might have changed before she returned.' He studied the photographs as he spoke. The one in the right-hand fold was, presumably, Pablo in his late teens – the smoothed down hair, cocky grin, and set of the head

183

made it likely Dolores's brief description of his character was correct.

'He has never done this before.'

'At his age, life is about doing things for the first time.'

'You really think that?'

'I do.'

'You don't believe he is dead?'

'Of course not.'

'Sweet Mary, I pray you are right.'

'I'm certain your prayers will be answered.' She seemed to have calmed sufficiently for him to question her. 'Suppose now you tell me the things I need to know?'

'I've said, I know nothing.'

He smiled. 'Believe me, in no time at all we will find you know a great deal more than you believe. Shall we be comfortable and sit down?'

'It will be better next door.'

They went into a smaller room, beyond which was a small garden. The most notable feature in the room was a flat-screen television, far too large for the area. She saw him looking at it and misunderstood his interest. 'Pablo bought it for me just the other day as a present because I watch so much. He is a good boy.'

And a very generous one, Alvarez thought as he sat. This set was about the size of one he had recently seen in a shop window and that had had a price tag of over four hundred thousand pesetas. 'María is Pablo's present girlfriend?'

'The sweetest girl! As I keep telling him, it is the person inside who really matters.'

'Why would you say that?'

She fidgeted with the arm of the chair. She looked out through the window at a tangerine tree which seemed to be having trouble living. 'When she was young, she had an accident with some burning fat and her face was damaged. Her family had money then and they took her to Barcelona to the best specialist in the country; he did all he could, but it wasn't enough. Not that she was ever a beauty: no one in her family ever has been. But she has the nature of a saint. Her mother has been bedridden for many years and she cares for her without a word of complaint. How many daughters will do that these days?'

'Few.'

'The young think only of themselves.'

Was she subconsciously basing her judgment on her own son? 'I'll have a word with María, so tell me what her address is.'

'I've phoned her many times, but she has not heard from Pablo.'

'Nevertheless, I need to speak to her. Where does she live?'

'On the other side of Mestara, in a big house.'

'And the name of the house?'

'Ca'n Magin. María's father owned much land and was an important man.'

Many years before, social importance had largely rested on the ownership of land; now, unless the land could be developed, there were many who regarded it as almost a liability rather than an asset. 'When Pablo left here yesterday, did he say where he was going?'

'I told you . . .'

'I know you did when we talked on the phone, but sometimes, when one's upset, one forgets things. So now I want you to think back very carefully and remember everything that was said before he went out.'

'Will I ever see him again?' she cried. 'Never before has he stayed away without a word.'

'Which is why you have to tell me all he said before he

left here so I can find him and tell him to reassure you. Perhaps he mentioned he would be seeing a friend?'

'I thought he must be with María. That he had finally understood it is the person inside who matters . . .' She became silent.

'He didn't specifically mention anyone? Or any place?' She shook her head.

'He has a car, you told me. Did he leave here in that?'

'Yes.'

'Can you remember its registration number?'

'No.'

Traffic would be able to tell him what that was. Then it would be a matter of fine judgment to decide whether to request an all-forces search for it. Because of the extra work involved in such a search, should Pablo return unharmed, the request would earn its originator much opprobrium. 'Let's get back to names. Can you remember any names of friends?'

She could not. It seemed Pablo seldom, if ever, confided in her.

He stood. 'When he returns, make certain you let me know immediately. Ring me at the post; if I'm not there, tell them they must contact me immediately.'

'You really believe he's coming back?'

'Don't I keep telling you just that?'

He left. It was a measure of how deeply he was affected by her fears that, despite his heartening words to her, he decided to drive to Mestara and speak to María even though there seemed little chance she could help him and this might make him late for supper.

He drove past the small and ancient church in which it was said there had been a holy visitation two centuries before, and out on to the main road. Should he, he wondered, have assured Matilde quite so firmly that Pablo would return safely? There were times when it was cruel rather than kind, to offer hope. Although it was a fact that, when most disappearances ended, the person concerned turned out to be safe and well, there were always one or two where the worst fears were confirmed. Why would Pablo have voluntarily disappeared from home for this length of time? There seemed to have been no bruising row between his mother and him. Indeed, such a row was highly unlikely, since she clearly saw her son as a reason for living and would almost always bend her will to his. Had there been a row between him and María? From what had not been said, it seemed likely the relationship was not as strong as she might wish, so was it really likely any row could be so traumatic for him as to force his disappearance? Had he found a willing foreigner on the beach? If so, wouldn't he have put her on hold and turned up for work in the morning, knowing that if he did not, his job would be at risk? Or could a man within hours become so infatuated with a woman that he threw aside every vestige of common sense? He would have said not, but was certain Dolores would have said, often . . .

Mestara stood amidst very many hectares of land which was renowned for the quality of its soil – the full potential of which had been realised by an Englishman who had introduced to the farmers, initially against their will, the modern system of irrigation which allowed high value crops in bulk to be successfully and repeatedly grown. The town was sufficiently far from the sea to have escaped most of the damage wrought by tourists and few gewgaws were sold at the Sunday markets, restaurants did not offer meals like mum made, and many family stores still survived; there were several flourishing businesses dealing in agricultural machinery and its repair.

Alvarez braked to a stop in front of Ca'n Magin and imagined himself the owner of this manorial house and its land, growing rich crops . . . He corrected his imagination. If he won the lottery – the only way in which he would ever be able to afford to possess such a property – he would buy a house not on the Pla but near to, or amongst, the mountains even though the cultivation of the land would be very much more difficult and less rewarding. Mountains were part of his life and when they were not close, he missed their brooding presence . . .

He crossed the drive, which was pitted with weeds, climbed the five marble steps into a grandiose porch, knocked on a wooden door heavy enough to face a battering ram. He was surprised to find himself knocking and waiting rather than entering and calling out, as he would normally have done. Social habits lingered.

A young woman, dressed conservatively, almost dowdily, opened the door. He introduced himself.

'Have you found him?' she asked, unknowingly echoing Matilde's words.

'I'm afraid not, Señorita, which is why I have come here for your help.'

Wordlessly, she opened the door fully for him to enter. The hall was smaller, though higher, than he had expected. On the walls hung several framed prints, but the light was too dim easily to make out their subjects; the few pieces of furniture were old and cumbersome, both in size and style.

'Do you think . . . ?' She came to a sudden stop.

'Most people who disappear soon turn up, unharmed, and only a very few do not.' Since she appeared to be in greater control of her emotions than Matilde had been, he was less positively optimistic.

'But why hasn't he told me . . .' There was the sound of a distant phone's ringing. She turned round, hurried across the hall and through a doorway.

Hoping this was a call from Pablo. She might be in

control of her emotions, but that didn't mean they were not deep and, when she had not finished the sentence, he had sensed a fear as great as Matilde's. How sincere were Pablo's feelings for her? Dolores had referred to him as wild and, by inference, often in trouble because he chased the women. Of course, one had only to smile at a young woman and Dolores's imagination soared, but the photograph of him in Matilde's house had seemed to portray someone who was, in old-fashioned terms, something of a cad. A cad wouldn't understand the value of a capacity for helping others; he'd only note a face that was badly scarred on one side, a figure that was too undecided for contemporary tastes, a lack of elegance, and he would weigh these so-called defects against the assets of house and land . . .

She returned, her expression downcast. 'It wasn't him.'

'I'm sorry . . . Señorita, I need to ask some questions because they may help me find him.'

She led the way into a very large sitting room, in semi-darkness because the shutters of the three tall windows were closed. She opened the shutters of the window nearest the door and sunlight streamed in to illume a room which probably had not been decorated or even rearranged in many years. There were several chairs with faded velvet upholstery, which stood on a carpet threadbare in parts, a display cabinet filled with ancient siurells – whistles in the form of clay figures – a battered cupboard, a table with a silver candelabrum in the centre, and on the walls a pair of Mallorquin bagpipes, a reproduction Talyotic bull's head, uninspired paintings of pastoral scenes, and large, framed photographs of stern looking men with full beards . . .

Alvarez sat on one of the chairs, which creaked as it took his weight. 'Will you tell me when you last saw or spoke to Pablo?' he asked.

'When he left here on Wednesday evening.' She spoke

quietly and in a controlled manner, but kept locking and unlocking the fingers of her hands.

'Did you make any arrangement to meet him yesterday?'

'He said he'd be here as soon as possible.'

'But you didn't worry when he failed to turn up?'

'Why do you say I didn't worry?'

'If you had, surely as time went by you would have rung his home to find out what had happened?'

She seemed to take a deep breath. 'Sometimes he doesn't come when he says he will. It's . . . it's not very interesting for him here.' She began to speak more quickly and with some colour in her voice. She could go out only when she could persuade their maid, who'd worked for them for years, to look after her mother, who had become so difficult that the maid had become less and less willing to stay. Naturally, Pablo liked to have fun and there was precious little of that in Ca'n Magin, more especially if her mother knew he was there, because she didn't like him and so kept calling for help, which meant he had to be left on his own. There were several times when she'd told him she'd have to stay at home the next evening because the maid refused to return and, although he'd said he'd still be along, he had not arrived; later, he'd told her he'd met a friend who'd suggested they went to a bar and he'd lost touch with time, or his car had broken down, or . . . 'I said I understood and he didn't have to worry.'

And Pablo hadn't the wit or the wish to realise that each time this happened she was hurt and her assurance it didn't matter, false. 'Can you give me the names of any of his friends? Matilde could only suggest Arturo Luque.'

'He never brings any of them here. And, when we go out, we don't seem to meet anyone he knows.'

Because he was ashamed to be seen in the company of a woman some would call ugly? 'If you could remember just one name, it might help. I could speak to him and he probably would know more names.'

'Do you think he spent last night with a friend?'

'It has to be a possibility.' If one included female friends.

She was silent for a while, then said abruptly: 'There's Alfonso. He makes me laugh.'

She had spoken as if that were unusual; perhaps it was. 'Do you know his surname?'

She shook her head.

'Does he live in Mestara?'

'I'm almost sure he does, but I do know for certain he works at the same restaurant as Pablo in Port Llueso.'

'Then I should be able to identify him without any trouble. And there's no one else you can remember?'

She again thought intently, her forehead creased, the scarred side of her face cruelly highlighted by the sharp sunlight. 'I'm sorry, but no, I can't. The only other name I remember is Marcial, but he died recently.'

'Marcial Ramos?'

She was clearly disturbed by the sudden sharpness in his voice.

'It's a bit of a surprise to hear his name . . . Did Pablo see a lot of Marcial when he was alive?'

'He went out with Pablo and me once or twice, but after a while I refused to be with him. Pablo said I was being stupid and we almost had a row, but I just thought . . . There was something nasty about him. Not because he was a bit stupid – he couldn't help that – but, when he looked at me, it seemed he was . . . It made me feel uncomfortable.'

'You didn't like him, but Pablo was very friendly with him?'

'They certainly saw quite a lot of each other. I couldn't think why because, when we were on our own, Pablo often used to sneer at him and say that his few brains were in his fingers, not his head.'

Alvarez chose his words carefully. 'Because he was good at making things?'

'I suppose so.'

'Did you ever see any of the things he made?'

'Only that motorbike of his which looked like a wreck.'

He thanked her for her help, promised to do everything he could to find Pablo, left.

As he drove towards the roundabout on the Palma/Playa Nueva road, he wondered why life should be so cruel that María could understand the true Marcial, but not the true Pablo . . . ? Was it a coincidence that Pablo had been very friendly with Marcial? Sometimes, coincidences stretched logic, yet he was certain that that was not the case here. Pablo's disappearance was in some way connected to Marcial's death, which meant that, in all probability, sooner or later a mother and a lover would be thrown into mourning.

Nineteen

When Alvarez hurried into the dining room, the family were eating bananas and baked almonds. Hastily and with suitable humility, he said to Dolores: 'I'm terribly sorry to arrive this late, but I had to go over to Mestara last thing to question someone and that took much longer than I'd expected.'

'Indeed!' She spoke in a disbelieving tone.

He sat. The atmosphere was frosty – so frosty that it called for supreme self-sacrifice. 'Don't bother about my meal. I'll make do with bread and cheese.' His place had been set and he reached across for the bottle of wine, filled his glass. He drank. Dolores remained seated.

'Was she a blonde?' Juan asked, and giggled.

'Be quiet!' Dolores snapped.

'But you said . . .'

'I have said, be quiet.'

In a wordless comment on injustice, Juan filled his mouth with the remaining almonds on his plate, hoping his mother would be annoyed by such bad manners. She did not notice.

'I'll get myself some grub, then,' Alvarez said. After a while he stood because it seemed she was not prepared to bring him the cheese to go with the bread which was already on the table.

'Your food is in the oven,' she said curtly.

'Why didn't you say so?'

'Because I had hoped it was unnecessary to say I will not allow anyone in my house to forgo a proper meal, even when that someone finds more important things to do than return home on time to eat what I have slaved in the furnace-hot kitchen for hours to prepare.'

'It's very kind of you,' he said meekly.

'It was not kindness, but a sense of duty.'

He expected her to go through to the kitchen to collect his meal. She remained seated.

In the oven was a covered plate; when he removed the metal lid, he looked down at a plateful of bacalla amb llet. He sighed. He liked salted cod in all its many guises, but for some strange reason, this was one of the few dishes Dolores could never cook well.

From the other room came Juan's voice. 'But you did say Uncle wasn't back in time because he was either boozing in a bar or chasing a blonde half his age.'

'I was not speaking to you, therefore you should not have listened. In any case, that is not what I said.'

'Yes, it is . . .'

'One more word and you go straight up to bed.'

Alvarez carried his plate through and put it down on the place mat, sat. 'This smells even more delicious than usual. All the time I was in Mestara trying to get the unfortunate woman to hurry up and tell me what I needed to know . . .'

'What a man wants to hear is not what he needs to know.'

'But in this case, it was. I wanted to hear where her boyfriend might be because I need to find him.'

'Then you weren't in a bar?' Jaime said.

'Would I waste time when I knew a meal fit for the gods of Olympus would be waiting at home?'

'When you talk like that, I'd say the answer's yes.'

Dolores turned to face her husband. 'You are so surprised someone should see fit to praise my cooking?'

'Surprised anyone talks like him. Gods of Olympus!'

'My meal is not good enough for them?'

'That's not what I said. Why won't you ever understand?'

'How does one understand unthinking ingratitude?'

'What's got you talking like that? I know your cooking's good, so I don't have to keep saying so.'

'Some men are born dumb, others should have been.'

'I suppose that's another of your mother's sayings?'

'And if it is?'

'I'd like to know how she gained such experience?'

'Are you suggesting something which I cannot put into words and speak them?' Dolores demanded furiously.

'All I meant was . . . If I spelled out the alphabet, you'd find something wrong with what I said.'

'Because you'd start with Z.' She went through to the kitchen.

Alvarez ate quickly, glad that Jaime's slow-wittedness had diverted Dolores's annoyance. He refilled his glass for the third time as Isabel began to clear the table around him, peeled a banana.

Dolores looked through the bead curtain. 'Where's Juan?' she asked Isabel. 'Why isn't he helping you?'

'He had to be excused.'

'The thought of work always weakens men's bladders.' She began to withdraw her head.

'By the way,' Alvarez called out, 'I have to go out when I've finished eating.'

She pushed her head forward. 'I am not surprised.'

'I need to question someone.'

'I am grateful I will hear neither the questions nor the answers.'

'It's work.'

'Because she is young enough to appreciate how old you are?'

'I am not old. I have to find out how a waiter can afford a television set that costs a fortune.'

Dolores hesitated, then came through the bead curtain and up to the table. She unnecessarily moved the salt and pepper mills. 'Would the person you have to speak to be Matilde?'

'It would. Hardly a curvaceous blonde half my age!'

'You have not found her Pablo?'

'Not yet.'

'She must be desolated.'

'She is.'

'Where can he be?'

'That only needs one guess,' Jaime said.

'To a one-track mind.' She returned to the kitchen.

He leaned forward and spoke in a very low voice. 'He's still shacked up with a woman? Some blokes have all the luck.'

'It's looking less and less likely his has been good.'

'What d'you mean?'

'Would that I knew.' He finished the banana, reached across for the bottle of brandy.

The sky had become tinged with violet, as frequently happened during the summer between sunset and dark, when Alvarez stepped into Matilde's house and called out. As she hurried into the front room, he said. 'I'm sorry, I haven't been able to find Pablo.'

Despair replaced the brief hope. 'He's a good boy.' Her voice rose. 'He'd never let me worry until I cannot eat or sleep unless something terrible had happened.'

He no longer denied the possibility that harm might have come to Pablo. To do so now would probably be to increase the pain later. 'We're doing everything we can.

I've spoken to María, but she knows no more than you. She gave me the name of another friend and I've had a word with him over the telephone, but he can't help.'

She abruptly sat on one of the chairs ranged against the wall.

'I need to know something,' he said quietly. 'Has Pablo recently had a lot of money to spend?'

'What's that matter?'

'I need to pursue a possibility.'

She stared into space and a world of fear.

'You told me he'd bought the new television for you. When was that?'

'He was proud to give me something so grand. He . . .' Her lips trembled.

'Try and remember how long ago he bought it.'

After a while, she murmured: 'Two, three weeks maybe.'

'Has he recently bought other things?'

She mentioned the music centre that was up in his bedroom; and then there was the new car he'd ordered, which wouldn't be delivered for a while because he wanted lots of extras.

'When did he buy the music centre and order the car?'

'Where can he be? Why hasn't he told me where he is?'

'We don't know, which is why I'm asking these questions. The answers may help me find him . . . When did he buy the music centre?'

'When he got the television. He laughed and said if I had a present, he ought to have one as well. He laughs like his dear father used to.' Tears began to trickle down her lined cheeks.

'Did he order the car at about the same time?'

She nodded.

His questions were exacerbating her distress, but they had to continue. 'That must have worried you, seeing him buy so many expensive things at the same time?' Someone of peasant stock would not watch with equanimity considerable money being spent.

'I told him, a peseta in the hand is worth two in the shopkeeper's.'

'How did he respond to that?'

'Told me there was no need to worry, we'd never be short of money again.'

'Did he explain why that should be?'

'When I asked, he just laughed.'

'Thank you for telling me all these things. Now, I must go and make more enquiries.'

She stared at him, her face taut from emotion. 'You will find him, won't you?'

'I will do everything possible,' he answered.

Twenty

As soon as he arrived in his office on Saturday morning, Alvarez dialled Traffic in Palma and when the connection was made, said: 'I need to know the make, model, and registration number of the car owned by Pablo Pino, whose address is 16 Carrer de Alfred Bonet, Llueso.'

The man at the other end of the line repeated the name and address. 'I'll get back to you on Monday with the details.'

'Why the delay?'

'What delay? Today's Saturday.'

'This is important. So much so the superior chief has named it priority.'

'And you know what takes greater priority than that? Making certain his weekend is all pleasure.'

'He's too miserable to know what pleasure is.'

'Aren't they all? OK, I'll be a martyr and let you know as soon as possible.'

Alvarez leaned back in his chair. Did he find out if the superior chief was in his office and explain the direction enquiries were now taking? Surely it was better to wait until he could present a rounded picture? In any case, it was time for merienda.

He was preparing to leave for lunch – a little early, but the previous evening he had put in overtime – when the phone rang. Traffic gave him the make, model, and registration number of Pino's car.

He drummed on the desk with his fingers. To ask, or not to ask, that was the problem: whether t'was more sense to speak up and suffer the doubts and objections or use silence as a cloak . . . Salas would undoubtedly find a dozen reasons to judge his half-formed theory nonsense and would expound on each one at an interminable length. If he were late for the meal for the second time within twenty-four hours, Dolores might well be so annoyed she would not be bothered to keep his food warm . . .

He phoned Traffic, spoke to a different man and, once more quoting the superior chief's authority, asked for an all-forces search for Pino's car. That done, he was able to return home in sufficiently good time to enjoy more than one brandy before the meal of Capo al Rei Jaume.

There was a large post on Wednesday. Alvarez stared uneasily at the several letters on the desk which had been left there by the duty cabo; experience said that when there were so many, at least one would demand action that would increase his workload. If only he could identify which one, he would drop it into the waste paper basket and later, if necessary, say in all honesty he had never read it.

Traffic rang. 'The Guardia have just reported that the car you asked to have a trace put on has been found in the airport car park.'

'Have they examined it?'

'Shouldn't think so. That would be showing initiative . . . What d'you expect to find – dope?'

'A body.'

'Then I pity whoever does open it up. After several days in this heat, it'll be as high as the sky.'

'Did they say if someone's standing by for orders?'

'You must be an optimist.'

'Could one of your blokes go along and check it out?'

'You must be an optimistic optimist.'

Alvarez finally accepted that he would have to make the initial examination of the car and asked if the other had been given the details which would enable him to find it amongst the many hundreds in the multi-floor building. He was given floor, letter, and number. 'Thanks for letting me know.'

'No problem.'

There never was when the work could be transferred on to someone else's shoulders. He replaced the receiver. The sooner he left Llueso, the sooner he would be back and, if he had to miss merienda, life demanded sacrifices. He seized on one small crumb of comfort – now there was not the time to open the post.

In the past few years, new roads had lessened the time of the journey between Llueso and Palma and, driving sufficiently steadily to be occasionally within the speed limit, he arrived at the airport car park forty minutes after leaving the office. He collected a ticket on passing through the barrier, drove up the oval spiral to the fourth floor, then three-quarters of the way along the outside line to an empty place. A few metres on was the dark-green Astra saloon, battered by the years and careless driving.

A visual examination showed the interior to be empty of everything but litter. The boot was locked. An old lag had shown him what could be done with a thin strip of metal and, forty-five seconds later, he lifted the lid. His relief at not finding a week-old corpse was profound. He used his mobile to ask Traffic to send a low-loader to collect the car for possible fingerprint examination. That done, he unlocked the driving door and unlatched the other three from the inside. In the back well was an empty plastic shopping bag and he used this to store all the litter and the contents of the glove locker. He returned to his own car and waited.

A low-loader arrived and he directed the crew of three to the Astra, adding that it was unlocked and whoever sat behind the wheel must wear gloves. They denied any of them had gloves. Certain they were liars, but unable to prove that, he put on one of the pairs of surgeon's gloves he always carried in his car, sat behind the wheel of the Astra, and steered it out of the bay as they pushed. They winched it up on to the low-loader, then left.

He drove in the Ibiza down to the exit barrier at ground level. Only then did he realise he had forgotten to pay the parking fee. All the pay machines were situated elsewhere and he had to leave his car and walk around the building. On his return, he was met by two irate drivers whose cars had stopped behind his and immediately become hemmed in by the oncoming stream of other exiting cars, the drivers of which had lacked the goodwill to halt and let them back up sufficiently to be able to make for the second exit lane. Typically aggressive, the two drivers threatened much until he explained the great pleasure it would give him to arrest them for disorderly conduct.

As a consequence of his trip to Palma, he overslept and did not reach the office until five thirty. He slumped down in his chair and stared at the unopened mail, which had not seen fit to disappear.

His thoughts moved on. Had Pablo driven the car to the airport or had it been driven there by someone else to give the impression that it had been he? Why would he have gone to the airport? To meet someone? Unlikely. To see someone off? Unlikely. Thanks to his sudden wealth, to fly off for a holiday with the long-legged, full bosomed blonde who haunted Jaime's daydreams? Perhaps. But, in this last instance, surely he would have told a close friend – if not María or his mother – at least that he was going, if not where and why?

Seeing is Deceiving

If humans always acted logically, how much easier police work would be . . . He sighed as he swept the letters to one side, then picked up the plastic shopping bag from the floor and emptied the contents on to his desk. Car papers, a very tattered instruction book, a dented container which had once held one of McDonald's best, four wrappers from Mars bars, many wrappers from boiled sweets, two pages from the *Diario de Mallorca*, a photograph that had been torn into many pieces, a receipt from a restaurant in the port – not the one at which he worked – a ballpoint pen which had been stamped on, two segments of orange peel, a chocolate with a soft centre stuck to an out-of-date lottery ticket . . . Carelessly untidy, Alvarez judged, overlooking the state in which the interior of his own car usually was. Nothing to affirm or deny that Pino had flown off the island . . . He collected up the pieces of photograph and arranged them in order, more to occupy his hands than because he thought the reassembled image could be of any consequence; and at first he failed to comprehend that indeed it was. The lighting was poor, the focus poorer, and the images not clear; the man standing by the bed and the woman on the bed were plainly naked, but their features were too fuzzy for them to be readily identified. On the nearer bedside table was an object whose unusual form was sufficiently clear to tickle a memory. But what memory? After a while, he dropped the bits of photograph into the plastic bag.

Dolores was in the kitchen, washing up the supper plates, cutlery, and dishes; she sang a cheerful song about two lovers for whom the skies were always blue. Judging her mood to be as benign as the words, Jaime and Alvarez did not hesitate to refill their glasses with brandy.

The television was switched on. Jaime said: 'Are you interested in what's showing?'

'Hearing someone tell me how hard his life is? I can do worse than him any day of the week.'

He switched channels. 'Ballet! A bunch of poofs larking about with flat-chested lesies.'

'The music's good.'

'If you like that kind of noise.' He changed channels a second time to bring up a nature programme. 'Can't think why the sharks don't eat the silly sods who go down and film 'em.' He switched off the television. 'There's nothing worth watching these days.'

'The programmes are always worse in the summer.'

'Yet the people don't get paid any less; they still make so much they daren't hide it all from the tax people.'

'A problem I wouldn't mind facing.'

'Having to pay over a fortune?'

'Being paid so much, I owed a fortune.'

'Sometimes you talk a load of nonsense. Who wants to pay them a peseta?' He drained his glass, looked towards the bead curtain. 'She's stopped singing.'

As if to contradict him, she resumed.

He poured himself another brandy, pushed the bottle across the table. 'There's a film on later that's suppose to be really hot. How about watching it?'

'I've had a tiring day.'

'According to Mateo, it's got scenes that would make the dead jump around.' When there was no response, he jerked his thumb in the direction of the kitchen. 'I suppose you're afraid she'll object.'

'Hadn't thought about it.'

'All we've got to say is there's a lot of violence and she'll be off to bed.'

'So will I.'

'Getting too old to enjoy life?'

'And are you in need of moral support – or should that be immoral support?'

'Bloody funny!'

The singing stopped a second time and Dolores came through the bead curtain and sat. 'Isn't there anything to watch on the telly?'

'Not yet,' Alvarez answered, 'but Jaime reckons there's a good programme later on.'

She turned to her husband. 'What is it?'

'I never said anything. These days, Enrique talks a load of cabbages,' Jaime answered, silently cursing Alvarez's sense of humour.

'It's sad how you men always misunderstand each other; that's why there are so many wars. Switch the set on and let's see what there is.'

A shark, mouth open and jagged teeth in great evidence, appeared to be about to eat the camera.

'I can't stand them,' she said. 'Just think of being eaten by one! Try another channel.'

'There's only some old fool telling everyone what a rough life he has. Probably has to exist on twenty million a year.'

'There must be something more interesting.'

'Ballet.'

'I like that if it's not some awful modern music. What ballet is it?'

'How would I know?'

'By switching it on.'

Jaime did so. A male dancer raised his partner with such apparent ease she might have weighed no more than thistledown.

'Isn't he strong and graceful?' she said.

Jaime, about to give his opinion, for once had the sense to remain silent.

When the ballet finished, Dolores yawned. 'I'm tired.'

'Then why not go up to bed?' Jaime suggested eagerly.

She stood. 'Are you coming up?'

'I reckon I'll hang on just a while.'

An advertisement appeared on screen for a medicine which promised to relieve all the trials of hay fever. One capsule every eight hours would abolish sneezing, blocked noses, itching eyes . . .

'Well I'm damned!' Alvarez said aloud.

'No doubt about that.' Jaime chuckled

'I've just had a possible revelation.'

She asked: 'Revelation about what?'

'Many things; things which had been tying my brain in knots . . . I'm going out.'

'This late?' She walked across to the stairs.

'If you're thinking what I think you're thinking, you're wrong.'

'I very much doubt that,' she snapped.

'I am not leaving here to chase an amorous twenty year old.'

She climbed the stairs.

When satisfied she was out of hearing, Jaime said: 'You're really going out?'

'I am.'

'What about the film?'

'I've more important things in mind.'

'So you've been lying. There is a bit waiting for you.'

'Not for me.' He left.

As he settled behind the wheel of the Ibiza and started the engine, he wondered why he suffered the overwhelming compulsion to act now rather than wait to confirm that the object in the torn-up photograph taken from Pino's car was almost certainly a puffer exactly similar to the one Hilary Palmer had shown him. She would hardly welcome his appearance this late at night to ask if she knew who else used similar puffers . . . Yet when there was the possibility of answering questions which had puzzled for a long time, it became very difficult to delay the possibility of learning the answers even by a few hours . . .

He passed through the belt of pine trees and above was Ca'n Greix. The thin line of light through shutters identified, he was reasonably certain, the sitting room. But, even as he watched, the room went dark. They were making for their beds. He braked to a halt. If it had been absurd to start, it was thrice absurd to continue. He would have to return in the morning . . .

The bungalow was long and thin, to gain the benefit of the view across the valley, and it was reasonable to assume that the bedrooms, facing south-east, extended beyond the sitting room. Lights went on in one room. He waited for lights to go on in a second bedroom. None did . . .

He was appalled by his sudden thoughts. Perhaps Salas was right and his mind was nothing but a sink of iniquity. Yet those thoughts provided a motive which accommodated the known and suspected facts.

Conscience certainly made a coward of him. When he opened the driving-side door and the overhead light went on, he was startled and shocked because an onlooker might have seen him and divined his intention. He cursed himself for a fool. There was no onlooker, he had every right to be there, no one could read his mind. Nevertheless, after climbing out, he did not slam the door shut, but carefully pressed it home because noise travelled far at night.

He climbed the slope, becoming more breathless with every laboured step. And it was only when he reached the relatively level ground on which the bungalow stood that it occurred to him that without the means of spying, it would be impossible to see anything other than the ceiling and the upper part of the bedroom and his target must surely be lower. But, even as he accepted the futility of his intentions, he discovered he had forgotten it was the heat of the summer and, if an air conditioning unit was not in operation, windows would be left open behind closed shutters. He could hear what was being said quite clearly. He experienced conflicting emotions of which shame was one, but none was as strong as the fear he would be sighted, would try to run, trip, roll down the slope and smash his head into a rock. Forever to be remembered as Eavesdropping Enrique.

Twenty-one

For the umpteenth time, Alvarez picked up the receiver; this time, he gained sufficient courage to dial. The plum-voiced secretary at her most abrupt, said: 'Yes?'

'It's Inspector Alvarez speaking. Is the superior chief in his office?'

'Yes.'

'I should like to speak to him.' Which was a complete lie.

He waited, uneasily certain that the coming conversation was going to be very unpleasant.

'I'm glad to have the opportunity to speak to you, Alvarez.'

'I am ringing to explain—'

'I have been informed that I authorised your request for an all-forces search for a vehicle. Unfortunately, I can recall neither your asking for permission to make this request, nor my agreeing to its being made.'

'Señor, the fact is—'

'I am glad we are to discuss facts, not inferences or assumptions.'

'In the circumstances . . . That is to say . . .'

'Then say it.'

'It seemed necessary to move very quickly.'

'Why?'

'Following the disappearance of Pablo Pino . . .'

'Who?'

209

He repeated the name.

'I now have to admit that once again memory deserts me and I do not remember any report from you regarding a case in which a person of that name was involved. Would you suggest it is age which afflicts me?'

Salas in ironic mode was even less bearable than usual. 'I think, Señor, it is just possible I may not have submitted my report because of the rush of events . . .'

'A problem to which, you would no doubt agree, all of us are subject.'

'Indeed. Perhaps if I detail all the facts now . . .'

'On that tried and trusted principle, better late than never?'

Alvarez briefly made his report.

'You base your suspicions that Pino has been murdered solely on the grounds that he was a friend of Ramos?'

'Because he's disappeared within a little more than a fortnight of Ramos's murder . . .'

'Is it not still an assumption he was murdered? There surely is not the proof he was.' Salas's mood changed. 'I find it very difficult to accept the conclusion of an officer who bases his reading of the case solely on an assumption and a coincidence, while rejecting the obvious probability – that the car was in the airport car park because Pino left it there when he flew from the island.'

'But he never told anyone – not his mother, his girl-friend, or his best friends – he was going away. I've checked with the local travel agents and he's not bought a flight through any of them. The only feasible reason I can think of for his acting as you suggest would be if he'd found a prospect and hoped to make good by throwing the money around; there's not the slightest hint of that.'

'Of course there isn't. What employer is going to accept a bribe to offer a job?'

There was a silence.

'Well?'

'I'm afraid I don't quite see the point of that question, Señor.'

'I can hardly put it more simply.'

'But Pino wasn't looking for a job.'

'Then why did you say that was the only reason you could suggest for his flying abroad?'

'But I didn't . . . Perhaps you mistook my use of the word "prospect".'

'Then in what abnormal sense were you using it?'

'I meant a young lady who needed to be impressed before she'd come across.'

'Why would she have to be persuaded to come to the island?'

'Not that kind of coming across.'

'Clearly, we speak different languages.'

'Come across in the sense . . . You know.'

'After even a brief conversation with you, I begin to doubt I know anything.'

'I meant, to have sex with him.'

'I suppose,' Salas said wearily, 'I should have realised you were finding reason to wallow in immorality.'

'The point I was trying to make, Señor, was that, although this was a possible reason for his car being at the airport, I don't accept it. In my opinion, the car was left there in order to give me that false impression.'

'I doubt there is anyone so misinformed as to believe he can direct your mind along any recognisable path.'

'If Pino has been murdered, at least part of the motive surely is to be found in the nature of Ramos's death and why his body was moved to make it appear that he died somewhere other than where he did. I think I have identified that motive.'

'Which is what?'

'Ramos was a peeping Tom . . .'

'There is no need to refer to matters best forgotten.'

'I don't think we can forget, since that's at the heart of all that's happened. Ramos was using his home-made equipment to peep. In addition, he was sometimes videoing what he saw and this allowed him to take still frames from the tape. People of his nature do gain added pleasure from . . .'

'Enough!'

'Pino was a friend of Ramos. He soon learned what was going on and was shown some tapes. He may, from time to time, have taken part with Ramos in the actual peeping – he seems to possess such a character. In Pino's car at the airport there was a lot of litter and amongst this I found a photograph which had been torn into several pieces. I put these together and it shows a fuzzy picture of two people who are naked in a bedroom. I could not identify the two concerned because their faces were too indistinct. Later, however, I realised there was an object in the photo which might identify them, given the help of someone who lives in Beniferri urbanización. So I drove there to have a word with them but, when this house – bungalow – came in sight, the light in what was almost certainly the sitting room went off. Because it was late, it seemed obvious they were going to bed. There was no good reason to disturb them then, so I decided to return another time but, before I started to leave, I noticed only one room was now illuminated and it was reasonable to assume that was a bedroom.'

'One normally goes to bed in a bedroom.'

'There was no light in a second room.'

'It's my understanding that it is only the English upper classes who frequently occupy separate bedrooms after their heir is born in order that the husband can return to the unmentionable lifestyle he enjoyed before his marriage.'

'Well, I was sufficiently intrigued to . . .'

'Surely not even you can have demanded to know the nature of their sleeping habits?'

'No, Señor. I decided to try to find out, without disturbing them, whether they were sharing a bedroom.'

'My God!'

'So I walked up the hill to the bungalow . . .'

Salas's voice rose. 'You peered into their bedroom?'

'No, Señor. I just listened.'

'You what?' he shouted. 'This is beyond belief! I shall make an immediate recommendation you be examined by a psychologist. On receipt of his report, I shall ask for your resignation on the grounds of ill health. Obviously, I should prefer the truth to be told, but it is quite unthinkable that the Cuerpo should have to bear the odium of your actions.'

'What I heard . . .'

'You will keep to yourself.'

'. . . made it clear they were making love.'

'This is the most disgusting report I have ever had to listen to. You will never, ever, put a single word of it down on paper.'

'I haven't finished.'

'On the contrary. You are beyond question finished.'

'The people living in that bungalow are Señora Palmer and Señor Wade.'

'Due to the lapse of all moral standards in the world of today, a liaison is not unusual.'

'Are you forgetting that they are brother and sister?'

There was a long pause. Then Salas slammed down the receiver.

213

Twenty-two

Alvarez's reluctance to speak to Salas on Friday morning was even greater than it had been on the Thursday. It seemed this reluctance was shared.

'He is not in his office,' the plum-voiced secretary said.

'When will he return?'

'It is impossible to say.'

'Do you have a telephone number for contacting him when something very important turns up?'

'No.'

'I need to speak to him urgently.'

'It will have to wait.'

There was something about her manner – not that she had been any less curt than usual – which convinced him she was lying. 'When you next speak to Señor Salas, will you tell him I'm worried about what to say to the press in connection with the Ramos case.'

She cut the connection. Two minutes later, the phone rang.

'What's going on?' Salas demanded.

'Señor, I have had a journalist asking what progress we are making in the Ramos case.'

'Why?'

'I suppose the editor reckons it's a matter of interest to the public . . .'

'Why are they suddenly showing an interest?'

'I've no idea.'

'You have been speaking to the press!'

'Of course not, Señor. My lips have been sealed since I spoke to you yesterday . . . What am I to tell them about the case?'

'Nothing.'

'That may not be the best move . . .'

'I do not require an inspector to tell me what course to take.'

'Perhaps I should refer any reporter to you . . .'

'You will do no such thing.'

'Very well . . . Señor, as I now have the opportunity of speaking to you, I should like your authorisation to ask for a disclosure of details of the bank accounts of Señora Palmer and Señor Wade.'

'Out of the question. The moment they learnt of this, they would demand to know the reason and that would inevitably mean the disclosure of your actions in this disgusting case.'

'Yet if I am right about them . . .'

'A presumption I should prefer not to be made.'

'They're unlikely to cause trouble because they'll not want to exacerbate our suspicions; and, more probably, they'll be eager to offer an explanation.'

'An explanation of what?'

'The large sums of cash one or the other, perhaps both, of them have recently drawn.'

'Why should they have done that?'

'To pay the blackmail being levied by Pino.'

'What proof is there he was blackmailing them?'

'There can't be any other explanation for Pino's sudden wealth.'

'There can be a hundred and one.'

'Not if their accounts do show large withdrawals of cash.'

'Could you show a direct relationship between their withdrawals and Pino's receipt of the money?'

'Not direct, no. But the inference would be so strong . . .'

'How many times do I have to remind you that police work demands facts, not inferences?'

'If there are several inferences which clearly meld together, they can become almost as strong as fact. And if we show it was very likely Pino had blackmailed them because he knew they were committing incest . . .'

'Quite unprovable.'

'Señor, there can be no doubt in view of what I heard . . .'

'That will not be disclosed in court. Can you really believe I would agree to your publicly admitting to having eavesdropped?'

'Not to agree might, I suppose, be construed by some as a perversion of justice.'

'Nonsense.'

'There would be no culpability in ordering an officer of the Cuerpo not to disclose information of a criminal offence?'

'There is no crime until it is proved a criminal act has been committed. Without your evidence that will not be possible.'

'But . . .'

'The matter is closed.'

'And is Pino's disappearance and murder also to be swept under the carpet?'

'How dare you make such an insulting inference. Nothing is being hidden. It is a matter of judgment. Where is the proof that Pino has been murdered?'

'He has disappeared without a word . . .'

'Which proves only that he is typical of modern youth and has no regard for anyone else's feelings. Has his body been discovered?'

'No, Señor.'

'Is there any evidence, apart from his disappearance, to suggest it is likely he is dead?'

'I'm saying his disappearance, and the manner of that, is as good as finding his body.'

'You are unaware that every year in Spain hundreds of people disappear and their disappearance is evidence of nothing but stupidity or instability, as is proven when they reappear?'

'This case is more complicated . . .'

'With you in charge, that is inevitable.'

'I'm convinced he's dead, murdered because he learned through Ramos that brother and sister were indulging in an illicit relationship; after Ramos's death, he used that knowledge, backed by one or more still photographs of the couple unambiguously engaged in—'

'Control your imagination.'

'He blackmailed the two of them. This placed Señor Wade in an impossible situation. If he refused to meet the demand, the relationship would be exposed . . .'

'Exposed in what manner?'

'Publishing a video or still photograph taken from one which Ramos had obtained on a previous visit to the house.'

'Did you not tell me that the two figures in the torn-up photograph are not sufficiently clearly focused to be immediately identifiable and that it was some object in the bedroom which led you to believe it was their house?'

'That's right.'

'Is this object in much clearer definition than the people?'

'Not really.'

'Then your identification is at best very doubtful.'

'But that's relatively unimportant when you remember what I heard.'

'What you say you heard may well be, due to your innate perversity, what you wished to hear, not what was actually spoken.'

'Until I listened, I had no suspicion of what they were doing . . .'

'Then why did you listen? You claim to be able to judge what was happening from words casually spoken?'

'What they were saying was hardly ambiguous. Shall I repeat what I heard?'

'Certainly not.'

'Señor, I am trying to look at things from Pino's viewpoint. Some of the photographs are clear enough or he can successfully bluff that they are: a guilty person is always ready to believe the worst. So Wade accepts he and his sister are faced by a criminal charge and subsequent social stigma. Yet he isn't well off and, although his sister has money, from the manner of their lifestyle I'm certain she cannot be considered rich. Blackmail never ceases and for them there would come a time when they could no longer meet Pino's demands; then, he would expose them. There was only one way of escaping disaster. Murder.'

There was a long silence.

'Shall I get on to the banks and ask for the information?'

The line went dead. Alvarez replaced the receiver. Since there could well be considerable work involved, it seemed only sensible to defer any action until after the weekend.

On Tuesday, Alvarez learned at which bank Charles Wade and Hilary Palmer held accounts. After a slightly prolonged merienda, he made his way along the shaded side of the road to the Sa Nostra bank. The air-conditioned interior offered a welcome, rare degree of comfort. He spoke to the assistant manager, whose desk lay behind one of the glass screens designed to provide privacy within an open layout.

'What exactly is it you want to know?' The assistant manager was a short, balding man with swarthy features which spoke of distant Moorish ancestry.

'Whether either or both Señor Wade and Señora Palmer have withdrawn large sums in cash in the past month?'

'What do you mean by "large"?'

'Hard to be precise, but probably in the hundreds of thousands of pesetas.'

The assistant manager tapped out instructions on the computer keyboard, read what appeared on the screen. 'Señor Wade regularly withdraws fifteen thousand a week: that has not changed.' He called up further details. 'Señora Palmer regularly draws thirty thousand a week and, once again, there have not been other cash withdrawals. That, of course, excludes the usual direct debits for electricity, telephone, and rates.'

Alvarez scratched the back of his neck. 'How would someone here get his hands on large sums in cash without their appearing in his bank accounts?'

'Basically, using an offshore account which is dedicated to secrecy and regards with deep antagonism any attempt to make it divulge information about its customers' accounts. Then the simplest thing is to ask that bank for the required sum in high value peseta notes, which it will supply without question, and one brings them here in the luggage. Thanks to mass air travel and the European Union, it is only common sense which now finds it difficult to cross borders.'

'What if the person doesn't want to be seen to leave the island in the first place?'

'He can use a plastic card and withdraw the maximum permitted amount from a cash machine as often as necessary. A very tedious task if one requires a large total, but effectively secret unless an investigating authority examines the records of all possible machines – a task to be compared with the cleansing of the Augean stables and no Alpheus and Peneus to assist. Then, of course, there are the people who come into contact with foreigners and who own or work in hotels, night clubs, restaurants, etcetera, and who are not averse to receiving foreign currency abroad in exchange for pesetas handed over here. It is only the honest who find difficulty in moving black money.'

Fifteen minutes later, Alvarez settled behind the desk in his office and thought with nostalgic longing of the cool of the air-conditioned bank as he altered the set of the fan to try to gain greater benefit from the threshing blades. He used a handkerchief to mop his forehead and neck. Sooner or later, preferably much later, he would have to phone Salas and admit he had learned nothing from the bank. Salas's scorn would flow. He would sarcastically point out that to the contrary, he had learned something important. Since no large sums in cash had been withdrawn from either account, there was no evidence to support the proposition that Wade and his sister were being blackmailed. No blackmail, no motive – a punctured theory.

He lit a cigarette. The photograph of the couple had been so fuzzy that, if one were realistic, one had to agree that the couple could only be identified when reasonably certain who they probably were. No one would consider producing the photograph in a court of law as evidence which could stand on its own. Wade was far from a fool and must have decided there was every possibility no better definition could ever have been obtained in the circumstances in which the equipment was used. So why would he have panicked to the extent of murdering Pino? The thought of social stigma and persecution? Hadn't it just been conceded that no good identification could be made? Would a man risk murder to avoid suspicion? Take it one stage further. If there were no prosecution, but rumour aroused suspicion, this could easily be escaped by leaving the island and settling somewhere else where it was most unlikely they would ever meet anyone who had known them in Mallorca. Common sense said the solution was far too extreme for the problem. Yet Pino had disappeared. Could the theory be as hopelessly wrong as Salas suggested? Could Pino, in truth, have taken off with a beach pick-up, callously not bothering to tell his mother or María he would be away? Would he turn up weeks later, unashamed, convinced his mother would forgive him and he'd have no trouble in re-engaging María's affections . . . ?

He had been convinced he knew the truth, even if he lacked the proof. Now, he was so much less certain. He stubbed out the cigarette, reached down to the bottom right-hand drawer of the desk. Segura had written that there was no problem which could not be erased by bribery, suicide, or liquor. He poured himself a very large brandy.

Twenty-three

A s the months passed, Port Llueso began its winter hibernation. By the beginning of November, many bars and restaurants and most of the tourist shops were closed, prices in those stores which remained open were reduced, it was possible to park, and the beauty of the bay could once more be enjoyed. At the end of the month, there was a sudden, sharp change of weather and a long torrential downpour flooded village roads, and the torrentes, dry in summer, became raging floods of water which threatened to wash away bridges and would have drowned anyone unfortunate enough to fall into one.

December was the month in which the young had reason to remember foreigners with gratitude. Until relatively recently, Christmas Day had been a fiesta, but no presents had been given because these were reserved for Three Kings, when, in the evening, the Magi went around the village on their gaily caparisoned horses, followed by decorated mule carts, throwing boiled sweets to the crowds while their assistants hurriedly carried named presents, earlier donated by parents, from the carts to doorways. With the coming of the foreigners, in particular those from Britain, Christmas Day had been observed by them in traditional form and presents had been given. It should have been no surprise that, in no time at all, Mallorquin children soon decided to honour all traditions, thereby ensuring gifts on both days.

On Christmas Day, Juan was given a mouth organ by an elderly cousin. It wasn't long before Adolfo's gift was consigning him to warmer regions.

'Enough!' Alvarez said, as he sat at the table in the kitchen and dunked a piece of coca in hot chocolate.

'I'm trying to learn how to play, Uncle,' Juan protested.

'Then I suggest you walk to the top of Puig Akar to complete your education.'

'It's too windy up there.'

'When you're making that row, there's too much wind down here.'

Dolores, who was preparing lunch, stopped dripping olive oil into the mortar and turned.'Why not find somewhere else to play, Juan?'

'Why can't I do it here?'

'Uncle Enrique doesn't enjoy the sound.'

'Who cares what he likes?'

'What did you say?' she snapped.

'I don't see why he—'

'And I don't allow rude manners in my house. Up to your bedroom and stay there until I say you can come down.'

'That's not fair. Uncle often makes noises I don't like.'

'Up immediately.'

His expression one of angry resentment, Juan stamped his way out of the kitchen. When halfway up the stairs, he blew a discordant blast on the mouth organ.

Alvarez dunked another slice of coca.

'You could be a little more forbearing,' she observed as she peeled another three teeth of garlic.

'It's difficult to forbear a row like that.'

'I know. But perhaps you could try?'

He drank some chocolate, replaced the mug on the table. 'Did Cousin Adolfo have any children?'

'No, much to his regret.'

'He'd likely have regretted it much more if he had.'

'Now you're talking like a misanthropist.'

'Just a mouth organ hater.'

'It is a terrible row,' she agreed, 'but it is giving him such pleasure.'

'Which makes him unique.'

She looked up at the electric clock on the wall. 'You're going to be late.'

'No cause for hurry. Salas has granted himself an extended holiday and it's one of his favourite sayings that lowly inspectors should learn to follow the example of their superiors.'

He had arrived at the post half an hour late, so he left half an hour early to ensure balance. He walked into the house, took off his short overcoat and carried it through to the dining room, where he hung it on the old-fashioned coat and hatstand which had belonged to Dolores's family and which she kept for sentimental reasons even though she disliked it.

As he sat at the table and leaned over to open the door of the sideboard, Juan hurried in from the kitchen. 'Uncle.'

'Yes?' He failed to find the bottle of brandy he sought, but brought out a glass.

'I'm sorry, Uncle.'

'Sorry about what?'

'That I was very rude to you earlier. Mum says it was all my fault for upsetting you by playing the mouth organ too loudly and too long.'

'It's history, so let's forget it.'

'But I have to say how sorry I am.'

He was agreeably surprised. Juan's apologies were usually curt and said with poor grace. 'Then thank you.'

He leaned over again until he could visually examine the bottles in the cupboard.

'Are you looking for something, Uncle?'

'I thought we hadn't finished the brandy, but I can't see it. I must remind your mother to make certain we don't run out of it again.'

'It doesn't matter.'

'It certainly does!'

'No, it doesn't, because I've a present for you.' Juan brought his hand from behind his back to reveal he held a full bottle in it.

Alvarez was able to read the label. 'Hors d'Age! How on earth did you manage to afford that?'

'I've been saving and mother gave me extra because I said I must give you a very special present to show how sorry I am.'

'I'm really touched!'

'I've opened the bottle so I can pour you a drink right away.'

'I'll need some ice. Perhaps you could go through . . .'

There was a call from the kitchen. 'I'll bring it.'

It seemed Dolores, who might have been expected to suggest with a touch of aggression that he fetched what he needed, was also seeking to apologise – for her negligence in not making certain there was brandy in the cupboard.

She came through the doorway, ice bucket in one hand. 'I can't think how you can like ice at this time of the year,' she said, as she put the bucket down on the table.

He noticed her eyes were sparkling, as they did when she was inwardly laughing. In so good a mood, lunch must surely prove to be a Lucullan feast.

'How many bits of ice do you like, Uncle?'

'A couple will do fine.'

Juan picked out two cubes of ice and dropped them

into the glass; he poured a brandy that even by Alvarez's standards was a large one, passed the glass across.

The colour of the drink seemed strangely tinged, but it was so long since he'd had the pleasure of drinking brandy of that quality that he merely presumed he'd forgotten its true complexion. He drank . . .

Careless of manners, he spat. 'It's been poisoned!' he shouted.

Juan laughed and Dolores chuckled.

He thought he must be in the grip of a waking nightmare; a few agonising moments of life left and they could only laugh . . . 'For God's sake, call the doctor.'

Dolores said: 'There's no need to bother him. It's only lemonade with a touch of vinegar to darken it.'

'Lemonade . . . Vinegar . . . Are you all crazy?'

'It's Dia dels Innocents.'

'When you said it was poison . . .' Juan laughed too much to complete the sentence.

When young, Alvarez had often played tricks on others on the day reserved for fooling people. He now understood why victims had not been nearly as amused as he.

'You looked like you were going to be sick,' Juan managed to say before he once more laughed.

'Enough is enough,' Dolores said. 'You spoil a joke when you stretch it out too far.'

They heard the front door shut.

'There's your father,' she said. 'So I'll dish the meal.'

'Can't I first play the trick on him? Juan asked eagerly.

'Why not, since it won't take long?'

Jaime came into the room, pulled out a chair, sat, frowned as he looked along the table. 'If you've finished the bottle . . .' he began, speaking to Alvarez.

Juan interrupted him. 'Do you want a drink?'

'Of course I do.'

'I've bought you a very special coñac.'

'Why?'

'Because you're such a wonderful father.'

He said, as he leaned over to bring a glass out of the sideboard: 'It's taken you long enough to realise that. Come on, then, don't waste time.'

When Juan finished pouring, Jaime held up the glass and stared at it for several seconds. Then he said: 'You think your father's so stupid he'll drink this innocentada?'

Alvarez found it even more infuriating that Jaime had not been fooled than that he had.

He awoke. With Salas away on what appeared to be a prolonged Christmas break, there was little need to hurry to return to the office. He could allow himself ten, fifteen minutes to enjoy the extra pleasure which came from knowing that each one was stolen . . . For once, that pleasure failed to please as he suffered the embarrassment of recalling the amusement of Juan and Dolores and the sniggering scorn of Jaime when told what had happened. Why, he asked himself, hadn't he remembered to be on his guard because it was the Dia dels Innocents? Why hadn't he queried Juan's expression of remorse far more critically? Dolores's inner amusement should have warned him . . . Of course, even the finest mind could be hoodwinked. There was the classic case in which a group had been told they would be watching the filmed reenactment of an armed bank robbery in which one cashier was shot and killed. They had been shown a sequence in which there was a robbery, three shots were fired, but all four cashiers were shown, clearly if briefly, to be unharmed. Almost all the watchers had said that one of them had been killed . . . Juan had said it was a bottle of Hors d'Age and the label had named the contents as that, so he had accepted without question what he had been told and what he read. The human mind was conditioned to expect those circumstances it was told to expect . . .

That truth triggered his mind suddenly to flip back in time and he remembered the circumstances surrounding Robina Wade's torture and murder. After a while, he wondered how it could have taken until now to understand how those horrific circumstances had conditioned the minds of all those who had learned about them . . . ?

Did he now assume that he knew the truth? Since he couldn't yet be certain that he did, to act could be a mistake that would cost him very dearly. He had to find some way of lowering the odds until certainty was only one move away . . .

He sat at his desk and helped himself to a brandy from the right-hand bottom drawer. His courage heartened, he phoned.

'Señor Wade, it is Inspector Alvarez speaking. I'm sorry to have to trouble you once more, but I have to ask a favour.'

'Which, if possible, will naturally be granted.'

He imagined the pleasantly-featured face. Could there really be black brutality behind the mask? A ridiculous question! Eichmann had never looked to be more than a small-minded clerk. 'I have had a phone call from Señor Fenton . . .'

'Who?'

'Detective Inspector Fenton. You remember him?'

'Yes, of course. I didn't catch the name initially.'

'He has asked me to speak to Señora Palmer and so . . .'

'About what?'

'The very terrible murder of your wife.'

'How does he imagine she can possibly help his enquiries?'

'I can't be certain. He has merely given me several questions he would like me to ask her.'

'What are they?'

'I think I must put them to her, Señor.'

'I see . . . Well, I'm sorry, but that's not possible.'

'Why is that?'

'She isn't here.'

'She is temporarily not with you at home, or she has left the island?'

'She has friends who spend a lot of time in the West Indies and they invited her out there and, being very generous, offered the flight as well. She was dubious about leaving me on my own – naturally I said I could cope and she must seize the chance – so she left a few days ago to fly to London and then on to Tobago. I gather it's the dry season out there now, so I suppose they're enjoying what they'll call winter and, back in England, we'd call high summer. The friends have a yacht so presumably they'll be spending a lot of time on that.'

'You can get in touch with her?'

'If she's at their home, yes; if everyone's on the yacht, no.'

'Perhaps it would be best if you wrote to her.'

'Saying what?'

'That Detective Inspector Fenton very much wishes to have a word with her. Since she is not here, his request to me becomes invalid.'

'I really can't begin to understand why he believes anything she can tell him will help.'

'Nor can I, but then, of course, I have no idea in which direction his enquiries have recently moved.'

'Don't the questions give some sort of an indication?'

'Not really.'

'Then there's nothing I can do.'

'Apart from writing to your sister.'

'Yes, of course.'

'And you might say that when she returns to England and before she comes on here, she might like to contact Señor Fenton directly. It would save time and trouble for everyone.'

'I'll suggest that.'

'Thank you, Señor.'

Alvarez said goodbye and rang off. He drummed on the desk with his fingers. Was her declared absence proof? Hardly, since she might truly have gone to the West Indies. But he was prepared to bet that she had not. He phoned the Guardia at Palma airport and asked them to keep watch for a passenger by the name of Hilary Palmer; if she tried to pass through emigration, she was to be turned back on the pretext that her passport appeared to be one of a number stolen from the Madrid embassy and it would have to be checked . . . Yes, he would take full responsibility . . .

Twenty-four

B y Wednesday morning, Alvarez had sufficiently overcome the excesses of welcoming in the New Year to make his way across the old square to Club Llueso for a merienda coffee and brandy. Not that he really enjoyed either. He had been so certain he had uncovered the answers, yet each passing day seemed to prove he had not even identified the questions. Hilary Palmer had not fled the island, warned that she was to be questioned and guiltily certain what those questions would be. Right now, she was lying in the sun, an iced daiquiri by her side, the gentle slap of the Caribbean waters on the beach providing background music. And the further thought that in fact it was early morning out there and she was still probably in bed brought no relief to his doleful thoughts.

He left the club and crossed the square, almost deserted because the northern Tramuntana was blowing and it had fingers of ice. He reached the post, climbed the stairs, slumped down behind his desk. Failure was always unwelcome, but it became doubly so when one had been congratulating oneself on seeing what so many others had missed. How could he have been so big-headed?

The phone rang. A pompous member of the Guardia detail responsible for security at Palma airport said that Señora Palmer had been stopped at the emigration desk and her passport had been impounded. She was furious and threatening diplomatic mayhem, so unless Alvarez would confirm his instructions, she would be allowed to proceed. He confirmed them after a short, barbed comment on those who were unwilling to accept responsibility.

The vixen had broken cover. All his sighs for shattered hopes, his moments of self-deprecation, had been premature and groundless. He had proved, as Dolores's mother doubtless had once said, A dowdy sparrow could be as smart as a golden eagle.

He phoned Fenton in England.

'Great to hear from you, Enrique, but please don't spoil the pleasure by telling me you've brilliant sunshine and people are swimming.'

'There's a cold wind, it may soon start raining, and anyone who swims will quickly die from hypothermia.'

'Your misfortunes make ours more bearable . . . What can I do for you?'

'I rather hope I can do something for you.'

'You've learned something from Wade that will start up our investigation again?'

'I think so. What I now have to say begins at the end.'

'I enjoy variety.'

'My nephew made a fool of me at the end of last month. Because of that, I realised something which is so obvious it is frequently overlooked. We expect what we expect.'

'Difficult to find fault with that.' Fenton's tone expressed some perplexity.

'If I am told I am to be given a bottle of coñac and shown a bottle which declares itself to contain a very excellent one, I assume that what is poured from it into my glass is that very coñac.'

'Quite. But to be frank, I don't see what bearing that can have on this case.'

'When the police entered Wade's house, he was on the floor, so securely bound there was never any question he might have tied himself up – is that not so?'

'It is.'

'And his physical condition reinforced his claim that he had been in the bonds for a considerable time?'

'As far as could be medically judged, from the time the intruders broke into the house.'

'So it seemed he had been tied up by the intruders who had abducted his wife?'

'Of course.'

'When the body of a female was found which bore signs of torture, she was provisionally identified as Robina Wade by the mole, the scar, and the few clothes she was still wearing; her husband was asked to make a visual identification, which he did. When the illegal transfer of bank funds was uncovered, it appeared she had been tortured to make her reveal the details of the security system at the bank at which she worked. Because so large a total was involved, you decided Mrs Wade's identity had to be confirmed?'

'There had to be room for the possibility of suspicion. That was why we took the corpse's fingerprints and samples of her hairs. These were compared with prints found in the house and hairs taken from a hairbrush. They matched with no room for doubt.'

'So the dead woman had to be Robina Wade?'

'What other conclusion can one come to?'

'Hugh, please understand, I am not attempting to criticise. Had I been in your position, I must have made exactly the same assumption, since logically no other was possible.'

'Yet you're saying it was wrong?'

'We suffered a peeping Tom who was found dead in circumstances which made me doubt he had died where his body was found. In the course of my investigations, I discovered Ramos had fallen while being chased after peeping at homes in Beniferri.'

'That name seems to ring a bell.'

'It's the urbanización in which Wade and his sister live . . . Just over a fortnight later, a man called Pablo Pino disappeared and has not been seen or heard from since. He was friendly with Ramos and perhaps went peeping with him; what is certain is that I found in his car left at the airport a photograph taken in the course of peeping. This showed two naked figures, clearly about to engage in sexual exercise. The quality of the photograph was too poor for them to be convincingly identified, but by chance there was also visible an object very closely resembling something which Señora Palmer had shown me. As a consequence of this, I was near enough to their bungalow when quite by chance – sometimes one is fortunate – I heard sufficient to make me certain the couple in the photograph were Señor Wade and Señora Palmer.'

Fenton swore in amazement.

'Until my nephew made a fool of me, I assumed they were guilty of incest and nothing more. But then, as I have mentioned, I had cause to realise how often one sees what one expects to see. When a wife is missing and a body is identified by her husband, her hair, and her fingerprints, it is naturally accepted that it is her body. Yet that can be to overlook the fact that there has been no "independent" identification, which in this case had to be a most unlikely happening, since is a friend or a relation also going to be subjected to the very distressing experience of viewing the body when this seems quite unnecessary, since confirmation has been obtained scientifically? Yet, if one looks at the facts backwards, one realises that what has not been proved is that the hairs and the fingerprints in the house came from Robina Wade.'

'The body was not Wade's wife?'

'Accept that and questions no longer remain unanswered. Since Ramos's death was accidental, why was his body moved? Why should Pino be murdered if he had tried to blackmail with photographs that would never be accepted in a court of law . . . ? A criminal investigation into the supposed incest would clearly raise the risk of uncovering the truth – that Hilary Palmer was really Robina Wade – and this had to be avoided at all costs.

'To go back to the beginning. Wade lured a woman – one must assume a prostitute, since her disappearance would cause little or no concern – to his house and she was there long enough to make certain she left her fingerprints on surfaces that had been cleaned of Robina's prints and that the hairs in the hairbrush were hers. Then she was tortured to make it appear she had been forced to divulge the secrets of the bank security systems, finally, mercifully, she was murdered. Robina tied up her husband very securely, left the house for some prepared hideout and there used her computing skills and security knowledge to transfer money to accounts abroad that could never be traced.

'Wade was asked to identify the body. He did so, certain that, unless there was a reason to suspect his identification, no one else would be called to do so.

'Robina Wade, armed with false papers, flew to somewhere abroad and remained for a while, then came here and, using a little of the stolen money, bought the house in Beniferri. When Wade later joined her, as her brother, they were careful to lead a comfortable but far from luxurious life, most of the expenses being paid by her, as he needed to appear relatively hard up . . . And remember that, when you were here and we made an appointment to speak to

Wade, he made certain his "sister" was not present – he feared you would recognise her from photographs you might have seen.'

'You could be right,' Fenton said slowly, 'but it seems to me there's no proof of what you claim; there's only the fact that, if you're right, you have answers to questions which have been puzzling you.'

'That is true. I understood I needed something to show these were more than false assumptions which explained what I needed to be explained, which is why I told Wade I wished to speak to his sister, because you had asked me to put several questions to her. I hoped they would panic, believing, as guilty people do, that they were in much greater danger than was the case. Wade told me that his sister was in the West Indies and he could not say when she would return. Today, Hilary Palmer tried to leave the island by plane.'

'I'll be damned!'

'Would you not agree that there should be an independent identification of the dead woman if that is still possible?'

'I would. And because the case has not been cleared up, the body is still in cold storage. I'll arrange an identification that can't be questioned by Doubting Thomas.'

'The superior chief,' the plum-voiced secretary said in her curtest tones, 'wishes to speak to you.'

Seconds became minutes.

'What the devil is going on?' Salas demanded.

'If, Señor, you mean why has Señora Palmer's passport . . .'

'I have just been addressed in the most insolent manner by an abogado who threatens to bring an action against the Cuerpo. He says Señora Palmer's passport was confiscated, as she was about to board a plane, on spurious grounds and this has led to severe emotional and financial problems. When I told the little turd it was nothing to do with me or my command, he insisted the passport was seized on your orders. Is that true?'

'Yes, Señor. The facts . . .'

'You claimed you had the authority to make that order?'

'I judged that necessary . . .'

'I would not accept your judgment as to whether it's night or day. Do you have the intelligence to begin to understand the consequences of what you have done?'

'On this island, the murder of Pino will be solved even though the body has not yet been recovered and the reason for removing Ramos's corpse from where he accidently died will be established; in England, a brutal murder will, to the gratification of the British police, be solved and they will doubtless express their thanks to the Cuerpo.'

'How can you claim all that?'

Alvarez was not normally boastful, but he presented his work in such a light that at the conclusion Salas could only say, in tones of utter surprise: 'I suppose I have to commend you,' before he rang off.

237

Twenty-five

O n Friday, Alvarez returned from his siesta, settled behind his desk and thought with pleasure that next day, Saturday, the family had been invited to lunch with cousins – the slightest blood tie, however remote, made for cousinship. Juana was nearly as good a cook as Dolores – not that one made such a comparison in Dolores's hearing – and there was every reason to believe the meal would be a memorable one. Oblades amb bolets? True, turbot was expensive, but Juana's husband, Emilio, was a crafty man who ran an agency that rented villas and there wasn't a trick he didn't know – and there were some he shouldn't – about making pesetas out of tourists.

The phone rang.

'Enrique . . . Charles Fenton here.'

'You have news?' he asked eagerly.

'I do. But I'm afraid you're not going to like it.'

Alvarez felt as if the icy winds that blew around the peak of Puig Major had suddenly swept into the room.

'The body was that of Robina Wade.'

'Impossible!'

'But fact. By chance, there was a break-in at the Wade's house some time before the murder. I spoke to the DC who carried out the investigation and he remembered Robina Wade. When he saw the body, he identified it immediately.'

'You're telling me I've been hopelessly wrong?'

'I'm afraid that that's the way it is.'

'But if Wade wasn't guilty of murder, why would he have lied about his sister's having gone to the West Indies?'

'In some, perhaps many, people's minds, incest is almost as abhorrent as murder.'

'He surely must have realised that couldn't be proved from a photograph which didn't sufficiently clearly identify the two persons concerned?'

'Some of the photos that were taken may have been very much sharper; the one that was torn up was destroyed for the simple reason it wasn't good enough.'

'The lack of definition was the fault of the equipment, not the operator.'

'Wade may not have been thinking clearly. We both know how guilt can befuddle the mind.'

'To the extent that Wade thought it necessary to murder Pino?'

'His body has been found?'

'No.'

'Then where is the proof he has been murdered?'

'I'm certain he has. And why did Wade not leave Ramos's body where it fell when it was so obvious the death was accidental? The answer has to be, he had an overwhelming fear of the consequences of its being found there.'

'Can you say beyond any doubt it would not have been the fear of having their sexual activities exposed? It would have meant social exclusion, since they were English, not French.'

'In moving the body, he was risking being thought guilty of murdering Ramos.'

'All that's certain, Enrique, is that it wasn't fear of being exposed as the murderer of his wife which drove him to act as he did.'

'Did Hilary Palmer buy the house with inherited money as she claimed?'

'That question occurred to me and I made a few enquiries. Hilary Palmer and her husband moved to Crete and lived there for eight years before they were involved in a car crash – he died and she was quite severely injured. He left her everything, which must have included their house; she sold that before moving to Mallorca.'

Alvarez said mournfully: 'I've made an overcoat out of a rat's tail.'

'I won't go along with that. Your theory held water right up to the time it became certain the dead woman was Robina Wade. So, when I say I'm sorry to have torpedoed everything, I'm not just offering you useless sympathy, I'm also bemoaning the fact that we're back to square one over the murder of Robina Wade when we thought it had been cleared up.'

'I should have paid more attention to my horoscope in yesterday's paper.'

'What did it say?'

'I would suffer disappointment and must look forward to the future.'

'That could suggest things are going to improve.'

'Like most oracular pronouncements, I expect it's deliberately double-edged. "Must look forward" probably means I can't escape the necessity of informing the superior chief of the results of the identification.'

'Will it help at all to say I was equally surprised, because I agreed with your interpretation of events?'

'Perhaps it may do. It is very kind of you to suggest that.'

Several minutes later, after Fenton had said he was an optimist and therefore hoping something would crop up necessitating his return to Mallorca, the call came to an end.

Alvarez slumped back in the chair. The more a man congratulated himself, the greater hostage he offered fate. Salas would express himself in great detail . . .

Always make the theory fit the facts, never the facts, the theory. Yet surely he hadn't started with a theory – that had come slowly, as the facts accumulated . . . Were the facts not facts? Until the body of Pino turned up, there could be no certainty he was dead, let alone murdered. Yet could it be coincidence he had disappeared after blackmailing Wade? Where was the proof he had blackmailed Wade? The signs of luxury spending? They proved only that he had suddenly come into a considerable sum of money.

Only fools or cowards sought escape in alcohol. He was both, so he leaned over and opened the right-hand bottom drawer, brought out bottle and glass, which he placed on the top of the desk. As the brandy began to warm him, he decided he was being too harsh on himself. There *had* been actions and words which suggested hidden currents, facts which had appeared to deny straightforward explanations . . .

It was common sense not to present an unwelcome report to one's senior until one could no longer refrain from doing so. He would not phone Salas just yet . . . Might there not be some further action he could take, some fact he could pursue, which would enable him to make the report more acceptable? He could think of nothing. He poured a second drink. And it was as he was finishing it that he suddenly identified something which had never been verified, because this had not seemed necessary. Even now, it was difficult to know how it could possibly be pertinent, but it wasn't only the drowning man who clutched at a straw.

He sat upright and refilled his glass before he lifted the

telephone receiver. There were strict rules governing the making of telephone calls abroad but, in an emergency, rules were made to be broken.

He phoned Fenton.

'What brings you back on the line so smartly?'

'To ask if you learned in which hospital in Crete Hilary Palmer was treated?'

'As a matter of fact, yes, I was given the name of the place.'

'What was it?'

'Hang on and I'll check my notes.'

There was a brief wait during which Alvarez stared at the far wall and wondered why he was trying to make concrete without cement.

'Sorry to hold you up. It had the somewhat uninspired name, the British Hospital, and it's in Canea. So now tell me, why the interest?'

'I think perhaps it is no more than the need to find something else which has to be done before I phone the superior chief.'

Fenton laughed. 'Then I should have told you it would take several days to check the name of the hospital!'

When the call was over, Alvarez phoned directory enquiries and used both his easy charm and quiet authority to persuade the woman to whom he spoke to provide the telephone number of The British Hospital in Canea. When this was given to him, he dialled it.

His hope that those who worked in a hospital of that name would speak English proved justified. The woman's English was as fluent as his own. She cheerfully admitted that the hospital records were not kept perfectly and therefore she might well be unable to find any reference to Hilary Palmer's stay in the hospital – more especially remembering the time-lapse – but she promised to do her best.

As the hours passed, hope faded and he found great difficulty in recalling how he had ever believed there could be a point to making the phone call to Crete. Obviously, *in vino* non *veritas*. Added to which, since it had been a woman to whom he'd spoken, the probability had to be that she had not bothered to make even a cursory search amongst the hospital records.

He was going to have to phone Salas and admit he'd made a griffin's tale of the case. On Monday.

On Monday morning the calms of January might have arrived – the sky was cloudless, the sunshine warm, the wind a mere zephyr – yet for Alvarez the world was bathed in grey. He stared at the telephone and tried to conjure up a believable reason for further delaying the inevitable . . . It rang and he was so certain the caller was Salas that it was a long while before he picked up the receiver.

'Elisabeth Papazoi here. As you requested, I have searched the records. Unfortunately, they are not in the best order and it has taken a long time to uncover any information.'

'I'm sorry to have given you so much trouble,' he said politely.

'Please do not be concerned . . . Mr Palmer suffered many external and internal injuries and died very soon after admittance. If you wish to have a list of those injuries, I will fax it to you.'

'Thanks, there's no need.' Far better not to know what horrors the human body could suffer.

'Mrs Palmer, who was wearing a seat belt, was not very seriously injured, but while she was in hospital it was discovered that she was suffering from a tumour in her left breast. This proved to be malignant and she underwent a mastectomy . . . I am afraid that that is all I can tell you. I hope it is of some help.'

He assured her the information would be very useful, but, after replacing the receiver, gloomily accepted he had learned nothing of the slightest relevance; nothing that would make it less likely Salas would soon point out that resignation would be far less harmful than dismissal to the Cuerpo's reputation.

When a man teeterd on the edge of an abyss into which he must fall, there was only one thing to do. He made his way to the Club Llueso.

'I've seen corpses look more cheerful than you,' said the barman.

'That's because they're already dead.'

Alvarez sat at one of the window tables and gloomily reflected that troubles never came singly. Hilary Palmer had suffered the death of her husband and then cancer. Had she raged against such injustice? Could this in some way have been responsible for her acceptance of an incestuous relationship, as if the breaking of moral and legal boundaries was a way of getting her own back on fate . . . ?

He returned to the bar and asked for another brandy and coffee. Back at the table, he wondered how she had summoned up sufficient courage to accept that she was suffering from cancer? Would he ever be able to do that? Perhaps, he thought with an inward shudder, he was about to find out. One of the billions of cells in his body was preparing to turn traitor. Which part of his body was he going to lose . . . ?

He silently swore, using one of the more colourfully obscene Mallorquin expressions. He stood and hurried across to the outer door.

'Where's the fire?' the bartender called out.

'In my head!'

'Is that why you haven't finished your coñac?'

'There isn't time to drink it.'

The barman was too astonished to swear.

Alvarez, breathless and sweating, reached the post and raced up the stairs to his room. He sat and opened the second left-hand drawer of the desk, brought out the envelope which contained the torn pieces of photograph found in the car. He fitted these together with fingers which shook from excited tension. His memory was correct. The woman had both her breasts. She was not Hilary Palmer . . .

He slumped back in the chair, mopped his forehead with a handkerchief. Who could she be, why was it so essential to conceal her true identity when neither was she Robina? Had Wade met her here, on the island? Very unlikely. The risk of someone's identifying her would have been too great. Why were they presenting themselves as brother and sister when social mores no longer condemned unmarried couples who lived together? That a peeping Tom had been watching and recording their actions would have been cause for angry annoyance, but why had this become so great that the place of Ramos's death had to be concealed regardless of the risks this must entail? Why had Wade paid blackmail money and then murdered to conceal the relationship? One possible answer was obvious. He had been involved in the theft of millions of pounds, even though all the evidence had clearly seemed to name him victim, not perpetrator . . .

Suppose he coloured certain facts with the characters of those concerned, might he finally be able to deduce or guess the truth?

Wade had had a job that provided an average income; Robina had probably not earned more, but at work she had dealt in millions of pounds. Any man might fantasise about enjoying some of those millions; a greedy, dishonest man would wonder if there might be some way of actually doing so. Had Wade considered persuading her to become an accomplice in the theft? Almost certainly not, since anyone so inherently trustworthy would be horrified by the suggestion, not tempted. So, he had begun to see her as the potential victim whose murder would ensure his success and this meant he had to enlist the help of someone with a very different outlook on life.

Maitland had described Anna Tait in terms which – remembering his dusty, repressed character – suggested a sexually attractive, morally careless woman. Wade had sought her favours, ironically not solely for the obvious reason. He had identified her as a woman so jealous of those who enjoyed the lives of luxury she read about each week in glossy magazines, she would be prepared to do anything, risk everything, to join them.

Robina had possessed a rare sense of sympathy for the misfortunes of others. He saw this as the weakness which offered the chance of success . . . In crime, as in warfare, planning could be as important as execution. He had persuaded Anna to understand they must move very slowly, and this meant bringing their affair to a temporary end so there could be no chance of its being exposed. It had to be Robina who was seen to promote the friendship with Anna, thereby eliminating the possibility that he had initially played any part in the relationship. The surest way to do that was to engage Robina's sympathies, but this would not be a simple task, because Anna's personality must challenge all her conservative values. But it could be done by tweaking her conscience . . .

Anna shared a secret with one of the staff, knowing her confidence would quickly be betrayed; it was soon common knowledge in the bank that she was having an affair with Keith, a married man. Naturally, Robina strongly disapproved of such a liaison, but one day when she and Anna were together on their own and Anna began to sob and wish she were dead, she instinctively offered a measure of comfort. Anna tearfully explained the cause of her misery. Initially, she had been drawn to Keith by his unhappiness, trapped as he was in a marriage which had become loveless due to his wife's alcoholism. At first at his wish, soon equally at hers, they had been together whenever possible. When he told her how much he loved her, she'd known golden happiness. Yet she had resisted his desires until the afternoon when he had talked about suicide – frightened, she had suddenly seen her moral stand as cruel, since it was in her power to offer him a happiness that must move his mind away from such a horror. Before they had sex for the first time, he had promised to marry her as soon as he gained a divorce. She had never doubted him, not even as time passed; then, very recently, he had told her he had gained his divorce and, because of financial considerations, was going to marry a wealthy widow, but he still loved her and they could . . . She'd not seen him since and would not in the future.

Robina acknowledged that Anna's behaviour had been so far removed from what it had seemed to be, one had to be bereft of any understanding or sympathy to condemn her. Yet she had condemned, even if only in her own mind, because of mindless prejudice. The knowledge burdened her with a sense of guilt which she tried to relieve by offering friendship even while recognising that normally she would have been friendly, but would have resisted that friendship.

Anna had resigned from the bank and, for many months afterwards, Wade had carefully played the part of a loving husband, so that subsequently no one would wonder if there might be a connection between her departure and the robbery and murder; that, when sufficient time had passed, she had stealthily returned to Rexly Close, where Robina had been tortured by her husband to divulge the necessary codes, before she was murdered; that she had securely tied up Wade before making her way to a temporary base where there was the computer equipment she needed to make the transfer of money . . .

Wade had correctly judged it would be a long time before the police lost interest in the missing millions and this raised the problem of how to begin to enjoy the fruits of the theft and murder without arousing sharp suspicion? Perhaps it had been an unresolved question until he'd learned that, following her illness in Crete, his sister had died . . .

Anna had arrived in Mallorca as Hilary Palmer and had bought a nice, though not noticeably luxurious, house. She had invited her 'brother' to live with her, to help him forget the past as well as ease his financial straits . . . From time to time they had left the island, ostensibly for a quiet visit somewhere – in fact, once beyond the ken of any inquisitive investigator, to enjoy a touch of the luxury they had so cruelly pursued . . .

Alvarez sat forward, lifted the receiver, and dialled with an enthusiasm that would have been impossible not long before.

'Yes?' Salas was at his most abrupt.

'Señor, a short while ago I spoke to Inspector Fenton in England to discuss the Ramos/Pino case. He was kind enough to agree with my judgment.'

'That surprises me, having always understood the British police enjoy reasonable standards of intelligence.'

'However . . . one has to accept that facts can turn out to be very ambiguous. Or, would it be truer to say, they are susceptible of ambiguous interpretations?'

'I imagine this nonsense means your investigation is now in complete chaos. Presumably, Pino, far from being murdered, has appeared alive and well?'

'He is still missing, Señor, which suggests ever more strongly he is dead.'

'After hitting the rock, Ramos recovered sufficiently to drive to Cala Blanca, where he fell and died?'

'I think not.'

'Then it is now certain he was not the peeping Tom it unfortunately gives you so much pleasure to assert he was?'

'There can't be any doubt he was one.'

'Then what have you got totally and absurdly wrong?'

'The dead woman in Wade's house was not a prostitute.'

'Who was she?'

'His wife.'

'What's that?'

'Robina, his wife.'

'Good God! You spend endless time, but doubtless little effort, pursuing a line of investigation which is based on a disgusting assumption, only to find that assumption to be totally wrong. You confiscate the passport of a foreigner whose only misfortune was to meet you, thereby precipitating a potentially destructive international incident, without a shred of justification for your action.' Salas's voice rose. 'Since it is you, undoubtedly there is worse to come. Have you arrested Señor Palmer? Have you used illegal force to try to make him confess to something of which he is completely innocent? Is he now in hospital?'

'Señor, I don't think you understand . . .'

'I do not begin to understand how a man lacking any ability ever came to be accepted in the Cuerpo, or how it has taken until now for that absurd mistake to be rectified. As of this moment, you are suspended . . .'

'Señor, the dead woman was Robina, but Wade's "sister" on the island is not Hilary Palmer, but Anna

Tait, almost certainly his mistress in England – of course, to have direct proof of that is difficult, as you will quickly appreciate. Hilary Palmer was ill in Crete and probably died there some time ago . . . It is only because I was so certain the facts of the case were not as simple as they appeared to be, and Ramos was a peeping Tom, that I have been able to uncover the truth. Would you not agree with me that it turns out to be fortunate I decided to have the passport of the woman who calls herself Hilary Palmer confiscated, since she must remain on the island until her true identity is established?'

Salas could hold his angry annoyance in check no longer. 'To agree with you is to sup with the devil. Even if correct, you have ravaged justice, yet, like a harlot, she dare not complain.'

Alvarez, deciding that in view of his success he might allow himself an amusing comment, said: 'I thought, Señor, you did not know how harlots behaved?'

It proved to be an ill-advised decision.